D0427594

IF YOU FOLLOW ME

CALGARY PUBLIC LIBRARY

OCT   2016

By the same author
With Hymns and Hearts and Voices
Fisher of Men
Casting the Net

The Dunbridge Chronicles

BOOK 3

IF YOU FOLLOW ME

Pam Rhodes

LION FICTION

Text copyright © 2014 by Pam Rhodes
This edition copyright © 2014 Lion Hudson

The right of Pam Rhodes to be identified as the author of this work
has been asserted by her in accordance with the Copyright, Designs
and Patents Act 1988.

All rights reserved. No part of this publication may be reproduced or
transmitted in any form or by any means, electronic or mechanical,
including photocopy, recording, or any information storage and
retrieval system, without permission in writing from the publisher.

All the characters in this book are fictitious and any resemblance to
actual persons, living or dead, is purely coincidental.

Published by Lion Fiction
an imprint of
Lion Hudson plc
Wilkinson House, Jordan Hill Road
Oxford OX2 8DR, England
www.lionhudson.com/fiction

ISBN 978 1 78264 079 0
e-ISBN 978 1 78264 080 6

This edition 2014

A catalogue record for this book is available from the British Library

Printed and bound in the UK, August 2014, LH26

To Richard,
My first proof-reader,
my sternest critic,
and my lovely husband.

WHO'S WHO IN DUNBRIDGE

Reverend Neil Fisher – curate at St Stephen's.

Reverend Margaret Prowse – former rector of St Stephen's.

Iris Fisher – Neil's widowed mother, Harry's neighbour.

Harry Holloway – elderly widower, Claire's great-uncle.

Claire – Neil's fiancée; Harry's great-niece; gardener employed by St Stephen's.

Sam – Claire's young son.

Ben – Sam's Australian father.

Felicity – Claire's mother, who lives with her second husband David in Scarborough.

Peter Fellowes – churchwarden; recently married to palliative care nurse, **Val**.

Cynthia Clarkson (Cyn) – churchwarden; husband **Jim** and sons **Carl**, **Barry** and **Colin**, the eldest, married to **Jeannie**; **Ellen** – Colin and Jeannie's baby daughter.

Wendy Lambert – Neil's keenest admirer; leader of St Stephen's worship group.

Sylvia Lambert – Wendy's mother; St Stephen's choir leader.

Brian Lambert – Wendy's father; organist at St Stephen's.

Barbara – runs St Stephen's playgroup.

Brenda – Sunday school teacher.

Boy George Sanderson – octogenarian leader of St Stephen's bell-ringers.

Clifford Davies – former professional pianist in variety; organist at the local crematorium.

Graham Paterson – Neil's friend at the Wheatsheaf; fellow member of the darts team; Deputy Head of Maths at Dunbridge Upper School.

Debs – Graham's wife; best friend of **Wendy Lambert**.

Bob Trueman – local farmer; chairman of the Committee of Friends of St Stephen's.

Shirley McCann – matron of the Mayflower residential care home.

Sylvie – care worker at the Mayflower.

Artie Simpson – resident at The Mayflower, son Ian

Dr Saunders – a partner in the local GP practice.

Victor – previous rector of St Stephen's for more than twenty years.

Bishop Paul – head of the team to which Neil belongs.

Hugh – retired local minister.

Rosemary – non-stipendiary industrial chaplain.

Michael Kerridge – retired minister.

Lady Romily – chairwoman of St Stephen's Ladies' Guild.

Major James Molyneux – organist; wife **Sue**; son **Daniel**.

Audrey Baker – head of the church flower team.

Pauline Walters – member of the church flower team.

Ernie and Blanche Perkins – elderly parishioners.

Sonia Roberts – battered wife of **Reg**; mother of **Rosie**, **Jake**, and **Charlie**.

Beryl – catering organizer at St. Stephens; husband **Jack**; son **Paul**.

Maria – from Romania.

Matt – Captain of Dunbridge rugby team; fireman; Paul's friend.

Madge – bell-ringer.

CHAPTER 1

"The trouble with you, Neil, is you're just like your father." Iris eyed her son across the table with obvious disdain.

"I can live with that," Neil replied, tucking into his roast dinner.

"You procrastinate. He did too. It drove me to distraction. There were things to be done, plans to be made, but he had no sense of priority when it came to putting arrangements in hand."

"But Neil spends every day organizing things," commented Harry, helping himself to another spoonful of Claire's home-grown runner beans. "A curate with no rector? He's a one-man band. I bet he'd love to procrastinate, if only he had the time!"

"I am well aware of the demands of his working life." Iris's voice moved up a couple of decibels. "It's his private life that's a disaster. I mean, how long is it since Neil asked you to marry him, Claire?"

Neil felt Claire's leg brush against his under the table.

"Six weeks."

"That's my point," continued Iris. "Six weeks on and nothing's been decided. When are you going to get married? In fact, are you even properly engaged? There's been no announcement – and no ring! Whoever heard of an engagement with no ring?"

"Ah, well," said Neil, "that I can explain. We have looked, haven't we?"

Claire nodded. "We've just not found the right thing yet."

"Why not?" demanded Iris. "There are plenty of jewellers' shops with hundreds of rings. Why haven't you got this sorted, Neil?"

"That's my fault," said Claire. "I'm choosy."

"Of course you are, my dear. As the bride, you have every right to be, but it seems to me the groom needs a bit of a shove to get his act together. Just like his father. If it weren't for me constantly pushing him in the right direction, we'd never have got anywhere."

"We saw some lovely rings, too many to choose from, but really I've felt from the start that I'd quite like to have an old ring, something with a bit of history to it."

"History?" Iris sounded appalled. "But what if it's not a happy history? Why lumber yourself with other people's misfortunes at this stage in your marriage?"

"Because I think I'll only be drawn to the right one for me. One that's belonged to someone who loved and was loved. I'd like to think of someone's loving commitment, and everything she felt and went through, bringing richness to my own feelings and experience."

"Sounds a bit fanciful to me."

"I know just what she means," said Harry softly. "Those last awful days when Rose was so ill in the hospice, I held her hand for hours, though I've no idea really whether she knew I was there. She was so thin and frail by then – her wedding ring looked enormous on her hand, but I took a lot of comfort from seeing it there. I could picture her face when I placed it on her finger all those decades ago. When I thought about what that ring meant to us, I was so thankful to see it there still – a bit battered and tarnished, but as full of love and promise as it was on our wedding day."

Claire laid her hand over Harry's, sharing a moment of silent understanding with her great-uncle. Suddenly, Harry pushed back his chair, excused himself and quietly left the room.

"That was nothing to do with me!" stated Iris, once he'd disappeared out of sight. "I didn't upset him. You need to be more careful, Claire. He's not as strong as he'd like to think he is."

"When it comes to his physical health," interjected Neil, "you may be right – but there was no weakness in what we saw just then."

"He was remembering a sad time," added Claire, "but I think what he said about his marriage to Aunt Rose was really touching."

Iris sniffed.

"Well, I think you should be more careful when you're dabbling in emotions. You're supposed to be good at counselling, Neil. Your skills were sadly lacking there. Thank goodness you're still a curate. Let's hope they've got time to give you a bit more training in people skills."

At that moment, they all fell silent as Harry came back in and sat down next to Claire.

"Here. This is for you."

He handed her a small box covered in deep red velvet, faded and frayed with age. Glancing up at Harry with curiosity, Claire gently lifted the lid to reveal three sparkling diamonds on a gold ring that was bent and thinned from years of work and wear.

"It's Rose's engagement ring. She wore it every day from the time I asked her to marry me until the day she died. Please don't feel you have to wear it if it's not right for you, but I know she would have wanted you to have it."

Deeply moved, Claire gazed down at the ring for some moments before she smiled up at Harry.

"Thank you, Uncle Harry. This is definitely the right ring for me. I'll wear it with pride, and hope that Neil and I can look forward to the same joy in marriage that you and Rose shared."

"Well!" said Iris, abruptly cutting through the intimate atmosphere. "I don't think that ring will last two minutes when you're gardening, Claire. You need something sturdier." She turned to Neil, suddenly hesitant. "How would you like to have your father's wedding ring too? It's quite wide and thick. Do you remember? Not the modern style nowadays, I realize that, but there'd be enough gold in it to add some to the band of Claire's engagement ring, and perhaps put the rest of the gold into your two wedding rings."

There was an air of vulnerability about Iris as she spoke, as if she was uncertain of his reaction.

"I think," said Neil quietly, "I would like that very much."

"So would I, Iris," added Claire. "What a lovely idea. Thank you."

"That's settled then."

Iris pushed back her chair and started to pile up the dinner plates.

"These plates won't get done on their own, Neil. I'll wipe, you wash. You need the practice if you're planning to be half decent as a married man. How many times have I told you to rinse the crockery so it doesn't dry streaky? And for heaven's sake, remember that rash you get. My Marigolds are on the hook above the sink. Use them!"

* * *

Attendance at church was traditionally low in August with so many families away on holiday. However, as Neil stood at the back of the church after morning worship on the following Sunday, most of the people lining up to greet him were familiar faces.

Beryl was first to the door. As leading light of the catering group she was rushing to rally her team of ladies who served refreshments in the hall. Neil was especially pleased to see Maria, a young Romanian girl, going out with her to help. The previous summer he'd caught her stealing from the church Bring and Buy sale, and discovered that she was homeless. Abandoned by the cousin who had promised to find her work, she knew no one in England. Neil had found her a place in a nearby hostel, and Jim, the manager, thought she'd benefit from being part of a caring community like the congregation at St Stephen's. They had benefited, too, because Maria was sincere and hardworking. Since then, she'd come across to the church almost every day, helping out at the children's playgroup, baking cakes with the Ladies' Guild and anxiously standing by to serve coffee or tea to anyone who might need it at any time of day.

"Good morning, young man. Not too bad today, I have to say."

Neil's thoughts were interrupted by a tall, distinguished-looking man standing before him. Major James Molyneux and his family had recently moved to Dunbridge after his retirement from a long career in the army. From the first day James and his wife Sue had arrived for Sunday worship at St Stephen's, he had made his presence felt. His devotion to his Christian faith was in no doubt. His in-depth scrutiny of every detail of each service was a little taxing, though, because it soon became clear that he expected his church services to be run in precise military fashion, just like the rest of his life. As a newcomer, he was unaware of the depth of sadness felt by the whole congregation when, earlier in the year, their rector Margaret Prowse had suddenly retired after the shocking death of her husband Frank, leaving Neil to cope alone. James seemed unprepared to make allowances for the shortcomings of the young, inexperienced priest who had suddenly been catapulted from curate training into full responsibility for this busy parish. He expected the priest-in-charge to know his job and *be* in charge. He didn't understand Neil's natural shyness, or his panic whenever he was faced with a new challenge. He didn't know that Neil trembled whenever James approached him with that slightly disapproving expression which always meant criticism would duly follow.

"Thank you, sir," mumbled Neil, cursing himself for his nervousness.

"Wrong hymn choice, of course," continued James. "There are so many more suitable texts that come to mind before that old chestnut Psalm 23. The trouble is that clergy often resort to it because they can't be bothered to find something more appropriate to the reading of the day. But then you compounded the crime by shunning the *only* melody to which those words should ever be sung, 'Crimond'. That new modern version is a poor substitute."

"Actually, Stuart Townend's 'The Lord's My Shepherd' is one of the most popular hymns in the country at the moment..."

"Exactly! That just goes to show how far standards are dropping."

"I wouldn't say that..."

"Don't let your standards drop just to make yourself trendy and popular. Stand up for what you know is right."

"Actually, I..."

"Constructive criticism, young man, that's what I'm giving you. You'd do well to listen to the considered opinion of someone who's been organizing church services since you were in short trousers."

"Ignore him, Neil," said James's wife Sue, joining them. "He's a grumpy old man who's not in the army now, and he doesn't have the right to tell everyone what they should be doing and expect them to hop to his command."

They were an incongruous couple. Sue was a foot shorter than her husband, short, round and blonde, while James was tall and wiry, his thinning grey hair smartly slicked into shape.

"If you want some of Beryl's ginger cake, James, you'd better get to the hall pronto!" she commented, linking her arm through her husband's. "See you there, Neil!"

Next in the line were Brenda, a Sunday school teacher, and Barbara, the grandmother who took charge of the St Stephen's playgroup in the church hall on weekday mornings.

"Thanks for including that lovely version of 'The Lord's My Shepherd', Neil," said Barbara, not slowing her pace as she headed for the church hall. "That made my morning!"

Congregation members filed past: first the team of bell-ringers, enthusiastically led by "Boy George" Sanderson, a sprightly octogenarian who felt it was his duty to make sure his hardworking team were rewarded with first pick of the cakes on offer in the hall. Then there was Bob Trueman, chairman of The Friends of St Stephen's and stalwart fund-raiser, followed by Shirley McCann, the manager of the Mayflower care home, who could only come to church when the staff rota allowed her time off. Other faces were less well known to Neil, but he greeted them all as chattily as possible, while keeping in mind that he had to lead a service at their sister church of St Gabriel's in three quarters of an hour, and that he'd love a cup of coffee before he had to set off.

"Good morning, Neil." Geoff Whalley, the local funeral

director, was an occasional visitor to St Stephen's for Sunday morning worship. Neil suspected that it was not so much his faith as his shrewd business sense that made him visit several of the largest churches in the area in strict rotation. Not that Neil minded. He respected Geoff: he was caring and sensitive, supporting the mourners as they made funeral plans. Some people felt he got too involved. Well, it *was* unusual to come across a funeral director who cried at every funeral he attended, but Neil had come to recognize that Geoff just loved his job. He loved the sentiment. He loved the ceremony. And he felt the sadness so much, he simply joined in. Who could possibly mind that?

"See you next week at the crem? Are you doing Williams *and* Fogharty? Tuesday morning and Wednesday afternoon, if my memory serves me well."

"I am, Geoff. I'll ring you about them both in the morning."

"Can you ring me too, Neil, when you have a moment?" Churchwarden Peter Fellowes and his new wife Val were next in line. Their marriage in April that year had been cause for great celebration for the whole St Stephen's community. Mild-mannered Peter had been married for years to Glenda, a blowsy, ambitious woman who had finally walked out on him. Their path to divorce was fraught with problems caused by Glenda changing her mind once she'd realized what she was losing, but eventually Peter was able to propose to Val, and now their long years of friendship were crowned by a happy marriage.

Neil smiled at them both. "Yes, I'd appreciate a chat. The timetable's all over the place at the moment, with only me available to do everything."

"That's what I wanted to talk to you about. Hugh's given me a few dates when he can help out, and Rosemary says she may be able to fit in one or two services too. I've said all offers will be gratefully accepted."

"Definitely!" agreed Neil. He simply couldn't have got through the weeks since Margaret's sudden departure without the help of Hugh, recently retired to a nearby village after years of ministry in the Midlands, and Rosemary, who was an industrial chaplain for one of the large companies in Luton.

"Move along there, please!" said a voice behind Val in the queue. "Some of us are gasping for a cuppa. Can you do your chatting in the hall?"

Neil looked up to see the smiling faces of Jim Clarkson and his wife Cynthia, known to everyone as Cyn. It probably wasn't the most appropriate nickname for a churchwarden, but Cyn would answer to nothing else.

"Quite right too," agreed Neil, nodding to their son Colin and his wife Jeannie. They had only recently felt able to come back to church after the death of their longed-for baby, Ellen. Neil held Jeannie's hand for a moment in understanding, before the family moved on to allow Lady Romily, formidable Chair of the St Stephen's Ladies' Guild, to sweep past Neil with the slightest nod of acknowledgment.

Right at the end of the line, Harry stood back to allow Iris to speak to Neil first. Since Neil's mother had made the alarming decision to move from her home in Bristol to buy a house in Dunbridge, Harry had been a wonderful friend and neighbour to them both. Iris couldn't help slipping back into her usual role of overbearing mother, interfering in every aspect of Neil's life, but there were now moments when she forgot herself, and actually became a slightly uncertain, surprisingly thoughtful elderly woman who still had a lot of life in her. To prove it, she had entered into the goings-on at St Stephen's with gusto, which unnerved and pleased Neil in equal measure.

"Did you clean your teeth this morning, Neil? You've got a piece of cornflake, or something, stuck to your tooth."

"Have I?" Neil rubbed his teeth furiously.

Iris peered at him through narrowed eyes.

"Oh, perhaps not," she said, then moved on as if she had already forgotten him.

"Psst! Vicar! Can you spare a moment? Over here…"

Neil caught sight of the worried face of Mrs Baker, undisputed head of flowers, peering out from behind a huge pedestal-mounted flower arrangement. Curious, he moved over towards her, and her hand shot out to pull him in to join her in true cloak-and-dagger style.

"Look!" Mrs Baker's finger poked accusingly at some glorious orange flowers that had pride of place in the display. "What do you think of that?"

Neil stared at the flowers, hoping for a clue about whatever was making her so anxious.

"Er… they're lovely. Very striking."

"They're *lilies*!"

"Are they?"

"And everyone *knows* about lilies."

"I'm sure they do. They're beautiful."

"They're dangerous! Anyone with an ounce of knowledge about flowers knows that."

"They are?" Neil stared at the blooms in confusion.

"Their pollen kills cats."

"How?"

"It's deadly poison to them."

"I never knew that. Thank goodness we don't have cats here in the church."

"But a good flower arranger would know that. And she'd know that lily pollen *stains*. You walk past them quite innocently, then brush your clothes and hands against the pollen, and it never comes off. Never!"

"Oh," said Neil. He really didn't know how to respond to this tirade. "I suppose that means we shouldn't be using them," he finally agreed.

"Of course we should be using them. They're perfect for displays in church. Huge blooms, low cost. I use them all the time."

"Right," agreed Neil, who had now completely lost the plot.

"I use them – but not like this! I cut the pollen off the ends of the stamens, like any experienced and professional flower arranger would."

"Ah, so we need some scissors."

"I *have* some scissors. I always carry them for emergencies like this. But I shouldn't have to be correcting such a basic mistake."

"You didn't do this arrangement, then?"

Mrs Baker stared at him accusingly. "Of course not! This is that Mrs Walter's work. This is what I have to put up with."

"Perhaps you could have a kindly word with her, then, just to remind her about the dangers of lily pollen?"

"I shouldn't have to. She says she's had experience with flowers, but I don't believe her. It's not just this. I think her claims about her past experience in the floral world are very suspect, very suspect indeed."

"Well, whatever her experience, it's wonderful that together you make such a valuable contribution to St Stephen's."

"She shouldn't be doing it. You need to tell her. Tell her I've been organizing the flowers at this church for twenty years, and I don't need someone who says she's been a professional telling me what to do – especially when she makes basic mistakes like this."

"Surely," ventured Neil, choosing his words carefully, "two people who share knowledge and interest in a skill like this have a great deal in common. Can't you find it in your hearts to divide up the work so that you can work together – but individually – for the good of the church?"

"I can't work with her. I *won't* work with her. Either you tell her to keep her nose out of the flowers at St Stephen's, or I resign!"

"Oh, come on, surely it needn't come to that…"

"You tell her, Vicar. Tell her I'm in charge – or on your head be it!"

And with that, Mrs Baker drew her scissors menacingly out of her jacket pocket, stomped off round to the front of the display, and started snipping off the offending stamen heads with all the venom of an executioner. Wincing at the sight, Neil realized his presence was no longer needed, so he tiptoed off in the hope he might escape before she turned her scissors on him.

Moments later, he had joined the others in the church hall. He glanced anxiously at the wall clock, conscious that he was now due at St Gabriel's in little over half an hour.

"You look like you could use this," said a familiar voice at his side, and he turned to see Debs, a flute player in the St Stephen's worship group, offering him a steaming cup of coffee, which he took gratefully. Debs had recently married Neil's best friend in the town, Graham, and they were expecting their first baby.

"Thanks for the invitation to your engagement party. We'd love to come."

"It's in the back room at the Wheatsheaf," Neil said. "Nothing posh. A buffet and a bit of music. Claire and I didn't want anything much, but people kept telling us we should mark the occasion with a bit of style."

"We'll definitely be there."

"Well, Graham told me he's only coming for the real ale. Actually, I'll enjoy that too!"

"How many are you expecting?"

"We've invited about fifty."

"Does that include Wendy?"

Neil was relieved that Debs had brought up Wendy's name.

"Honestly, Debs, I wasn't sure what to do. I certainly don't want to embarrass or hurt her in any way. I don't really know what her feelings are about me now. You're the one she confides in. What do you think?"

Debs looked thoughtful for a moment before answering.

"She's still upset about losing you. I do know that."

"So perhaps it's better left alone..."

"But Wendy's always been a very practical person. She wouldn't want someone who doesn't want her. She knows she deserves better than that, because I've told her so!"

"Thanks. I'm not sure how to take that."

"Look, she loved you. She saw a future with you, and honestly I don't blame her, because on the face of it she would have made a wonderful wife for you. The leader of the worship music group marrying the handsome young curate – sounds like a match made in heaven! But love doesn't always run in straight lines, does it? Of all people, I should know that. When I think of the merry dance Graham led me before I got him up the aisle! Claire may not seem such an obvious choice for you, but anyone can see that there's a real spark between you. I've watched you together. You laugh a lot. You're always chatting as if you're in a world of your own. You're content in each other's company. OK, so she's not a Christian..."

"I'm working on that!"

"... but she's kind, caring, talented and hardworking. And she loves you. That shines out of both of you."

"She makes me feel complete, Debs. I've not had loads of relationships in the past. I've never felt very confident around women. But loving Claire is the easiest thing in the world. It just feels natural and right. There's no question in my mind that she's the one."

"Well, that's all that matters."

"Yes, except that Wendy's feelings matter too. What should we do, then? Should we send her an invitation? After all, we're inviting her mum and dad. The three of them are so involved with the music here and I'm very fond of them all. I'd like to share our happiness with them – if they choose to come, under the circumstances."

"Do you know," said Debs thoughtfully, "I think I'd just send the invitations, and let the whole Lambert family decide for themselves. Wendy might decide to come with her mum and dad. She might prefer to give the evening a miss. But if she fancies coming along with me and Graham, we'll definitely look after her."

"Thanks, Debs. And remind Graham we're meeting up for the darts league match at the Wheatsheaf on Thursday night. Tell him I'm having bangers and mash there first."

"He can join you, then, because that's my late night on duty." Debs worked as a police officer in nearby Bedford. "He's hopeless at cooking for himself. If he's with you, at least he won't starve!"

"Shouldn't you be going, Neil?" prompted Peter Fellowes, pointing at the clock as he passed Neil and Debs. "St Gabriel's?"

"No peace for the wicked," grinned Neil, and with a last gulp of coffee and a wave to all, he headed off towards the car.

* * *

Two days later, a small white envelope was posted through Neil's letterbox. It was an acceptance to the engagement party on behalf of the Lambert family. Neil recognized Wendy's distinctive handwriting.

> *Dear Claire and Neil,*
>
> *Thank you for the kind invitation to your engagement party which, on behalf of my parents and myself, I am delighted to accept. By the way, would it be all right if I brought a friend along with me?*
>
> *Best regards,*
>
> *Wendy Lambert*

Deeply relieved, Neil immediately dashed off an email saying that the whole group would be most welcome, and he was looking forward to meeting her friend too. As he finished typing, he found himself saying a silent prayer of thanks. He wanted the best for Wendy, and hoped she would soon find a life partner worthy of her. Perhaps this friend? With that thought, he pressed the Send button with a flourish.

* * *

Later that week, Neil was in the church office when Beryl popped her head round the door.

"Good, you're here. Can I share an idea with you and see what you think?" She made herself comfortable in the battered armchair in the corner of the room. "What do you think about Maria?"

"She's lovely. I hardly recognize her these days. She's lost that timid look she had."

"She's really come out of herself, hasn't she?" agreed Beryl. "Did you see the cupcakes we had at coffee last Sunday? She made all those. I didn't even need to ask her. She just spent some time looking through the cupboards in the church hall, and pulled them together. She's a very talented cook."

"No wonder you get on so well, then," smiled Neil. "You've met a kindred spirit."

"It's more than that. I feel a bit like a mum to her. Oh, I know her real mum's back in Romania, but she sent her daughter off to a foreign country to live with a cousin who couldn't be trusted. What sort of mother does that?"

"A desperate one? It's difficult to understand how challenging other people's lives are in more unsettled parts of the world."

"I take that on board, honestly I do, but I can't help feeling a bit protective towards Maria. She's kind-hearted and capable. She deserves a chance – and I'd like to give it to her."

"What do you have in mind?"

"Well, you know our Lynne's left home now, so we've only got Paul living at home these days."

"He's the photographer, isn't he?"

"That's right. He works on the *Dunbridge Gazette*. Got a really good job."

"He's done well."

"But now Lynny's gone, Jack and I are getting a taste of empty-nest syndrome. We're rattling round the house, and I'm a mother hen with no one to cluck over."

"What about Paul? He's coming and going all the time, isn't he?"

"We don't see much of him, really. I probably shouldn't tell a man of the cloth this, but he spends most nights round at his girlfriend's house. And that's why, with the house feeling so quiet, Jack and I have had a natter, and we'd like to ask Maria to come and live with us."

"That's a lovely idea, Beryl."

"I've not said anything to her yet, because I'm not sure what the protocol is here. At the moment, she goes back to the hostel in Bedford each night, then she catches the bus early every morning to help with the playgroup. It'd be so much easier if she lived in Dunbridge, but would the hostel people allow that? Who do we have to ask?"

"I'll check with Jim, but I should think he'll be delighted."

"And you'll ring me when you know?"

"You're really excited about this, aren't you?" said Neil, looking at the flush on Beryl's face.

"I am. We both are. Maria's been popping in to see us quite a bit when she's not busy at the church, and she and Jack get on really well."

"And Paul won't mind having someone move into his sister's room?"

"They've got to know each other quite well. Maria's shy, but Paul's like a big brother to her, and that's brought her out of her shell a bit."

"It sounds like a wonderful solution. Thanks, Beryl. I'll give Jim a ring now."

* * *

Graham got to the pub before Neil on Thursday evening and had already ordered bangers and mash for them both, before the rest of the Wheatsheaf darts team arrived to welcome their rivals from the Dog and Duck at the other end of the town. There was hot competition between the two teams, who had taken turns at winning previous tournaments. That night's match was the first of two to be played, one at each of their home pubs. If one team won both matches, they would be outright winners of the League. If the teams won one match each, there would be a deciding game at another pub in the town to name the triumphant winner.

It was a good night. The pub was full of darts enthusiasts from around the town. Neil and Graham both played well, with Graham having more success as the evening wore on, and in the end, the home team won comfortably to cheers all round.

After the match had finished, while the bar was still packed with a very buoyant crowd, Neil spotted a familiar face in the corner of the room. Among a group of young men who were becoming rowdier by the minute, was one lad Neil knew was nowhere near the age allowed for drinking in public. He detached himself unobtrusively from his friends and moved over to stand beside Daniel Molyneux. Neil was aware that, as James and Sue's only son, there was a lot of pressure on Daniel to live up to the high expectations and standards of his military father. He also knew – from snippets he'd gathered from Graham, who taught at Dunbridge Upper School – that Daniel was far from a star pupil. It wasn't that he was lacking in intelligence. He simply refused to conform to the work regime of the school, constantly falling behind with project work, missing lessons, and sometimes bunking off school altogether.

When Daniel finally noticed Neil standing beside him, his face lit up with recognition and he threw an arm around Neil's shoulders. His breath smelled of alcohol and his clothes bore the unmistakable odour of cannabis.

"Hey, guys," he called to his equally drunk friends, "this is my mate Neil. You'll never guess what he does for a living!"

"He's learning to play darts," slurred one of the group.

"Not learned much yet, judging from tonight."

"Nowhere near!" guffawed Daniel. "Shall I tell them, Neil? Shall I tell them you're a vicar?"

"I'm a friend of your mum and dad's at the moment, and I don't think you're supposed to be drinking in here, are you?"

"Don't tell them, then!" retorted Daniel. "Don't upset my dad. No one dares upset my dad. See, the truth is *everything* upsets him. Mum upsets him, you upset him – and I upset him most of all."

"Come on, Dan. Why don't I walk you home?"

"I don't know," Daniel continued, his eyes glassy from a combination of alcohol and sudden emotion. "I don't know whether Dad hates me because I don't want to join the army, or because I'm just a disappointment 'cos I'm not remotely like him. Doesn't matter which, really, because he hates me anyway, whatever I do. So it's not worth doing anything."

"Of course he doesn't hate you, Dan. Mind you, he might not be best pleased if he knew you were this drunk – and high too, I suspect – when you're not supposed to be drinking in pubs at all."

"You're drinking here and you're a vicar. If it's OK for you, it's OK for me."

"It's OK for me because I'm ten years older than you, I've only had a pint, and I'm five minutes' walk from home," commented Neil. "Come on, Dan, let's go outside for a while. The fresh air might sober you up a bit."

"Before my dad sees me, do you mean? Well, I know what he'll say and I know there'll be hell to pay, so I'm not going home. I'm going to stay with my mate Kieran."

"Do your parents know that?"

"I might have mentioned it to Mum. Can't remember."

"Where does this Kieran live?"

"Dunno. Kieran!" Dan yelled across to the other side of the bar. "Where do you live?"

When no answer was forthcoming, Daniel mumbled that he couldn't see Kieran now, and he'd catch him later.

"Did you have a coat, Dan?" Neil was alarmed to see Dan swaying precariously as if he was about to collapse. "You definitely need to get out of here. Did Dan have a coat, anyone?"

A girl with long dark hair looked at Dan's pale face with alarm, then produced a jacket from under one of the bar stools.

"I think this is his," she said. "Do you want me to take him home? He lives just round the corner from me."

"Are you going now?"

"Yes. Come on, Dan. We're leaving."

"Betsy," moaned Dan. "You do like me, I know you do."

"Not when you're drunk, Danny Boy." Betsy linked her arm through Dan's, turning down Neil's offer to help the two of them out. "No need. I'll get him home. I seem to be doing that a lot lately."

Neil watched as the diminutive young woman skilfully manoeuvred the staggering Dan across the room. He wondered if James would be standing behind the front door waiting to lecture his son as soon as he stepped inside. Poor James, to have an only son who caused him such worry. And poor Dan, to have a dad who would never ever think his son was good enough, however hard he tried.

* * *

Just over a week later, Neil was in the Wheatsheaf again, arriving arm in arm with Claire to celebrate their engagement. While he'd been busy at the church, she and a few friends had worked most of the day to decorate the back room; it was completely transformed with balloons, streamers, table decorations and fairy lights.

"Wow! This looks wonderful. Just another example of how talented my fiancée is, and what great taste I have in women," laughed Neil.

"Absolutely right," came the reply as Claire wound her arms around his neck to draw him close. "You're not having any second thoughts, are you? After tonight, there'll be no turning back, because it'll all be official. You're definitely sure it's me you want?"

Neil gently drew her away from him so that he could see the earnest concern and vulnerability in her expression.

"Claire, it's you I want. It's you I need. It's you, and only you, I'll love and adore every day for the rest of my life."

"What about when I'm ratty or disorganized or have spots all over my face? Will you love me then?"

"Provided you promise to love me even when I'm feeling overwhelmed and inadequate at work, leave my dirty washing on the floor or nod off after meals when you want me to be doing other things."

"It's a deal!" grinned Claire. "But go easy on the dirty washing, or I might change my mind."

The room filled up quickly. First to arrive were Claire's mum Felicity, and her step-father David, who had travelled down from Scarborough to spend a few days in Dunbridge celebrating the engagement. Iris followed them, along with Harry, and Claire's five-year-old son Sam. Sam ran into his mum's outstretched arms for a quick hug before he broke away to delve into a plate of crisps he'd spotted.

"I shall enjoy being a dad," said Neil softly, watching Sam scurry away.

"Well, it'll be nice for him to have a proper father at last. He already thinks you're great because you're good at Lego and like red jelly almost as much as he does. But Neil," she said, nuzzling her head into his shoulder so that she could whisper in his ear, "from now on, Sam having two parents instead of just one won't only be wonderful for him. It'll be great for me too. It's hard being a single mum."

Neil pulled her closer. "And you've done a fantastic job, since before he was even born. You've been Mum and Dad to Sam, and just look at him now. He's a credit to you, he really is."

She looked fondly over towards her son, who was shovelling handfuls of crisps into his mouth as fast as he could. Neil's gaze followed hers.

"Well," he grinned, "I might need a bit of tuition in this parenting business, because I reckon he's got the right idea. I'd like to demolish that whole plate of crisps by myself too!"

Before long the room was crowded with their friends, old and new, local and from further afield, all wanting to congratulate the couple and share their happy occasion. The buffet was delicious, the fruit cup packed more than a punch, and the disco was soon pumping out favourite tracks that got everyone, from the youngest member of the St Stephen's church choir to Uncle Harry and Iris, up and doing their thing on the dance floor. Even Neil, who had two left feet when it came to dancing, found himself with Claire in the middle of the crowd, singing along and thinking that, without a doubt, this was the happiest night of his life.

* * *

Wendy carefully applied a coat of lipstick, studying the finished result critically before she closed her make-up bag and sprayed a cloud of her favourite perfume around her. The new dress had been a good investment, she decided, admiring the way the bodice clung tightly while the skirt swirled around her legs. Her heels were high and elegant. Yes, she thought, checking her image in the long mirror in the hall, she looked good – and tonight of all nights, she *needed* to look very good indeed.

Her house guest came out of the living room, letting out a low whistle as he took in her appearance.

"I must say you're not looking bad yourself," she laughed as she picked up her bag and keys. "Are you quite sure you're not too tired for this after your journey?"

"No, I'm really looking forward to it. I hope we aren't going to be too late."

"I think our timing will be perfect," said Wendy, smiling to herself. "Come on, let's go. This should be fun!"

* * *

There was a ripple of admiring applause when the engagement cake was wheeled in. Once again Beryl had excelled herself. In one corner of her iced masterpiece was a very lifelike image of Neil, in full clerical garb, stretching his arms towards Claire, who was depicted in wellie boots, her sandy-coloured hair short and spiky, surrounded by flower beds and a vegetable patch full of leafy plants. The happy couple cut the cake with cameras flashing all round them, and there was a general call for the groom-to-be to make a speech.

"Unaccustomed as I am to public speaking..." he began, to much laughter from the crowd. "Many of you here will know that speaking in front of a crowd has never been something that comes easily to me – which is a strange thing for a vicar to say! Tonight, though, is the exception, because it's the easiest thing in the world for me to say, with all my heart, that this wonderful woman at my side is making me the happiest man alive. She is completely bonkers, of course, because she hasn't worked out yet just what she is taking on – and I'm hoping none of you will put her right until I've managed to whisk her up the aisle, and make her mine forever. All I know is that blessings don't come better than this…"

And to the cheers of the crowd, Neil leaned down to place a tender kiss on Claire's willing lips.

As he raised his head, Neil caught sight of a couple of latecomers making their way towards the centre of the room. Wendy looked beautiful in a shimmering dress that suited her perfectly, but Neil couldn't help wishing she hadn't arrived at such an intimate moment. He searched Wendy's face for a sign that she was hurt or uncomfortable about what she'd seen. On the contrary, he was relieved to see she was smiling broadly as she walked straight up to him, her companion following in her wake. It was at that moment that he noticed Claire's face had completely drained of any colour as she stared at the man by Wendy's side.

"Hello, Claire," said Ben. "It's good to see you again. Where's Sam? Is he here – and has he got a hug for his dad?"

≫ CHAPTER 2 ≪

"What's he playing at, Mum? Why now? He's not been interested in us for years, so what's he up to?"

"Well, he has tried to be in touch…"

"You didn't invite him, did you? I know you've been sending him letters and photos all these years behind my back. Did you put the idea of coming back into his stupid head?"

"Of course not!" Felicity was clearly hurt by the accusation.

"You've fallen for all his fancy talk, though, haven't you – about caring for Sam, even though he's never bothered to see him before? You've just accepted everything he's said about how well he's doing now, and how he's such a mature, wonderful grown-up these days. You've fallen for that hook, line and sinker – and look where it's got us!"

"I don't know why he's here, Claire. Until you talk to him properly, we won't know. Stop guessing, and talk to him!"

"He's *your* best friend. You talk to him."

"You created Sam together. You are his parents. It's you two who need to be not just *talking* but *listening* to each other – no one else."

The fight seemed to go out of Claire. Her shoulders drooped and she slumped down on the sofa, her cheeks flushed with tearful frustration.

"Supposing Ben's come for Sam, Mum? Is he going to try and take him away from me?"

"He can't do that – and I don't think he would."

"I didn't think I'd ever see him again, and here he is. What's his plan? What's going on in that conniving mind of his?"

"He gave me his mobile number. He wants the two of you to meet up properly."

"I don't want to meet him."

"I think you have to, Claire, for Sam's sake."

"I'm about to get married! It can't have been a coincidence he turned up at our engagement party. Whatever must Neil think?"

"Neil only cares about you and Sam. He's right beside you, whatever you decide."

"Perhaps Neil and I should see Ben together? We're a unit, after all. We come as one."

"Why not talk to Neil and see what he thinks?"

"What do you think? Is it a good idea?"

"I don't know, Claire. Conversation might be a bit stilted if Neil's there. I wonder if you might get more out of Ben if there's just the two of you talking things through quietly together."

Claire fell silent then, thoughts clearly racing round her head before she spoke again.

"I will talk to Neil," she said, "but I think you're right. Ben and I need to be able to talk freely. I can't do it on my own, though. If we meet here at the house, will you stay in the background, just in case it all goes wrong and I want to get him out quickly?"

"Of course I will, love."

"I'll go and find Neil, then. Tell him what I've decided."

"He'll understand. I know he will. He loves you, Claire, and above all he wants what's best for you and Sam."

At that, Claire stood up to be drawn into her mother's open arms.

"I'm sorry." Her voice was muffled against her mum's shoulder. "I've been awful to you, and I know it's not your fault. It's as if I need someone to blame, and you're in direct line of fire."

"I've only ever meant well, darling. When Ben contacted me asking for news of Sam, I didn't know what to do. I knew you'd hate the idea, but there was Sam... Ben may not be much of a dad, but he *is* Sam's father. I didn't feel I had the right to shut the door completely on the possibility of them having a relationship in the future, whatever that might be."

Claire sighed heavily. "I know."

"And you're scared..."

"Terrified."

"Of how this visit might develop?"

Claire nodded.

"How you'll feel if Sam actually *likes* his dad?"

She nodded again.

"And how you'll feel if you find *you* still like Ben too?"

Claire sank further into her mother's arms, her whole body shaking at the very thought.

* * *

Wendy glanced at the dashboard to check the time. The traffic was unusually slow that morning, but she'd probably still manage to get everything essential done before she began lessons at nine. Not many people were lucky enough to indulge their passion and their hobby during their everyday working life, but Wendy found her role as a music teacher at Fairlands School, about ten miles out of Dunbridge, completely fulfilling.

The pupils certainly contributed to her enjoyment of her job. It was a private school, and the girls mostly came from loving homes with supportive parents who encouraged regular music practice along with their other extra-curriculum activities like riding, dancing and gymnastics.

As the traffic slowed yet again, her mind drifted – as so often lately – to the delicious memory of her triumph on the night of the engagement party. Her stage management had been subtle but masterly. The image of Claire's ashen, shocked expression when she realized who had just walked in brought particular pleasure. Her heart was warmed by the confusion and worry on Neil's face as he began to piece together the possible impact of Ben's arrival not only on Claire and her son, but on their own future together. Well, that would teach him to go for someone who was complicated, immoral, pagan, and immature!

Wendy sighed as she remembered the glorious months she and Neil had spent together before Claire set her sights on him and enticed him away. Had he got any brains at all? Was he using them – or was he just being a typical, weak-willed, illogical man when it came to relationships? What possible comparison could there be between Claire and herself? Wendy was a committed Christian who had grown up at the heart of church life, so skilled and competent in music that she had single-handedly brought together the music group that now contributed so much to the worship at St Stephen's. What Claire could offer was frankly worth very little to him in terms of his vocation. The very idea that a Christian minister could carry out his responsibilities with a wife who didn't share his faith was clearly absurd.

Wendy hadn't actually seen Neil since the night of the party, but if he had pieced together her own instrumental part in creating the upset, he'd made no sign of it. She guessed he must be curious about Ben's unexpected arrival. Probably neither Neil nor Claire realized that when Ben was in Dunbridge six years earlier, Wendy had known him too, through the local squash club. It hadn't been difficult to find him on Facebook and invite him to visit England again.

For a moment, Wendy recalled her first sight of Ben less than a week ago as he had strode through the arrivals gate, broad shouldered, long limbed, relaxed and smiling, spotting her immediately among the waiting crowd. Their friendship had been instant. Conversation on the long journey back from Heathrow flowed freely, even though he should have been exhausted after almost twenty-four hours of travelling. When she told him there was a party that evening to which they'd both been invited, he was definitely up for going. She had mentioned casually that Claire might be there, but had omitted to point out that it was her engagement party. Less is more, she had decided. Why burden him with too much information so early in his visit? There would be plenty of time for explanation when and if he asked for it.

One pleasing and obvious change was that Ben was now very much more mature than the young man who had scuttled back to Australia six years earlier. He'd talked about his wish to reconnect with Claire and his son, and his obvious sincerity and longing to put things right was both moving and reassuring. How could Claire resist the man she'd once loved, who had returned to make amends and rebuild the relationship between them? And he looked like a young Adonis, with his tanned face framed with dark blond hair. Perhaps he would persuade Claire and Sam to go back to Australia with him. She could find plenty of gardens to work on out there. And if she flounced off, leaving Neil broken-hearted, who would be there to comfort him and love him through the heartache?

With a contented sigh, Wendy turned her car into the school gate and headed for the car park.

* * *

In spite of the fact that he was snowed under with work, Neil was finding it very hard to get out of his mind the image of Sam's dad appearing so unexpectedly at their engagement party. It was the impact on Claire that worried him most. He'd been shocked by the strength of her reaction when Ben stepped back into her life that night, and even more concerned as he realized that, along with her anger and indignation, he could see real fear. Fear about what? About Sam? About Neil, and what his feelings might be? Or, more worryingly, was she fearful of her own emotions? This was a man she'd once loved with a passion. Could that passion ignite again? Neil shuddered when he compared the muscular, good-looking Ben with his own very ordinary appearance.

Every time that terrifying thought crept into his head, he deliberately tried to block it out as unrealistic and unhelpful. Claire had promised to marry him. Her commitment was deep and sincere. Whatever else he had to worry about, it certainly wasn't the love he shared with Claire.

Still, he struggled to know how he should support her through this. He could see that her thoughts were in turmoil, so he made sure she knew he was right beside her, loving her and wanting to help in any way she needed him. Better not to push. It would be wrong to make demands or voice his own concerns when it was her welfare – and Sam's – that mattered most. She must be in no doubt that nothing could change his love for her. No worries there.

He tried to put such thoughts aside when he called on Mrs

Walters, a necessity after the rather alarming discussion he'd had behind the pedestal display with Mrs Baker. He didn't know Pauline Walters well, but he found her surprisingly good-natured about the formidable leader of the flower-arrangers, and the way in which she made her feelings and her floristry credentials very clear at every possible opportunity.

"Her bark's worse than her bite, really," she laughed. "Honestly, I don't take it very seriously."

"It must be hurtful, though," ventured Neil.

"Well," agreed Pauline, her expression becoming more serious, "I was quite hurt by it – until I heard how unhappy her life has been."

"Oh dear. I'm afraid I don't know much about her, which I should do, of course, as she's such a stalwart member of our congregation."

"Apparently, for years she owned a very successful flower shop in Blackpool with her husband. Then, out of the blue, her husband just didn't wake up one morning. He'd had a heart attack in the night and she was racked with guilt at the thought that she'd been asleep beside him and hadn't realized a thing. But she was even more upset when the will was read. She'd assumed she still had their business to keep her employed and solvent, but it turned out that her husband had left his share of their property to the children of his first marriage, which she hadn't known anything about. He'd been estranged from his first wife and their two sons for years, but once the two young men knew there was money on offer, they insisted on selling their share of the business, and she couldn't raise the capital to buy them out. So she was left with no husband and no flower shop – and a huge great chip on her shoulder."

"What made her come to Dunbridge?"

"Well, they didn't have children, so she had no family ties

in Blackpool. Her sister lives here, I think. Not a churchgoer, so I don't know her."

"What a sad story!"

"Exactly. So every time she slings an insult at me, I bite my tongue. I think of how shattered I was when my Ken died. At least I've got a family. Our Pattie's great, up in Gloucester with her husband and two kids. And my son Greg, married to Tina. She's a Canadian who was working over here for a while, but they live near her family in Ontario now. I've been over to stay with them. It's a great life for them and little Zoe. Thank God for Skype, that's all I can say. They call me a couple of times a week."

"So is there anything I can do to help ease the flower-arranging situation?" asked Neil. "Would you like me to have a word with Mrs Baker – and if so, what on earth should I say?"

"Don't worry. Her criticism's all water off a duck's back to me. I'll smooth it over with her. If I have a real problem, I'll let you know, I promise."

"Just be careful of her scissors!" grinned Neil.

"You too. Remember you're about to become a married man!"

Neil walked back from Pauline's house through the market square, which was bustling with stalls and customers. On one side of the market he noticed a group of three people laughing together over coffee at a table outside a café. It was Maria he spotted first, before he recognized one of her male companions as Paul, Beryl's son. He must have been taking a break from work, because his camera with its huge lens was slung over the back of his chair. The other man was plainly fascinated by everything Maria said, and Neil could see that her face was prettily flushed by the pleasure of his attention.

It was Maria who waved first.

"Reverend Neil! We here! You with us!" Maria's English was becoming better day by day, but she still missed out or mixed up words in her delightful Romanian accent.

Neil glanced guiltily at his watch, wondering if he had time to join them for a quick cup of tea. In the end, he decided that whether he had time or not, he was gasping – and he could always say this was pastoral work.

"Neil, this is Matt," said Paul, introducing a bear of a man, who looked huge even when he was sitting down. "We're both in the rugby team. Matt's the captain."

Matt smiled, about to speak, when Maria got in first.

"Matt does fires."

Seeing the confusion on Neil's face, Matt laughed. "I'm a fireman."

"Based in Dunbridge?" asked Neil. "Are you kept busy enough here?"

"Well, we rescued a cat this morning and put out a chip pan fire last night. We get lots of those. There's the occasional road accident on the motorway. And we do a lot of talks and training about fire prevention."

"Busy enough, then."

Matt grinned. "Either run off our feet or got our feet up. Doesn't seem to be much in between."

"And Maria, how are you?" asked Neil. "Have you moved into Beryl's house yet?"

Maria's face lit up when she smiled. "Beryl and Jack – they good people."

"I'm good people too!" added Paul.

"All good people!" laughed Maria. "Is nice. My room myself. Very nice."

"She's got Lynny's old room," said Paul. "She's made new curtains and painted some of the old furniture in the garage so it looks really stylish. *Distressed?* Isn't that what they call it when you do up old bits of furniture?"

"Don't look at me," shrugged Matt. "No idea."

"I like paint," beamed Maria.

"She's very artistic," explained Paul, "and she's settling in so well, it seems as if she's always been there."

"Feels home."

"Mum and Dad love having her. Mum's gone into overdrive playing mother hen…"

"Beryl teach me cakes."

"This girl's cakes are legendary," said Paul. "As if that's not enough, she's even got a brother in Romania who plays rugby, so she's quite a fan of the game. That's how she met Matt."

"She stands on the sideline yelling at us in Romanian," said Matt. "We might not know what she's saying, but we certainly know what she means."

"Well, I'm really glad it's going so well," said Neil, draining his cup of the last mouthful of tea. "Got to run. It's been lovely to see you all."

He pushed back his chair and stood up. As he crossed the road he almost walked into two of the most elderly members of St Stephen's congregation, Ernie and Blanche Perkins. They were walking arm in arm, her handbag dangling over her free elbow, while he carried a battered shopping bag over his.

"Steady, Neil," cried Ernie. "You're always in a rush, lad. You'll meet yourself coming back, if you're not careful."

"I often do, Ernie," agreed Neil. "How are you both?"

"Not bad for a couple of old 'uns. We've clocked up nearly eighteen decades between us!"

"Fresh vegetables," interjected Blanche. "That's the secret. Good food, good thoughts…"

"... and a good argument every now and then!" finished Ernie, his face creasing up with delight at his own joke.

"A good slap round your ear, if you don't mind your manners," admonished Blanche. "This is your vicar and he's about to get married, so don't try and put him off the whole idea, you daft old duffer!"

"Oh, I'd never do that. I wouldn't be what I am today without my lady wife."

Blanche looked at him fondly.

"I'd have some money left, for a start!"

Blanche's handbag caught him fair and square in the stomach, and he dramatically clasped his sides as he laughed out loud.

"I apologize for the rudeness of my husband," said Blanche. "Some little boys never do grow up."

And with that, she hooked her arm through his in a gesture that left no room for resistance, and Ernie was dragged away feigning indignation but chuckling loudly.

* * *

"The thing is," said Claire, weaving her fingers in and out of Neil's as they sat together on the sofa late one night, "I'm just so angry with him. From the very start, when he left me to bring up Sam on my own, I think it was anger that propelled me. It gave me the energy I needed to be the best mum I could be. It's as if I wanted to have the closest possible relationship with Sam, just to prove how well I've managed to cope *in spite* of Ben, rather than *because* of him."

"But at the start, were you angry because he walked away from his son, or because he walked away from you? Did he break your heart when he left?"

"Yes, he did. I suppose there was a lot of shock and fear in my reaction, which probably made my feelings all the more poignant and tragic, but he was my first real love. I adored him. I couldn't imagine a time when we wouldn't be together."

"Even though you knew his home was in Australia?"

Her laugh was hollow. "Sounds stupid now, doesn't it? Stupid and naïve. But yes, I wanted it to be forever. I even imagined we would go back to Australia together."

"But he didn't ask you."

"No – and that might have been just because the baby was on its way, or most probably it was because he just never considered our relationship to be as serious as I did."

"And now? Could you feel that way about him again?"

Claire pulled back so that she could look closely at Neil.

"I'm engaged to marry you. Of course I don't feel anything for him, except fury and contempt."

He drew her to him then, kissing her softly first on the lips, then on her forehead as she settled back into his arms.

"So, when are you going to see him?"

"Mum's organized it for tomorrow night. I'm dreading it."

"Does he want to see Sam?"

"Of course, but we've asked him to come after eight, so Sam will be in bed. I managed to keep them away from each other at the party. I don't want Sam involved in this until we've got a few home truths clearly explained. Unless I'm totally sure of Ben's motives, I just won't let them meet. I won't have my boy upset or confused because his father is selfish enough to think that what he wants takes priority over Sam's needs."

"I'm worried that I can't be here with you, even if I only stayed out in the kitchen while you talk – but I'll be taking the confirmation class that evening."

"I know, and I can't tell you how much it means to me to know you care. But I probably do need to see Ben alone, as much as I'm dreading it. Come round as soon as you've finished tomorrow night. He'll be long gone by then."

"I love you," whispered Neil, his lips touching her ear.

"I love you too, so very much. And please don't worry, my darling. There is nothing at all that Ben can do to change my feelings for you. I just want him to go – and stay out of our lives for good."

* * *

Neil found it difficult to concentrate the next day, with the meeting between Ben and Claire looming. He was trying to make some sense of his diary bookings for the following week, when churchwarden Cyn popped her head around the church office door.

"You look harassed!"

"I could do with about four more hours each day," grimaced Neil. "I might just manage to fit everything in then. Or maybe if I could find a way to be in two places at the same time? That might work too."

"Would a bit of good news help?"

Neil laid down his pen. "Let me guess. You've finally managed to find enough volunteers to fill in the gaps on the Readers' rota?"

"I'm working on that, but no."

"You've persuaded Boy George to stop singing his own, very loud version of a bass harmony line which doesn't bear any relation to what the rest of us are singing during the hymns? Either that, or he's promised to learn to sing in tune…"

"An even better idea, but no."

46

"Mrs Baker has declared that she will not use her pruning scissors to commit any dastardly deed against Pauline Walters – or me?"

"I'm not sure about that. She does have a very peculiar gleam in her eye…"

"OK, one last go, then I give up. Lady Romily has decided I am actually OK and she's not going to report me to the higher echelons of the Anglican Church because I'm hopeless and irritating beyond belief?"

Cyn laughed. "The jury's out on that one. No, my good news is much better than all of those put together. Jeannie's pregnant again – and it all happened naturally! It's a miracle, really. No IVF this time."

"Well, praise God for that! How wonderful!" agreed Neil. "And is she well? I mean, is there any reason to wonder…?"

"A perfectly normal pregnancy, so the doctor says – but then last time the pregnancy with Ellen seemed completely normal, although Jeannie felt lousy for most of it. The doctor seems very confident and reassuring this time, though, so we're just praying for a healthy, happy baby. Colin and Jeannie'll make terrific parents."

"They certainly will," said Neil, who felt the mood of the day had been lifted and lightened by this heart-warming news. "When's it due?"

"Mid-March."

"That's definitely something to look forward to. Oh, by the way, Cyn, is it you who's drawing up the service sheet for the Harvest Festival on Sunday?"

"Yes, I am. Do you know what you want yet?"

"I've written out the list of hymn numbers somewhere," said Neil, rummaging through the papers strewn across his desk. "Ah, here it is. I've made a note of the readings too. And

I'd like to do something special right at the start of the service: I want everyone to stand and say a Bible verse together. It's just right for Harvest. I don't think I got round to putting it on that sheet, but it's Genesis 8, verse 22. Can you make a note of it?"

"Consider it done," said Cyn. "Must rush. I'll have that ready for Sunday morning." And with a wave in his general direction, she was off.

Neil immersed himself in paperwork for some time before he heard a timid knock on the office door. He looked up to see an anxious-looking woman, probably in her early thirties.

"Do come in!" he invited. "Excuse the papers all over the desk. I'm trying to catch up."

"Look, you're busy. I'll come back another time."

"No! This is perfect timing. I'll even put the kettle on. I'm parched. Tea for you, or coffee?"

"Let me make it," she volunteered. "I shouldn't be disturbing you."

"Believe me, you've done me a favour. And while I'm brewing up, you can tell me what's brought you here."

"I'm Sonia Roberts; Mrs Roberts, that is – or was… We're not together any more."

Neil switched the kettle on, then sat down beside Sonia. She was plainly distressed.

"Is that difficult for you?"

"Difficult being on my own with three young children, yes. But difficult being without a man who communicated with me, and the kids too, with his fists? No. It's a relief to be away from him."

"Where did you live when you were together?"

"The other side of Bedford."

"And he's aware of where you're living now?"

"Yes." Her voice was little more than a whisper.

"How were you able to move away? Did you have help?"

"I went to the police. They got me a social worker. She put the kids and me into a hostel for a few weeks, then we were given a place here."

"And how's that working out?"

The shadow of a smile crossed her face.

"Nice. It's a nice house with curtains and carpets and most of what we need. Social services have helped a lot, and people have been really kind. We left without anything. Didn't even get chance to pick up the kids' clothes, and when the social went round, he said there weren't any – and they believed him because there was nothing there. He was so angry. He must have got rid of anything to do with us."

"We've got quite a lot of children's clothes and toys here, if they would help at all. How old are your children?"

"Rosie's six. Older than her years, really – looks after the other two, and me as well half the time. Then there's Jake, he's four, and Charlie's twenty months. Into everything, Charlie is. I need to watch him like a hawk."

"How have they coped with the upheaval of moving?"

"They love it. They're safe now, and they know it. They were scared of their dad." She suddenly looked very near to tears. "It was horrible, seeing how frightened they were whenever he was around. I could cope with the beatings he gave me, but when he started on the kids…"

"What's happened to him? Are the police charging him?"

"They say they are, but he's been released back home now I'm not there, so I'm not sure what's going to happen."

"And are you worried about him turning up at your new home?"

She nodded, unable to speak.

"Do the police here in Dunbridge know about your situation?"

"Yes. They send a patrol car round more often than they usually would. Sometimes they knock, just to make sure we're all right."

"That's good."

She seemed uncertain of how to answer, as if she was far from sure that she and her children could ever be completely protected.

"How can I help, Sonia?"

"Do you believe in curses?"

"Why do you ask?"

"Well… there were times my husband was so drunk and angry, all I could see when I looked at him was pure evil. And that last night, when he split my lip and pushed me down the stairs with the kids watching and screaming, I told him I was going to take them as far away as I possibly could. He pulled me right up close to him, so I could smell the beer on his breath, and he spat out such awful words. He said he was putting a curse on me. He said I was his property and he'd make sure I'd never have a moment's peace if I left him."

"That sounds to me more like the threats of a cruel, uncaring man than any sort of curse."

"But suppose he meant it? Could he have meant it? Could he have put a curse on me?"

"Sonia, honestly, I don't think so. He's a bully – not just with his fists, but with his words too."

"He really scared me…"

"… as he meant to, and he's succeeded."

"But if he has put a curse on me, surely you can do something about that? You're a man of God. Couldn't you come and say some prayers at the house, just to protect the children and me?"

"Yes," said Neil immediately. "That's an excellent idea, and of course I'll come. I think you need our prayers for many reasons that have nothing at all to do with curses. When would you like me to call round? Where are the children now?"

"They're with our neighbour, Sharon. Children make friends so easily, don't they? She's a nice woman, with a couple of kids the same age as Jake and Charlie. She offered to keep an eye on them for me."

"Well, let's go straight away, then."

Neil looked round the office for the things he needed. Thankfully these were unusual circumstances and he didn't need them very often. But he was prepared. Her face lit up with relief as he grabbed his stole, a hand-sized crucifix, a canister of blessed water and his car keys, then gently guided her towards his car, parked behind the church hall.

The house was one of four in a row of terraced houses probably built about twenty years earlier. There was a note of pride in Sonia's voice as she showed him around the rooms – they were sparsely furnished, but neat and tidy.

Neil poured the holy water into a shallow dish and placed his stole around his neck. He gave Sonia the cross to hold in front of them as they stood close together in the small living room.

"In the name of the Father, the Son and the Holy Spirit," he began, making the sign of the cross. "Father, we ask for your loving protection around this house which is home for Sonia, Rosie, Jake and Charlie. They have lived in danger and in fear, and they have fled here in search of safety and peace. They have looked evil in the face, and are now frightened and alone. We pray that you will surround them with your loving arms, and send your angels to stand guard beside them. Heavenly Father, we ask you to comfort them, reassure them, guide and protect them, so that they come at last to the certainty of knowing that they have moved from darkness into your light. And Lord, we ask for your blessing on Sonia, who is coping with so much on her own as she tries to build a new home and life for her children. Let her know your love, Father: constant, unconditional and everlasting. We ask this in the name of your Son, Jesus Christ our Lord. Amen."

Neil opened his eyes to find that tears were streaming down Sonia's face as she stood silently beside him.

"Come with me," he said, taking her hand as they moved together from one room to the next, sprinkling holy water in each, as Neil asked for God's blessing on every corner of the house. Step by step, he could sense a growing relief and reassurance in Sonia until, by the time they returned to the living room, there was a quiet calmness about her.

"I'd like to bring the children to church," she said at last. "I used to go myself when I was a kid, but Reg always wanted me at home once we were married."

"You'd all be welcome. I wonder... do you know about the playgroup in the church hall every weekday morning?"

Sonia's face lit up at the suggestion. "They'd love that! Can they all come? They haven't sorted a school place for Rosie yet, but I expect she'll start next week. They're climbing the walls with boredom, with no toys here."

"Bring them along, then. How about tomorrow morning? It opens at half-past nine. I'll tell Barbara to expect you."

Her smile suddenly dropped. "Oh, I didn't ask how much it costs..."

"Nothing at all, until you've got yourself a bit more settled. I think at the moment you need some good and caring friends, and you'll meet plenty of those at St Stephen's."

"I don't know what to say – how to thank you..."

"No thanks needed."

"I do feel stronger now. Reg might come and find us, but he's not in charge here. This is our house. For the first time, I don't feel I'm on my own. I've got neighbours and friends, a church to belong to and a playground for the kids. We can be safe here. This is a new start."

Neil took her trembling hands in his.

"Yes, it is. You are most welcome here, Sonia."

She smiled at the thought, and it struck Neil that she probably hadn't had much to smile about for a very long time. Then she stepped back so he could pack everything together and take his leave.

⇒ CHAPTER 3 ⇐

"You'd better come quick, Neil!" Peter Fellowes put his head round the vestry door to find Neil was preparing for the Harvest service, always one of the most popular of the year. "The flower ladies are at loggerheads – and they've got secateurs, so this could get nasty!"

Neil arrived at the altar to find Mrs Baker angrily tugging out flowers from a carefully arranged display that Pauline Walters had put in place.

"Them's coming out – and these is going in!" she screamed, as she laid a bunch of replacement (and, to Neil's inexperienced eye, virtually identical) blooms beside the vase.

"For heaven's sake, Audrey," pleaded Pauline. "Remember where you are! Does it matter if they aren't *exactly* the colours in the order and shape you had in mind?"

"We had a plan – and you've ruined it! And don't you *dare* call me Audrey! Only my friends call me that."

"Mrs Baker, then," begged Pauline. "I didn't mean to offend you. It's Harvest! There's so much to do. I was only trying to help."

"You never help. You just interfere. You obviously know nothing about flowers, but you seem determined to ruin everything for everyone."

Mrs Baker's accusation echoed around the arched ceiling

of St Stephen's as Pauline, plainly close to tears, turned on her heel and hurried out of the building.

Neil stepped in, his eyes fixed on the sharp secateurs that Mrs Baker was still wielding angrily.

"Mrs Baker," he said quietly, "it's never acceptable to speak so rudely to another member of the congregation, but especially not here beside the altar."

"She shouldn't have been so pushy and selfish, then, should she? You go and explain to her about what's not acceptable. She's the one who needs the lecture. I told you, didn't I? I told you she was trouble!"

"Whatever's been said, whatever the rights and wrongs of this, we'll get together and talk it through thoroughly once the service is over."

"Fine," snapped Mrs Baker. "Clear off and let me get on, then! I've got a lot to do before the congregation arrives."

"I think the church looks splendid exactly as it is," replied Neil, surprising himself by the note of authority in his voice. "We won't have any arrangement here in the altar area…"

"You can't do that. We always have a display here."

"And until a few seconds ago, there was a perfectly splendid arrangement already in place."

"She'd done it wrong. I told her to…"

"And I'm telling you that there will be no more flower-arranging now. Thank you for all you've done, but I'd like you to take a break to compose yourself before the service."

Mrs Baker's eyes flashed with anger as she gathered up the armful of flowers she'd brought with her, then stomped off down the aisle without a backward glance.

"Well done, Neil, you handled that brilliantly. You've got the makings of a good school teacher!"

Neil hadn't noticed Wendy arrive.

"All I could see were those secateurs. My knees were knocking, really."

There was an awkward silence for a moment before Wendy spoke again.

"Look, I've been meaning to catch you to apologize for the other evening. I'd completely forgotten about Claire knowing Ben when he was here before. He didn't say…"

"Well, of course not. You'd never have brought him if you'd known," agreed Neil.

"I hope it didn't cause too much of an upset."

"It's not been easy, especially for Claire. There's a lot of sorting out to do."

"Of course."

"I didn't realize you knew Ben."

"Yes, from the squash club. We often played together during the year he was here. We'd lost touch completely, but then he flashed up on Facebook. We started chatting – you know, just in a general catching-up sort of way – and he said he was planning to make another visit. It would have been rude not to offer to put him up when I've got a perfectly good spare room."

"Well, yes, I can understand that. I just wish the timing hadn't been quite so… sensitive."

"I am sorry, Neil. If there's anything I can do to help, just let me know. After all, Ben is my house guest. If you need a go-between, or if you'd like to talk things through, I'm a good listener, and I'm only ever a phone call away."

"Thanks for that. And you? You're all right, are you? We don't seem to have talked much lately."

"I've been really busy. School work, of course, and the social life has been quite hectic too. You know how it is…"

"I'm glad. You deserve to be happy, Wendy."

"Neil!" called Cyn from further down the aisle. "You didn't

get chance to check these service sheets, did you? Are you OK for me just to put them out along the pews?"

"Fine, Cyn, thank you!" he called back. He turned to speak to Wendy, but she had already gone to set up the music stands for the worship group.

Fifteen minutes later the church was filling up rapidly. Neil got into his robes, and pulled out his Bible to check the verse he wanted the congregation to say together right at the start of the service: "As long as the earth endures, seedtime and harvest, cold and heat, summer and winter, day and night will never cease."

At exactly half-past nine, the choir, sidesmen and Neil processed down the aisle to the congregation's enthusiastic rendering of "We Plough the Fields and Scatter", and made their way to the front of the church. Neil stopped in front of the altar steps, lifting his arms in praise as the hymn came to a triumphant end.

"The Lord is with us!" he cried. "Hallelujah!"

"Hallelujah!" was the obedient reply.

"Let us start our Harvest service by reminding ourselves of the promise we hear in Genesis. It's written at the top of your service sheet. Let's call it out loud and clear!"

Moved by the moment, Neil didn't immediately notice the puzzled looks being exchanged around the church as the congregation hesitantly read out the verse printed on the sheet: "Ham, the father of Canaan, saw his father naked and told his two brothers outside."

Shocked, Neil looked down at the service sheet. It should have been Genesis 8, verse 22. To his horror, he realized they had just read out Genesis 9, verse 22! In her hurry the other day, Cyn had got it wrong.

He sighed as his sense of euphoria at the start of a glorious Harvest service slipped away. What with warring flower ladies and naked fathers, today had not started well...

* * *

He looked taller. Six years had added strength and broadness to the boyish frame she remembered. The man who walked uncertainly into the living room had darker skin and blonder hair than he'd had then – probably the result of working long hours in the hot Perth sunshine. His voice seemed deeper too.

"It's good to see you, Claire."

She was standing by the mantelpiece, her eyes almost level with his as she replied. "I never expected to see you again."

"I'm sorry. I've left it too long."

"So why now? What do you want, Ben?"

"To see my son."

"The son you've shown no interest in for the whole six years of his life?"

"That was wrong. I should have done more."

"There was no need. Sam and I have managed just fine without you. He's well and happy. He doesn't need you. Neither of us does, so you can just turn round and go home again."

"I'd like to see him, get to know him…"

"And then disappear again for another six years? That's not going to happen, Ben. You can't walk in and out of my little boy's life on a whim. I won't allow it. I can't."

"I've wasted six years, I admit that. I don't want to waste any more. Sam is my son as much as he's yours…"

"How dare you! How dare you think that your contribution to the fact he was born makes you important to him! He doesn't know you. He's never heard of you. He's never asked about you. You are irrelevant to him – and as long as you live thousands of miles away on the other side of the world, you will always be irrelevant in any real sense."

"You're right, and I know it's not good enough. That's why I want to start being a presence in his life. The very least I'd like to do is provide for him…"

"We can manage. We don't need your help."

"… but most of all, I just want to get to know him, and for him to get to know me."

"What? So that he can spend every other weekend with you in Australia? So that you can stand on the sideline watching him play football on Saturday mornings? Or read him stories at night? Or comfort him when he has a bad dream? That's what real dads do. You can't do that. You can never be a real dad to him – so don't mess with his feelings by dipping in and out of his life at your convenience. A proper relationship with you can never work, so don't inflict it on him just because it's something you've suddenly decided you want."

"It's not sudden. I've never stopped thinking about him – or you."

"Liar."

"Call me what you like, but you're wrong. I've been a coward and a fool, but not a liar."

"You told me you loved me. That was a lie."

"I did love you very much, and you know it."

"All I know is that you couldn't get on a plane quickly enough once you knew I was pregnant."

"I was scared."

"Nowhere near as scared as me."

"I was still a student, miles away from home. I panicked."

"And you think I wasn't panicking too, flat on my back with morning sickness every day? I didn't know anything about being a parent either, but I didn't have a choice. You did. You chose. You ran – and as far as I'm concerned you lost all your rights in the process."

"You can say that, but it's not true. I do have rights as Sam's dad."

"Don't threaten me, Ben. Don't think you can just demand to have what you want. If you really were worth something as a parent, your priority would be what's right for Sam. Can't you see how confusing this could be for him?"

"That's why I want to do it right. I know you're angry, and I deserve it. But I can't build any sort of bridge without your help. So I'm begging you, Claire. Please. Please."

She caught the note of despair in his voice, saw the pleading in his eyes. She hadn't expected that. She'd been prepared for argument, persuasion, even some sort of defence of his indefensible behaviour – but this caught her unawares. She closed her eyes as weariness crept through her body and brain. She'd thought of nothing but this conversation ever since he'd first walked into the party. Claire sat down heavily on the sofa, burying her head in her hands.

"I love him so much," she said at last. "He's my world. I can't bear the thought of him being hurt."

Ben looked at her wordlessly for a while, before he moved across to sit down beside her.

"You need to know," he started at last, "that this is not a flying visit."

She looked at him sharply.

"Work's going really well and I've saved quite a bit. That gives me a safety net, so I can allow whatever time it takes to sort this out properly. I feel as if I'm at a kind of crossroads. Whether you believe it or not, I have been thinking about Sam a lot for a long time. I can't simply get on with my life as if he doesn't exist. The thought that I've got a son somewhere, and I'm missing out on his life, a little boy who doesn't even know he's got a real dad, has been tearing me apart. I had to come,

Claire, and I have to do what I can to build a relationship with him. I know it's not going to happen in days or even weeks…"

"You're planning to stay longer?" Claire's green eyes flashed with shock.

"I'm allowing myself up to a year. I'm a car mechanic, a good one. I could probably get work here, if I needed to. My aim is to stay around Dunbridge and see what happens."

Claire looked as if she was about to reply, but she obviously thought better of it.

Ben turned to look at her as they sat side by side. "I know I can't build my relationship with Sam without first repairing my relationship with you."

"We have no relationship."

"Well, we should have. On whatever level we make it work, we need to be able to relate to one another as Sam's parents."

"I'm about to get married – but then you know that, since you chose to make your dramatic reappearance in the middle of our engagement party."

"Not intentional, I promise you. I didn't know it was a special occasion. Wendy just asked me if I'd like to go to a party with her that evening."

"So she set this up. The bitch!"

"She's been very kind to me."

"She's a calculating schemer. Did she tell you that she used to go out with Neil? Did she tell you that she's been like a woman scorned ever since he walked away from her? Watch yourself, Ben. There's nothing sweet and innocent about that one!"

Ben looked thoughtful for a moment. "Are you happy, Claire?"

"Blissfully, thank you."

"Neil seems like a nice guy."

"He's one in a million. He's great with Sam too."

"What's his reaction to me being around?"

"Not ecstatic."

"Tell him not to worry. I just want a chance to get to know our son."

Suddenly, he got to his feet. "Look, you've got a lot to think about. I'd better go."

Claire stood up, and then seeing the sadness on Ben's face made a decision that surprised her. "Sam's asleep," she said, her voice little more than a whisper. "Would you like to see him?"

Ben caught his breath. "Can I?"

She led the way upstairs to the back bedroom, which was bathed in dim light from a bedside lamp with racing cars revolving round it. Sam was lying on his back, one arm flung casually to the side of his head, the other clutching his beloved cuddly rabbit, Fred. It struck Claire for the first time, as she looked down at her sleeping son, how much had been inherited from his father. The shape of his nose, his long eyelashes, his thick, fair hair. Why had she never noticed before that he was so like Ben? The thought was an uncomfortable one.

She glanced at Ben in the half-light. He was transfixed as he stared down at Sam. He didn't say anything. He didn't need to. The depth of his emotion was plain to see as he gently reached down to touch his son's hair. For several minutes, mother and father stood side by side, listening to the gentle rhythm of Sam's shallow breath, watching a flicker of a smile cross his face as he dreamed.

"Night, son," said Ben softly. "See you soon, I hope."

He glanced round at Claire, holding her gaze in wordless thanks. Then he walked quietly out of the room. She reached the landing in time to see him turn at the bottom of the stairs and give a small wave of his hand before he closed the front door behind him.

* * *

Mayflower House had once been a gracious family home in a leafy, high-class corner of Dunbridge. The years had taken their toll, until it was rescued about two decades earlier by a Christian organization that ran more than two hundred residential care homes across the country. As one of the Mayflower's chaplains, Neil was a frequent visitor, often staying much longer than he should in the entertaining company of both the residents and staff he'd got to know very well over his two years in Dunbridge. That morning the garden was windswept, with golden leaves strewn all over the lawn. If he hadn't had so much on his mind, he might have stopped a while to enjoy his favourite season of the year in this well-loved garden. Instead, with a frantic glance at his wrist watch, he hurried into the main lounge, hoping he wouldn't be noticed as he slid in late.

The singalong was in full swing, ably led by three members of the Dunbridge Amateur Dramatic and Operatic Society. Clifford Davies on the piano was perfect for this audience, having played professionally when variety theatre was at its height. He had accompanied some of the most well-known performers of the day and, with a sherry or two inside him, could be both hilarious and outrageously indiscreet for hours, to the great delight of all who were listening. Neil knew Clifford well, as he was also the resident organist at the nearby crematorium, so their paths crossed often. Sometimes, when the hearse was late, or there was some other unexpected delay, Neil would catch sight of a dangerous gleam in Clifford's eye which made him worry that he might suddenly burst into a lively rendition of "I Do Like to be Beside the Seaside" to keep the crowd entertained.

Neil slipped into his seat and settled back to listen. Elizabeth Hanson, probably the only member of the choir at St Stephen's to have had any proper singing training, and her husband Ken, who had a wonderful bass voice, were belting out a selection of "Songs from the Shows". Their rendition of "Tonight" from *West Side Story* suspended belief just a little, as the two sixty-somethings gazed lovingly into each other's eyes in their roles as the tragic teenage lovers Maria and Tony. Mostly the audience loved it, especially the four lively lady residents in the front row who were known as the Gaiety Girls because they enjoyed everything. True, some members of the audience were asleep. Others were gazing out of the window as if they wished for all the world they were anywhere *but* in that room. But on the whole, the singing was going down well. Certainly Artie, sitting alongside Neil, was enjoying himself. He was a relative newcomer to the Mayflower, but he'd already made it very clear that he loved to sing. He didn't usually mind whether or not he had music to sing along to. He sang everywhere. He sang as he trundled down to meals with his walking frame. He sang in the bathroom. His neighbour in the room next to his grumbled that he even sang in his sleep. His voice wasn't particularly tuneful, so his singing was often accompanied by loud complaints from the other residents about the din he was making, but he simply turned a deaf ear, and carried on singing anyway.

When Elizabeth and Ken moved on to a selection of Doris Day songs, it brought tears to Artie's eyes. The early Beatles medley had him shaking his non-existent hair just as Paul McCartney had done in the group's early days. Then the duo came to their big finale, an emotive medley of Second World War songs, starting and finishing with Vera Lynn, but with a lively selection of marching songs in between. Bearing in mind how familiar all the songs were, it was quite a surprise when Artie not only stopped singing, but remained completely silent until the end.

"What's wrong, Artie?" whispered Neil. "Don't you know the words to these?"

As Artie turned to answer, Neil was alarmed at the unexpected bleakness in the old man's face.

"Oh, I remember them well enough," said Artie. "There are far too many reasons why I'll never forget that war."

"I'm so sorry. I didn't think…"

"Oh, give over, vicar! That's not the reason why I'm not singing. Those two up there are giving us the proper words. I can only remember the ones we lads really *did* sing: the ones we made up ourselves. Reckon I'd get thrown out before tea if I started on them, so I shut up now so that I can eat up later!"

* * *

At first he thought it was his alarm, but as the noise dragged him out of a deep slumber, Neil eventually realized the house phone on his bedside table was ringing. Peering through half-closed eyes at the clock, he reached towards the phone. Was it really only half-past six in the morning?

"Neil, I'm sorry to ring so early. It's Beryl here."

"Are you all right? What's happened?"

"It's been a busy night. You remember Sonia and her children: the three that came along to playgroup a couple of times last week?"

A shiver of fear coursed down Neil's back. "Are they OK?"

"Well, they're safe, but they very nearly weren't. There's been a fire – their house was completely gutted. Paul went down to cover the story for the newspaper, and Matt was there with the fire brigade. He said it looked as if someone had put a petrol-soaked rag through her letterbox."

"Oh, poor Sonia! She was so scared something like this would happen. Was it that husband of hers?"

"Almost certainly. The lady across the road saw him hanging about, plainly up to no good. Her description fits Reg exactly."

"Have they arrested him? Sonia won't have a moment's peace until she knows she and the kids are safe."

"Not yet, apparently. He seems to have done a runner, but that's only what I've heard."

"Where are they now?"

"Social services are supposed to be sorting them out later this morning, but no one official seemed to have any idea what to do with them last night, especially at the hospital. They gave them a check over, said they were basically all right, then told Sonia she could take the kids home. That's why Paul rang me. He knew I'd suggest they come here. Maria's been great. She gave them her room, and she was wonderful with the kids."

"They must be exhausted."

"And they've lost everything, Neil. Sonia hasn't got a thing except what they're standing up in."

"What time did this happen?"

"Gone eleven, apparently, so they were all upstairs asleep. The smell of burning woke her up, and she looked down to see the hall carpet was on fire and the flames were starting to catch on the bottom stairs. She couldn't get down, so she managed somehow to get the children into the bathroom, shut the door, and open the window wide enough to get them out onto the flat roof."

"She had to do that all alone?"

"I think she'd screamed so much that the neighbours were there to help by then. You can imagine how terrified she must have been – handing three small children down from that roof. Poor woman!"

"Shall I come over?"

"Yes please, if you could. Sonia's completely exhausted, but she's so shocked that she's unlikely to sleep. I've persuaded her to have a soak in the bath now, but she has been asking for you."

"I'll be right there."

Apart from the children, who were huddled together sound asleep in Maria's bed, everyone else in Beryl's household was wide awake when Neil arrived. Maria was in the kitchen handing out copious supplies of tea and toast. Paul's face looked gaunt from exhaustion as he sat at the table, his clothes stinking of smoke. Stopping to check that the young photographer was OK, Neil went into the lounge to find Sonia. She looked small and pale as she sat with her legs curled tightly beneath her in the corner of Beryl's sofa. Her eyes were glazed with shock, haunted by the horror of all she'd been through. Gently, Neil took her hand.

"Sonia. It's Neil."

She turned slowly to face him. "He could have killed them."

"Reg?"

She nodded. "His own children. I know he hates me, but how could he do that to his own children?"

"Did you see him?"

"I didn't need to. It was him. The moment I smelled the smoke and saw the fire, I knew." Her voice was husky from the choking smoke. Neil noticed how her hands continually twitched and trembled.

"I thought we were going to die."

"Thank God none of you were hurt, at least not physically."

"We *should* have died. You blessed us and the house. We should have died, but we didn't."

"And you're safe now. Beryl and her family will look after you while you get some rest. Do you think you could sleep a little? You look worn out."

"I was sleeping and he tried to kill us."

"You're safe here. He doesn't know where you are, and the police are dealing with him."

"Have they found him yet?"

"Honestly, I don't know, but I expect they have."

Sonia shook her head slowly. There was no way she would allow her eyes to close until she knew for certain that her ex-husband was safely under lock and key.

"Shall we pray?" suggested Neil, covering her small hands with his own. The two of them sat, their heads almost touching, while he asked for God's blessing on the family, praying for them to find peace and comfort after everything they'd been through.

"Rosie saw one of your angels."

Neil looked at Sonia curiously.

"I remember screaming out to her that I was going to get Jake and the baby. I put the two little ones in the bathroom and shut the door on them to keep them safe because I knew Rosie would be terrified and I had to get her too. But she didn't look scared at all. She was sitting up in her bed, smiling and looking over to the corner of the room. I yelled at her that she needed to come with me straight away, and she just smiled and said the man had told her it would be OK. I panicked then, because when she talked about a *man*, I thought she might mean that her dad had been in the house. But she just pointed to the corner and said she meant that man over there, the one all in white. I looked over and couldn't see anything, but I didn't hang about. I remember now, though, that she was waving at him as I picked her up."

Sonia turned to look intently at Neil. "Who was she looking at?"

Neil couldn't find the words to answer.

"Do you think she saw an angel? When you blessed the house, you asked God to send his angels to protect us. Do you think he did? We all got out without a scratch on us, and yet the house was completely gutted by the fire. How is that possible? There's only one answer. God was protecting us, wasn't he?"

"I believe he was, yes."

"And he'll keep Reg away from us, won't he? If he's protecting us, we're safe. We are safe here, aren't we?"

"Yes, Sonia, you are – and you can rest now because Beryl and her family will care for you."

With a big sigh, Sonia closed her eyes and leaned her head back against the soft cushion of the sofa. Neil watched the strained contours of her face soften, and her lips part as her breathing gradually became deeper and slower. Within seconds, she was sound asleep. Watching from the door, Beryl made her way across to them carrying a soft blanket, which she tucked gently around Sonia before she and Neil quietly slipped out of the room.

In the kitchen Paul was sitting at the table eating an enormous cheese and pickle sandwich.

"An angel?" asked Beryl, as she started to fill up the kettle and reach for the cake tin. "She said the same thing to me as soon as she got here last night. What do you make of that, then?"

"Well," said Neil thoughtfully, "the whole family have had a very traumatic experience, and Rosie's only six. It must have been terrifying for her."

"So you think she made it up, then, to help her cope with how frightened she was?"

"It wouldn't be surprising, would it? Did Rosie say anything about what it looked like, this angel she thought she saw?"

"She did, actually," said Paul, joining in the conversation between bites of his sandwich. "After Matt and the lads had got her down from the roof, they put her in my car for a while to sit in the warm until the paramedics got there. She was fine, surprisingly calm really, and she was chatting away about this angel for ages, as if it was a real person. And wait for this – when I asked her what it looked like, she said it was glowing white with big wings."

"Oh, for heaven's sake," retorted Beryl. "She's been watching too much television. Don't you think so, Neil?"

"I don't know. Maybe."

"You're not telling me you believe she actually *saw* an angel?" Beryl turned sharply to give Neil her full attention, seemingly unaware that she had a long, pointed cake knife in her hand. "I know you're a man of the cloth, but honestly, does that really seem likely to you?"

"Well, I've never seen one myself, of course, but I have read quite a bit about people who have."

"What, in this day and age? You're joking, aren't you?" asked Paul.

"What sort of people claim something like that?" demanded Beryl.

"Ordinary, down-to-earth people, I think. Quite often children like Rosie."

"So you reckon she might have been telling the truth?"

"I think she probably said what she thought was true – but how can we know? Especially tonight, when they're obviously shocked and exhausted."

"So if Rosie's still saying the same thing in a week's time, you'll think about it?"

"I think," said Neil, "that if we believe in the Bible where there are countless sightings and comforting visits from angels, why shouldn't we believe in them now?"

"So we might have had a real-life miracle right here in Dunbridge?" smiled Beryl. "Well, I must say that's one of the oddest things I've ever heard. After all that, I definitely need a cup of tea and a piece of chocolate fudge cake. How about you?"

≫ CHAPTER 4 ≪

Claire tried not to be too obvious as she stood by the French doors to peer out at the two of them in the garden. She'd been awake most of the night, worrying about this first meeting between Sam and Ben. She'd tossed and turned for hours, eventually coming to the conclusion that if she were a nicer person, she'd hope with all her heart that father and son might establish an instantly loving bond which would bring pleasure and fulfilment to them both. She wasn't that nice, though, because if she allowed herself to be brutally honest, she wanted it to fail. She wanted Sam to be angry with the father who'd abandoned him before he was even born. She hoped he'd tell Ben he wasn't needed or wanted, and that Neil was going to be his dad now. If he told this father he'd never known to leave him alone, then Ben might get the message, and decide to go back to Australia, get on with his own life and allow Claire and Sam to get on with theirs.

Looking at the two of them now, though, with Ben playing goalie while Sam tried to kick the ball between two fruit trees, Claire was struck by an unwelcome thought. As Sam yelled and whooped and giggled, they looked just like sons and fathers the world over. This shouldn't be happening. Ben didn't deserve Sam's unquestioning trust and friendship. But as she watched, she had an awful feeling that the safe world she had built for her son and herself was beginning to rip apart at the seams. When Sam suddenly lost his footing and took a tumble, her stomach lurched as Ben knelt down to rub grass off the boy's knee. Two blond heads almost touched, two faces broke into identical grins, then two long-legged bodies leapt up to re-start their football practice. *They're so alike,* thought Claire. *Why couldn't Sam just take after me, so Ben would be in no doubt that he's* my son? *He's always been mine. He always will be.*

She felt an arm around her waist, and looked round to see her mother standing behind her. The two women gazed through the window in silence before Felicity spoke.

"Sam likes him."

Claire nodded.

"And Ben seems to be taking things steadily."

Once again, there was no answer from Claire.

"Darling," said Felicity, pulling her daughter closer, "I know this is hard for you…"

Claire shrugged her shoulders dismissively, as if how she felt seemed irrelevant to everyone but her.

"… and you're doing brilliantly."

"I hate him being here. I hate him acting as if he's the perfect father."

"And you wish Sam hated him too."

"Yes. I do."

But another scream of excitement from Sam made it clear that the boy and his dad were having a wonderful time together.

"Where's this all going, Mum? That's what worries me."

"Ben's leaving, isn't he?" said Felicity. "He'll go back to the other side of the world, and that will be the end of it, I imagine."

"The end of him giving Sam any thought at all, if past experience is anything to go by. Out of sight, out of mind.

But then the other night Ben was talking about staying for months. How's that going to work when eventually he does his usual act of disappearing? How do I put the pieces back together in that little boy's life then?"

"You will, because you love Sam and you're a devoted mother. We'll help – and Neil too, of course."

"Neil." Claire shook her head with frustration. "He shouldn't have to put up with this. We've just got engaged. We're going to get married. We're planning our life together, our home, our family. Ben's timing's lousy. It's all such a mess."

"How's Neil reacted so far?"

"Oh, you know him. He appears to take everything in his stride – but it's a front. I know that. He's nowhere near as confident as he pretends. He's worried about this. He won't put it into words – certainly not to me because he doesn't want to add to my worries – but we both feel as if the rug's been pulled out from under us."

The women stared out at Sam, who was now talking non-stop as he and Ben sat down on a wooden bench to have a breather.

"I suppose," said Felicity at last, "you don't really have much choice except to get on with this and make it work for Sam as best you can."

"See how it goes…" sighed Claire.

"That's right."

"… until the inevitable happens, and it all goes horribly wrong."

* * *

The playgroup was in full swing when Neil popped his head round the door later that week. He couldn't help smiling as he caught sight of Maria sitting cross-legged in a circle of toys and children, obviously enjoying the fun as much as any of the youngsters. So what if her English wasn't always very clear? When it came to playing games, they all understood each other perfectly.

With a quick wave, he walked on towards the kitchen where small plates of fresh fruit and glasses of blackcurrant squash were being prepared for the mid-morning snack. It was Beryl he hoped to see, because she helped Barbara with the playgroup on three mornings each week. He found her ticking off lists of names and requirements on the counter by the serving hatch where she could also keep a watchful eye on the goings-on in the hall.

"Maria's doing well," commented Neil. "The children seem to love her."

"Actually we all love her. She's got a big heart, that one. I don't know how we'd manage without her when the playgroup's full like this."

"I see Jake and Charlie are here. I gather they've finally found a school place for Rosie."

"Yes, she's loving it and it's taken a lot off Sonia's mind to know she's settled. The local authority people were slow at getting their act together. I know they've got a lot of calls on their resources, but bearing in mind the emergency, I thought they might have pulled out the stops a bit. And then to offer them bed and breakfast, away from Dunbridge, much nearer to Bedford – which is the place they'd escaped from at the start of all this! With Sonia having no transport, and Rosie at school here, it just wasn't practical."

"But you've managed to find them somewhere more suitable?"

"Yes. You remember Paul's friend Matt, the fireman, the one he plays rugby with? Well, his parents are rattling around in a big house down by the river. Their two boys have both left home now, so they stepped in to offer Sonia and the children a place until they can find a house of their own."

"That's great!"

"They've got a couple of bedrooms upstairs and their own bathroom, and Sonia cooks for the four of them downstairs in the family kitchen. It's not ideal long term, but it certainly helps right now."

"And it'll be good for her to know she's not alone in the house, at least until that ex-husband of hers is finally put away for a very long time. Any news yet on when he goes to court?"

"He made a first appearance yesterday and pleaded Not Guilty, even though he's as guilty as sin! The magistrates must have thought so too, because he's been remanded in custody until the proper hearing in a couple of months' time. Meanwhile, Sonia's lost everything. Apparently Reg got rid of anything that belonged to her and the kids at the house she shared with him."

"So how on earth is she going to get a home together when she's got nothing at all?"

"Funny you should say that…"

Neil looked quizzically at Beryl.

"Don't ask!" she said. "My lips are sealed. Suffice it to say that the boys have a plan to raise money so Sonia can get settled again."

"Why do I get the feeling you're keeping me out of the loop because I'd probably think their plan is not the best of ideas?"

"I don't know what you mean!" retorted Beryl, her eyes dancing with indignation. "You'll just have to wait and see. Right now, this information is on a need-to-know basis – and you of all people definitely *don't* need to know! Don't worry, though, because when you see the end result, it won't matter if you don't like it, because at least half the population of Dunbridge most certainly will!"

* * *

Neil had always had a particular fondness for the Remembrance service which took place each year on the second weekend of November. As a boy, his parents had regularly taken him along to the local church where he grew up in Bristol. He knew Iris probably only went because it was the proper thing to do and anyone who was anyone would be there, but his father had had an enduring interest in all things military, which he loved to share with his young son. Dad had whispered in his ear about what the various banners represented, and what could be learned from each medal proudly pinned on the smart dark jackets of the British Legion members. Neil could never hear the haunting notes of the "Last Post" without being overcome with emotion at the loss of the father he still missed so much.

This year the poignancy of the moment hit him harder than ever. The soulful melody, played by a lone bugler, echoed across the town square, where a crowd stood in a circle around the war memorial. He looked down at his mother, who was standing beside him, and wondered if her thoughts were similar to his. To his surprise, she looked sombre and genuinely moved in a way that was at odds with her usual belligerent, dominating manner.

At that moment, he felt Claire's arm link into his, and they exchanged a quick smile. Harry, on the other side of Claire, was standing stiffly to attention, his eyes focused on the poppy wreaths, his eyes misted by memories. Perhaps he was remembering his own father, who had never returned from the Second World War. Perhaps, in his mind's eye, he was picturing old friends now lost through age and circumstance. Like his fellow members of the British Legion standing in the biting wind that day, there was a dignity and pride in his stance which allowed a glimpse of the steely determination and courage that had carried his generation and those before him through the horrors and the aftermath of the Second World War. He personally had been too young to fight but, like many of the old soldiers in their eighties who were standing to attention as the flag was lowered in Dunbridge that morning, Harry had joined up for National Service on his eighteenth birthday in 1950.

There were younger men marking the traditional silence too, each remembering the battles they'd fought – the Falklands, Iraq, Afghanistan. The years had passed. Different conflicts, other parts of the world, and lessons seldom learned. How many mothers on all sides had mourned their sons since Neil had been born? And how many more to come?

A movement to his right caught Neil's attention. James Molyneux, in full regimental uniform, was standing stern and upright beside his wife Sue, while Danny shuffled from one foot to the other with obvious boredom. He certainly looked considerably better than the last time Neil had seen him in the pub, but the contrast between the rod-like father and his uninterested son was dramatic. Suddenly, James turned his head towards Danny, his look wordlessly expressing deep anger laced with pure venom. For a moment, Danny met his eyes as if he intended to speak up for himself, but he plainly thought better of it, and slumped back into a position of fear and subservience.

The hot coffee and tea served in the Wheatsheaf after the service smelled pungent and welcoming as the crowd made their way inside to warm themselves in front of the big log fire. Neil looked around at the many faces he recognized. Boy George was already at the bar buying his customary Guinness ("for medicinal purposes only, of course!") while Madge and several others from the bell-ringing team squashed themselves around a table with Peter and Val Fellowes and Cyn and Jim Clarkson. Ernie and Blanche Perkins, the oldest married couple at St Stephen's, were there too, tucked into a comfy corner from which there were regular bursts of laughter to be heard as they talked over old times with several other members of the Legion.

Neil waved in the direction of the snug, where Shirley McCann, the matron at the Mayflower, was organizing hot drinks for half a dozen of her charges, including Artie who had memorably *not* joined in with the songs from the war years during their entertainment afternoon. Artie gave a broad grin as he returned the greeting, revealing a set of false teeth that seemed alarmingly likely to pop out of his mouth at any moment.

On the other side of the room Neil spotted another familiar group. He'd been aware of Paul taking photographs of the war memorial service for the paper earlier that morning, but now he had a pint of beer in his hand rather than a camera. Neil smiled to see Matt's arm resting protectively across Maria's shoulders. She was listening intently, obviously trying to understand as much as possible of what was being said, and looking up at Matt adoringly. So that was how it was! Not a bad thing, thought Neil. Maria deserved a bit of happiness after all she'd been through.

At that moment, Paul spotted Neil, but rather than waving a greeting, the young photographer instantly turned his back so that the three of them were jammed even further into the corner. Strange, thought Neil. Whatever they were talking about so urgently, they certainly didn't want to be disturbed.

"You should go, shouldn't you?"

His thoughts were disturbed by Claire, who had come up to plant a kiss on his cheek.

"Yes, I've got six home visits to make. If they want communion, it takes about half an hour. I should be back around three. You'll get Mum and Harry home, won't you?"

"Of course," she smiled. "I love you."

"You too."

It was as he fought his way over to the door that Neil heard someone call his name.

"Reverend Fisher!"

The voice was as unmistakable as the superior tone. Taking a deep breath before he turned, Neil saw Lady Romily standing alongside the town's mayor and several other dignitaries in a small private room to one side of the entrance hall. Obediently, he walked over to join her.

"You know Sir Andrew Bartlett, the Lord Lieutenant of Bedfordshire, of course…"

"Good morning, sir," gulped Neil, who until then had only ever seen the Lord Lieutenant at a distance during official functions. "Thank you for coming today."

"Stop talking and listen!" commanded Lady Romily. "Sir Andrew is planning a special service here in Dunbridge. *You* will organize it for him."

"Of course, Lady Romily. What did you have in mind?"

"Ask Sir Andrew, not me!"

Feeling his face redden, Neil looked at Sir Andrew to find the older man smiling.

"Well, you see, as Lord Lieutenant and the Queen's representative in the county, I like to follow the tradition set by my predecessors, of organizing a series of civic services in different towns throughout Bedfordshire."

"Dunbridge has not yet hosted one of these services,"

interrupted Lady Romily, "and it's about time our town took its place on the county map."

"Of course," mumbled Neil. "And you're thinking of holding the service at St Stephen's?"

"Lady Romily thinks we should," replied Sir Andrew, "and she can be *very* persuasive."

Smiling graciously in Sir Andrew's direction, Lady Romily continued, "You can't take the service, of course, Reverend Fisher, because you're still only a curate. We couldn't entrust such an important occasion to you when you plainly aren't experienced enough."

"Oh," said Neil, uncertain as to what was expected of him. "Then how can I help?"

"You'll be expected to do a lot of the background work, but we will be asking the Bishop of Bedford to officiate at the service."

Neil managed to contain his sigh of relief. "Bishop Paul will be excellent for the task. Do you need me to contact him?"

"Don't worry, Neil," said Sir Andrew. "I'll do that. Paul and I are old friends."

"And do you have a date in mind?"

"The last Thursday in June at three o'clock in the afternoon," said Lady Romily.

Seven months away. Without the benefit of a diary to hand, Neil's mind was racing as he tried to remember if there was anything planned for that day.

"Check the date and get back to me!" Lady Romily snapped out the instruction, immediately dismissing Neil by turning away to talk to the Mayor of Dunbridge, as if he were no longer there.

* * *

Ben carried Wendy's sherry and his own lager to the table they'd chosen in the Green Man, a popular country pub just outside Dunbridge. The pub was known for its excellent food, so when Ben said he would like to take Wendy out to thank her for her hospitality, she knew just where to suggest.

"So," asked Wendy, "how did the interview go?"

"OK, I think. It's quite a big garage, with full bodywork facilities as well as a service and repair workshop. They do a good trade in second-hand cars too."

"And what did you think of the people? Would you like to work there?"

"I'm willing to do anything that pays, quite frankly, but if I'm going to be here for a while, a proper job that uses my qualifications and experience as a car mechanic would suit me best."

"And you *do* intend to be here for a while?"

"Now I've met Sam, I never want to leave again."

"How does Claire feel about that?"

"Not over the moon."

"How sad," commented Wendy. "And how do you feel about her, the girl you loved all those years ago?"

He took a sip of lager, replacing his glass before answering.

"Apart from the fact that she clearly hates me, do you mean?"

"Oh, I wouldn't take that too seriously," said Wendy. "You're the father of her child. She *has* to sort things out with you, for his sake, especially as you and Sam already seem to be getting on so well."

"Claire was always quite fiery, with a mind of her own. That's one of the things I liked best about her."

"Maybe not so much now, if she's set her mind against you…"

"That doesn't worry me much. I've got time. I'm not going anywhere."

"I bet Neil is thrilled about that. The love of his fiancée's life turning up to ruin everything just as they've announced their engagement!"

"By the way," said Ben, "when you told me that Claire *might* be there on the night I arrived, you didn't tell me it was her engagement party, so she would *definitely* be there – along with her husband-to-be!"

"Didn't I?" asked Wendy, a mischievous gleam in her eye. "Sorry about that."

"So I guess you're still soft on Neil, then? I heard that you two were quite an item not so long ago."

"And probably will be again, once he's come to his senses."

"You don't think he and Claire will stay together, then?"

"Now you're back on the scene? Hopefully not."

Ben shifted in his seat so that he could look directly at her. "Let me get this straight. You want Neil back – and my coming here was all part of your plan?"

"Let me get this straight," repeated Wendy. "You want to be a father to your son – and I suspect from the way you talk about Claire that you'd rather like to play happy families with his mother too."

A slow smile spread over Ben's face. "You, Miss Lambert, are very perceptive. You are also an evil vixen. Remind me never to get on the wrong side of you!"

"And you, my dear Ben, are catching on quickly. We can help each other, you and I. You get the girl and your son – and I get Neil back when he needs my very comforting shoulder to cry on."

"I'll drink to that!" agreed Ben. "And look, here comes our dinner."

* * *

A little over a week later, Neil was driving back from a Churches Together meeting in Bedford. It was almost eleven p.m. before he got back to Dunbridge, and he was just about to turn into Vicarage Gardens when he spotted something unexpected, and frankly, at this time of night, rather irritating. He stamped on the brakes and backed up in order to see more clearly. Yes, he was right. Someone had left the lights on in the church hall. To his knowledge, it hadn't been used since the playgroup left at lunchtime, so those lights must have been burning all day. The last parish council meeting had got very heated when they discussed their spiralling utility bills, which resulted in a general directive that all gas and electricity on church premises should be used as frugally as possible.

With a sigh of pure exhaustion, Neil rummaged in his briefcase for the church hall keys, then parked as near to the hall as possible. He got out of the car and stopped in alarm. He could hear voices. And wasn't that a shadow passing across one of the windows? Could it be burglars? What on earth was there to steal? A few children's toys and a lot of coffee cups?

He was rooted to the ground for several seconds while he tried to work out what to do. He could hardly call the police – there might be a perfectly reasonable explanation. Probably one of the playgroup leaders had forgotten something and popped back in to collect it. Besides, he was the person responsible for all the church buildings. He should go and investigate, just to put his mind at rest. A couple of deep breaths later, his nerves were steady enough for him to creep quietly up the path and round the corner to the side door. It was open.

His heart thumping, Neil gingerly pushed the door a little further ajar. He could hear several voices – there must be a gang of them...

He tiptoed slowly through the small cloakroom where the children left their coats, and made his way towards the door to the hall. Holding his breath, and hoping the ancient hinges wouldn't creak, he nervously pushed the door open just enough to peer through. At that precise moment a completely naked man walked straight across in front of him.

"What the…?"

"Neil! What are you doing here?"

Neil stood open-mouthed and astounded at the sight before him. It was Beryl who had challenged him – sensible, down-to-earth, homely Beryl – but behind her was a scene that looked like the set of a porn movie. There were several men in various states of undress – and as the fog began to clear from his mind, he realized he recognized a lot of them, mostly because the small amount of clothing they were wearing gave him all the clues he needed. Standing before him was every member of the Dunbridge fire crew, one wearing a bright yellow helmet, another in his regulation wellie boots, others with just a jacket slung over one shoulder, a T-shirt or waterproof trousers worn so low that little was left to the imagination. Behind them, scattered across the floor of the hall was an assortment of tools – hoses, fire axes and gas masks – and right at the front, camera in hand, was Paul, his eyes wide with shock as he noticed Neil.

Neil's gaze, however, was focused beyond Paul to the pool of light in which a completely starkers Matt was bending over provocatively with his back to the camera at just the right angle to hide what should definitely be hidden – but only by a whisker. And standing in the shadows to one side of Matt was Maria, a powder compact and brush in her hands. Everyone in the tableau seemed as gobsmacked to see Neil as he was to discover them.

"I don't understand," he mumbled at last. "What the devil is going on?"

"It's for Sonia," said Beryl. "The fire lads were so upset by what they saw the night of the fire, and the way she and the children were left with absolutely nothing, they wanted to do something to help."

"It's a calendar," interjected Paul. "We can get it out in time for Christmas, and we reckon all the ladies of Dunbridge will want a copy."

"Well, how could they resist taking a peek at this lovely bunch of good-looking fellas?" asked Beryl. "I've already ordered twenty copies. I'm getting one for everyone I usually give presents to at Christmas."

"And it's all for a good cause," added Matt, hurriedly reaching for the coat Maria was holding out towards him.

"You don't mind, do you?" There was a note of pleading in Beryl's voice, and her concern was mirrored in the face of every other person in the hall.

It took a moment for Neil to find his voice. "It's for Sonia?"

"Yes. We want to help kit her out with everything she and the kids'll need when they get their house back."

"And there won't be anything – you know, bits and pieces – on show that shouldn't be?"

"I'm being really careful, Neil, I promise," said Paul.

"There's nothing smutty about this, Vicar," added Matt sternly. "The lads and I wouldn't be here if there were."

"This is art!" said Paul.

"This is charity," finished Beryl, "and you should be very proud of us all."

There was a dramatic silence as Neil struggled to word an answer, aware that every eye in the room was anxiously looking in his direction. And then he started to laugh, a deep, delighted peal of laughter that was gradually joined from every corner of the hall.

"If there's ever any come-back," he finally spluttered, "I will deny all knowledge of this."

"And if it's a huge success," interrupted Beryl, "as it certainly will be, you can take all the credit. We won't mind."

"It's nothing to do with me," said Neil, backing towards the door. "Just make sure you don't leave anything around for the playgroup to find in the morning. Switch off the lights and lock the door behind you."

An audible sigh of relief wafted around the hall.

"And if you're not going to get dressed, at least put the heating on. It's freezing in here!"

≈ CHAPTER 5 ≈

"Mrs Baker – Audrey!" called Neil as he walked in to set up the church for the funeral that was due to take place half an hour later.

The flower-arranger was deeply engrossed in balancing both sides of a dramatic pedestal display featuring the colours and flowers of the Christmas season: holly with bright berries, stripy ivy leaves, poinsettias and deep red chrysanthemums. She glanced over her shoulder, and when she saw Neil, returned to her work without comment.

"That looks wonderful!" he enthused, feeling as usual that he was on the back foot with Mrs Baker. She could be as prickly as the thorns in the roses she loved to arrange.

"I'm busy," was her curt reply. "If you're not going to tell me what you want, I'd prefer to get on, thank you."

"I was just wondering how you are," mumbled Neil. "We meant to have a chat, didn't we, but never got round to it?"

"I've got nothing to talk about."

"Well, perhaps we have. There's obviously some dissent in the ranks of our excellent flower-arranging team…"

"It's not me who's got the problem. Talk to that Pauline Walters! She's the one who needs to have a few facts pointed out to her."

"I can see there are conflicting opinions about how to organize our floral displays…"

"Look," said Mrs Baker, standing up so that she could speak to him eye to eye, "that woman is an amateur. I am a professional. She's only been involved for two minutes. I've spent years in charge of the flowers at this church with just the help of a few willing pairs of hands who work to my direction. She insists on doing her own thing."

"Surely, in a Christian community like this," countered Neil, "there's plenty of room for everyone to play their part along with others. We're a team here at St Stephen's."

"Tell her to be a team member, then, and stop trying to take over things that have nothing to do with her!"

"Actually," suggested Neil rather nervously, "we *all* need to be team members, and that goes for you too, Mrs Baker." He saw the woman's eyes flash dangerously, so he hurried on to say his bit before she stopped him. "We all recognize your expertise and experience, but others want to contribute too – Pauline Walters among them."

Mrs Baker let out a loud, derisive snort.

"Might I suggest that you divide the work up into sections?" he continued. "I know nothing about flowers, of course, but could you perhaps take full control of all the displays to the rear of the pulpit, then let others be responsible for different areas of the church? For example, maybe Pauline could help by organizing the displays on the window sills?"

There was a chilling coldness in Mrs Baker's glare. "No, you don't know anything about flowers, do you, Reverend Fisher? So I suggest you keep your nose out of things you don't understand!"

"Mrs Baker, I am the minister here at St Stephen's…"

"You're just the curate. You have no real power at all."

"I assure you, Mrs Baker, that I speak on behalf of the whole parish council when I say that this feuding and unpleasantness has got to stop."

"Right!"

Peeling off her gloves, Mrs Baker dramatically threw them down into her bucket and grabbed the handle before squaring up to Neil.

"You're on your own, then, you and the other stupid people on the parish council – and on your heads be it! Standards will drop – you mark my words. Don't say I didn't warn you, and don't come crying to me when the flowers are a mess all over Christmas. I'll be sitting at home with my feet up – not, and I repeat *not*, to be disturbed!"

A quarter of an hour later the first mourners started to arrive at the church, but Neil still felt shaken by his encounter with the belligerent flower-arranger. Cyn Clarkson was the churchwarden on duty that morning, and it was a relief to be able to pour out the whole sorry tale to her.

"She certainly is an odd character," mused Cyn, "but I can't help thinking she's quite a wounded soul underneath it all. You know what happened when her husband died? She lost her home and the flower shop business because he left his share to two sons she didn't even know he had!"

"So she's suffered an unfair loss. That means she's got something in common with just about every worshipper here at St Stephen's," replied Neil. "No one's exempt from difficult and emotional challenges in life, but most of us don't choose to take our grievances out on everyone else!"

"Absolutely right," agreed Cyn. "Would you like me to speak to her?"

"You can try, if you like, but she made it very clear that she doesn't want to speak to any of us ever again."

"Better let her cool off a bit, then. In the meantime, should I have a word with Pauline and the other ladies? You know, just to warn them that they'll have a lot more flower arrangements to organize than they were expecting, especially with Christmas just around the corner?"

Neil gave a wry smile. "The season of goodwill to all men…"

"Ah, but women are different!" grinned Cyn. "We're the first to be hurt, but usually the first to make amends too."

"Unless you're Mrs Baker…"

"Unless you're Mrs Baker."

"Right! Must get on," said Neil, realizing the church was beginning to fill up quite rapidly. "By the way, I forgot to ask about Jeannie. Is she keeping well?"

"She's absolutely blooming. So different from last time, when she had to stay in bed for weeks on end."

"When's the baby due?"

"The middle of March. Not long now."

"All right, Neil?" interrupted Brian Lambert, heading towards the organ. "Have you seen the guard of honour forming out in the porch? Must have been a popular chap, this one. Looks like we're going to have quite a crowd here. Oh, and they were asking for you outside."

"On my way!"

In the end, there was something immensely moving about the guard of honour. It was formed by a team of smartly dressed elderly gentlemen, all proudly wearing their medals, lining the way to guide the coffin of their old friend into the church. Neil recognized several of them as British Legion members he'd seen just weeks before as they stood with their banners around the war memorial on Remembrance Sunday.

It was no surprise when the first hymn was "Abide with Me": most of the congregation knew it so well that they didn't even need to glance down at the words. The grandson of the deceased man read the lesson, followed by one of his grand-daughters reciting a poem she'd written herself. By the time his son had managed to get through the moving eulogy, there wasn't a dry eye in the building.

Catching the mood of the occasion, Neil stood to give his sermon. He started in his usual way with reassurances about the care and protection of the God who loves us all, and he asked for God's comfort for those who mourned the loss of a wonderful husband, father and grandfather. Then he added his own thoughts as he drew the sermon to an end.

"I would like to thank all of you from the British Legion who formed such a magnificent guard of honour for your comrade today. I'm sure he was very proud to be part of that wonderful organization, and would have been deeply touched to know that his Legion friends marked his passing with such dignity and affection."

Ten minutes later, once the coffin had made its stately progress back down the aisle on its way to a short private service at the crematorium, Neil realized that Cyn had come to stand at his elbow.

"A word in your ear," she hissed under her breath. "This service was nothing to do with the British Legion. They're all from the bowls club!"

* * *

"So now you've got this job, you're planning to stay around here for a while, are you?"

Claire realized she didn't really want to hear the answer.

"That's my plan, yes," replied Ben. "I want time to get to know Sam better – if you don't mind, that is."

Considering that she had spent years being furious with him because of his lack of effort, she could hardly complain about him making such a commitment now. Instead, she changed the subject.

"And you're quite sure you're organized for today? You know where the cinema is?"

"Not really. It's on one of those out-of-town leisure areas, isn't it? What's the best way to get there?"

Claire launched into a convoluted explanation of how to drive to the cinema complex and where to park, before noticing that Ben's eyes had glazed over with confusion.

"I'm ready, Dad!" Sam came downstairs bouncing with excitement at the prospect of this first trip out with the father he was beginning to discover he actually liked quite a lot.

Ben suddenly turned to Claire. "Come with us!"

"No. This is an opportunity for you and Sam to be together. I'm with him all the time."

"Exactly. I bet Sam will feel a lot more secure if his mum's with him too."

"Oh, come on, Mum!" begged Sam. "That would be great."

"I'm busy, Sam. I've got things to do this afternoon."

"Well, that's very understandable," commented Ben, innocence written all over his face. "Don't worry about us. I'm not quite sure where the cinema is, and I'd hate to get lost with Sam in tow – but I expect we'll manage to find it somehow."

"Please, Mum. Come with us, please!"

Claire looked down at Sam's earnest expression with frustration. She was being outmanoeuvred and she knew it.

"Well, all right, just this once – but I need to ring Neil to let him know what's happening."

But Neil's mobile was on voicemail, and there was no reply from either the church office or his study at home. Feeling almost disloyal in a way she couldn't quite explain, Claire left a loving message for him, assuring him that she was only going along to appease Sam, and that she would be needing an extra big hug from him that evening to make up for the trauma she was about to go through.

Three hours later, she, Ben and Sam emerged from the cinema into wintry sunshine, having thoroughly enjoyed the fantasy film Sam had chosen to see.

"I'm starving!" announced Sam, looking hopefully towards his mum.

"Me too!" said Ben. "Your mum probably needs to get back, though."

"Can't we have tea now, Mum? There's that pizza place you love over there. Look!"

"I must say I could murder a pizza." Ben's expression was so deliberately non-committal as he spoke, that Claire felt an overwhelming urge to slap the smugness off his face. She didn't, though. She silently counted to ten before pinning on a smile and grabbing Sam's hand.

"We've got to make this quick, then," she said, "because I still need to do tea for Uncle Harry and Neil when we get home."

Sam looked puzzled. "Uncle Harry's going round to Grandma Iris's tonight for tea. It's Tuesday. He always goes on Tuesday – and Neil goes too. Don't you remember?"

"Well, we're still going to make this quick, Sam, do you understand?" said Claire through gritted teeth, as she marched the little boy off in the direction of the pizza restaurant, not caring whether Ben was following or not.

The service that afternoon was very slow. They waited ten minutes to order drinks, another ten minutes for a waiter to take their meal order and then more than a quarter of an hour for their pizzas to arrive. Later, Claire put it down to the half of lager – she probably downed it far too quickly on an empty stomach, in an effort to calm her tattered nerves – but she was gradually aware of her taut shoulders relaxing. She saw how delighted her son was when both his mum and dad helped him to fill in the puzzle sheet left on the table. And when she found herself laughing at something funny Ben had said, she allowed herself to acknowledge the unexpected thought that she was *almost* having a good time. She'd forgotten how quick-witted and entertaining Ben could be. She watched his hands as he helped Sam join dots to complete a picture on the sheet, and an unbidden memory crept into her mind of how those same hands had held and caressed her during the days when they were in love. She studied his face, noting how the unevenness of his smile added a rugged edge to his good looks. Seven years had changed him. She had known the teenager. This was the man.

At that moment, Ben glanced up to hold her gaze for several seconds before she looked away. Those blue eyes. She remembered them too, filled with love, the last thing she used to see before he kissed her – very much as they looked right now...

Abruptly she pushed back her chair and stood up.

"Come on, Sam. Time to go. You've got school in the morning." Still acutely aware of Ben's gaze, she had the unnerving sense that he could see right through her.

"I'll get the bill," he said at last, "and see you at the door."

Claire had taken her car to drive them all to the cinema, and on the return journey she said very little. Sam did most of the chattering. Occasionally, in the darkness, she sensed Ben was looking at her, but she doggedly ignored him. She didn't want to like him – and she definitely didn't want to remember why she had once loved him. She wanted him out of her car, out of their lives – and, most of all, out of her mind.

* * *

The *Undercover Firemen* calendar was a magnificent success. At first, the people of Dunbridge were shocked at the whole idea, then curious about how and where the photographs had been taken without a whisper of the plan getting out.

The *Dunbridge Gazette* broke the news story, announcing on its front page that the calendar was being printed, and that it would be on sale following a grand launch ceremony at the fire station. Their report featured not just a group shot of the fully clothed fire team, but also a photograph of Sonia and the children looking suitably forlorn, alongside pictures of their home following the devastating fire.

Iris was filled with indignation. To think such a thing could happen in Bedfordshire, one of the Home Counties! How could a respectable town like Dunbridge allow such pornography to be circulated among its residents? It was disrespectful to the women, harmful for the children and highly offensive to all good Christian folk. And just to make sure her opinions were heard loud and clear, she was first in the very long queue of mostly women waiting for the fire station doors to open on the morning of the launch.

When she arrived home after the event, she was surprisingly quiet about exactly what had changed her mind. Perhaps it was the time she took studying in minute detail every photograph, just to make sure it was perfectly acceptable and appropriate. Maybe it was the manic enthusiasm around her as calendars were grabbed, money thrown at the sales people, and bags stuffed full by ladies who insisted on having a photo taken with one of the uniformed firemen before they left. By the end of that morning, more than a thousand calendars had disappeared off the shelves, a dozen of them bought by Iris.

It was with some trepidation that Neil opened the first copy he managed to get his hands on. Would anyone be able to recognize where the photos had been taken – and would that mean accusing fingers being pointed at him? Beryl and the boys had insisted the end result would be *artistic*. Neil had spent several sleepless nights thinking about the range of meanings that word could have....

But as he frantically flicked through the pages, relief washed over him. The photos were wonderful – fun, imaginative, tasteful and thankfully discreet. Paul had done a brilliant job, especially on such a tight timescale.

And then, on an impulse, he began to write a note on the top copy: "Thought you might like to see the latest fund-raising triumph from the people of Dunbridge! Merry Christmas from Neil and everyone at St Stephen's." Then he scribbled Bishop Paul's address on the envelope and popped out to post it before he could change his mind.

* * *

It was alarming how the remaining days of December were being crossed off the current calendar with ever-increasing speed. The build-up to Christmas was manic as St Stephen's played host to one carol service after another for local schools, organizations, clubs and businesses.

Neil was exhausted. Since Margaret had left her role as rector earlier in the year, the workload that had fallen onto the young curate's shoulders had been overwhelming and almost unbearable – and yet there was no question that things had to be done. Services had to be celebrated, funerals led, baptisms and confirmations prepared for, meetings attended, plans made and ruffled feathers smoothed. During the rare times when Neil had enough energy to think about it, he knew that nothing would be possible if it weren't for the warm-hearted support from the team at St Stephen's. They all rallied round him – the churchwardens, the office helpers, the readers, the choir and worship group, the cleaners, the Sunday school and playgroup leaders, the Ladies' Guild, the fund-raisers, the flower-arrangers (although, just at the moment, he couldn't quite bring himself to include them in this list of helpers) – and, of course, the extended family of ordained ministers and lay preachers who were occasionally able to help him out with services when he finally had to admit that he hadn't yet mastered the art of being in two places at one time.

And it seemed that any sort of solution was still far off. When Bishop Paul rang to thank Neil for the *Undercover Firemen* calendar, he made it clear that the selection process had stalled for unexplained administrative reasons, and that it was unlikely a replacement rector would be found before the summer.

"And, of course, we need start thinking about your own future too. Your three years of curacy will be complete by next July, so no doubt you will be considering your options. Have you had any thoughts about where you might like to take on your own parish?"

"To be honest, I don't have time to think anything beyond the next task right now – where I should be, who I should have spoken to and what I have forgotten."

"And Claire? Have you two discussed where you would like your home to be? In fact, have you decided on a date for your wedding yet?"

"Sometime in the summer, we thought, but we've not settled exactly when. I'll have to go through the diary to see when we might fit it in."

"Well, I would be the first to admit that I've never been able to fathom the mystery of a woman's mind," said Bishop Paul with what seemed like a smile in his voice, "but that sounds a bit unromantic, even to me."

"Claire understands. She knows how busy I am."

"And she doesn't mind you being vague about your wedding plans?"

"I don't think so," replied Neil, suddenly uncertain. "I've not asked her about it really."

"Then perhaps you should, dear boy. Perhaps you should."

Those words echoed round Neil's head all day until he saw Claire that evening over a rushed cup of tea and a sandwich, fitted in between a visit to the hospice and the last confirmation class of the year. Sinking into her arms, he held her tightly, relishing the scent of her hair, the curve of her neck, the softness of her lips.

"Whoa! Where did that come from?" she asked when he finally came up for air.

"Am I unromantic?"

"Yes."

"Really? That's awful."

"Well, you're busy all the time. You can't help that."

"But I should never be too busy for you."

"I understand. It's not a problem."

"Why haven't we set a date for our wedding?"

"Because your diary is packed for years to come!"

"That's not good enough. We need to choose the date we want, and get things organized."

"OK. When do you have in mind?"

"Tomorrow? Next week? I just know I want to be with you always – fall asleep in your arms, and wake up beside you every morning. I'm longing for that, and yet I know I'm not doing anything to make it happen."

She wound her arms around his neck, pulling him closer so that their lips touched.

"Let's make some decisions, then," she murmured, nibbling his ear. "Later tonight?"

"We've got that big carol service in the church this evening. That could go on a bit."

"Tomorrow morning? I don't start work until eleven on Thursdays."

"A funeral visit at nine, the home communion run all afternoon, the hospital at four and the accounts to get into the post by five – and I haven't even started them yet!"

"Friday?"

"Funeral in the morning, school carol service in the afternoon, December diocesan meeting in the evening."

She pulled back slightly. "Not to worry. We'll find time. Hey, you'd better go! It's nearly six."

Claire watched him gather up his papers, saw the regret in his eyes as he pecked her on the cheek, and heard the front door slam before she slumped back against the kitchen work surface.

Notice me, Neil. Reassure me. Keep me close.

But how could she share with him the knot of worry that had her stomach constantly churning? How could she speak of her anxiety as she found herself once again being drawn under the spell of the man with whom she'd shared such all-consuming love in the past? How could she explain the inexplicable – to herself, let alone to Neil?

She caught sight of her reflection in the mirror. She looked wretched. How unfair, she thought, when she had done nothing at all to merit a sense of guilt. Could she be blamed for no more than a vague feeling, a sense of unease that something *could* happen?

She stared at herself sadly. If her misery was so plain, why couldn't Neil see it? Was she hiding it from him because she loved him too much to want to hurt him – especially as there was probably nothing at all to worry about? Or was it just that he didn't care enough to see? That he was too preoccupied with his own life to notice that she was struggling, and desperately in need of his love and reassurance?

And with that unthinkable thought, Claire buried her face in her hands.

* * *

It had long been the tradition in Dunbridge that the congregation of St Stephen's acted out the nativity story in the market square on the last Saturday of Advent, which that year fell on 23rd December, the day before Christmas Eve. Stalwarts like Peter Fellowes, Cyn Clarkson and Wendy's parents, Brian and Sylvia Lambert, had overseen the event for more years than anyone could remember, which was a great relief to Neil, who was so busy concentrating on the spiritual and pastoral needs of the congregation, he was glad to leave the stage management of the pageant completely to them. Wendy was a great help, too, bringing along children from her own school to increase the number of young people who could both act and sing in harmony. Bob Trueman, chairman of the Friends of St Stephen's, dug out the full-size stable from the barn where it was stored all year. Neil's best friend in Dunbridge, Graham, was even persuaded by his very pregnant wife Debs to borrow a set of large stacking boxes from Dunbridge Upper School to create staging high enough for the stars and angels to stand on.

On the couple of occasions when Neil had managed to pop his head into the church hall to see how the rehearsals were going, it seemed like total chaos. Mind you, when Neil had read the list of who was responsible for what, he did wonder whether they'd ever get as far as the actual production without killing each other. As a teacher, Wendy was responsible for supervising all the children; Sylvia was conducting the choir; Brian was playing the keyboard; Clifford was stage manager and director; and James Molyneux insisted that, as a former conductor of one of Her Majesty's military bands, his title was producer, which meant he could override absolutely everything and everybody.

"How's it going?" Neil whispered to Peter Fellowes as he stood in the one corner that didn't appear to be a battle zone.

"I never knew we had so many luvvies at St Stephen's!"

"Artistic temperaments running high, are they?"

"Just a bit! For heaven's sake, this story's not only two thousand years old, but we've been performing it in the square every year for the last two decades. We *should* know what we're doing by now!"

"So what's the problem?"

"Do you want the list? Wendy says we should include a few modern worship songs, but Brian refuses to play them because he and Sylvia think we should only sing traditional carols. Clifford sees it as showtime and would probably have a line of high-kicking chorus girls, if he had his way. And James! Well, we just call him 'He Who Must Be Obeyed'. He's got no sense of performance at all. He'd just like everyone to line up and stand to attention for the whole thing. It's a nightmare!"

"Have you got a job?"

"I'm head of props. Oh, you haven't got a shepherd's crook at home, by any chance, have you?"

"As it happens, I have. I needed it as a prop for a sermon once. I'll bring it in tomorrow."

"What about anything that looks vaguely like a manger? Ernie Perkins usually turns out Blanche's plant trough to provide the box we've always used before, but he's not at all well. Did you know that?"

"No, I didn't. I'll call in and see them."

"He's in hospital, I'm afraid. He's not far off ninety and he's had cancer for at least a couple of years. I gather it's not looking good for him at the moment."

"Poor Blanche. I'll follow that up."

"And you haven't got a manger?"

"Afraid not. Anything else you need?"

"Baby Jesus. We don't have any babies at our house, I'm afraid."

"Sorry, I can't help you there. Sam might be able to come up with a racing car or even his old teddy bear, but he doesn't do baby dolls."

"Props!" yelled James from the other side of the hall. "Where's the frankincense?"

With a shrug of his shoulders, Peter grabbed the coffee jar he was in the process of covering in silver foil, and rushed over to Danny Molyneux, who looked thoroughly miserable dressed up as one of the three Wise Men.

"Daniel!" snapped the booming voice of his father. "Stop shuffling and concentrate! It's your line next."

For just a moment, the look on Danny's face said it all: his embarrassment, indignity and fury at the way James publicly badgered and bullied him. But then, in a flash, the sullen indifference returned, and he ambled as slowly as possible over to the spot where his father demanded he should stand.

Finding the whole thing too painful to watch, Neil took that as his cue to leave them all to it. As he was making his way back to the vestry to pick up the carol service programme for the next day his mobile rang. He didn't even have time to say hello before Graham's familiar voice shouted down the line.

"Neil, mate, it's a boy! I'm a dad!"

"Graham, that's absolutely great. Is he OK – and Debbie too?"

"They're both bloomin' marvellous. Debbie screamed her way through the whole thing, so we're not surprised to find he's got lungs to match his mum's!"

"Have you chosen a name yet?"

"Jacob. We both like that."

"Very biblical. Congratulations, all of you! Let me know when you want the baptism!"

Graham let out a roar of laughter. "You know, Neil, Jacob changes everything. I'm a dad! Me!"

"Does this mean your days on the Wheatsheaf darts team are numbered?"

"It just might, mate. It just might."

* * *

For the previous two years, the day of the nativity pageant had been miserable and wet, so there was relief all round when the big day this year dawned bright but very cold. Neil joined the construction team who gathered in the market square at the crack of dawn to erect the stable, build a makeshift stage, sort out the sound and lights, set up instruments and tuck into a mountain of bacon butties and hot tea miraculously produced by Beryl and Maria just at the point when the early risers were starting to flag with exhaustion.

By ten o'clock the performers were all in place, hidden in various shops and side alleys until they heard their respective cues. Several hundred onlookers had gathered around the set, vying to get a front row position so that not a moment of the much-loved occasion would be missed. As Neil gingerly

stepped up onto the compère's box to announce the start of
the pageant, he was glad to see Iris and Harry sitting monarch-
like in two comfy garden chairs in prime place at centre front.
He couldn't actually spot Claire, but he knew she was there
somewhere with Sam. The thought of them both warmed
him through in spite of the biting wind as the first performers
stepped forward to take their places.

The square was filled with magic. It settled like a soft blanket
around the people gathered there. The music, the children,
the carols, even the donkey which, having carried Mary to the
stable, promptly wandered off and had to be rescued from
the vegetable stall in the market where he'd developed a taste
for Brussels sprouts – the whole thing was inspirational. The
most magical moment of all came when Mary was revealed
cradling her new son, and a gasp of recognition went round
the crowd as they realized that Jesus was indeed a newborn
baby. Baby Jacob's mum, Debs, watched fondly from a few
yards away, while Graham had the video camera whirring to
make sure every second of his son's first taste of show business
was recorded for the family archive.

Towards the end of the performance Neil realized with
some surprise that Wendy was standing beside him. She was
looking straight out into the crowd, compelling him to follow
her eye line. What he saw made his mouth go dry. Claire was
now standing behind Harry's chair, her arm around Sam,
who was completely absorbed in the production. Claire wasn't
watching her son, though. She was gazing up at Ben, laughing
at something he'd just said. The intimacy of the moment, the
closeness of the three of them, the perfect family unit they
made together, hit Neil like a hard punch in the stomach.

Why hadn't he seen that coming? Why didn't he know?
He answered his own questions immediately. *Because I've been*

too busy with my own life to worry about what's happening in Claire's world. What a fool I've been!

"Do you want me to have a word with him?"

Neil turned to look at Wendy. He'd been so engrossed in his own thoughts that he'd almost forgotten she was there.

"Ben. He's staying with me. Should I say something? Get him to back off?"

"Er – no." Neil struggled to clear his thoughts. "It's nothing. We're fine. No need to say anything."

"OK," said Wendy. "But Neil, remember you and I have always been friends. I'm here if you need someone to talk to."

If he had intended to answer, the opportunity was lost: he had to mount the compère's podium again to wind up the performance and thank everyone who had taken part. Group by group he introduced them all, as the audience responded with rounds of delighted applause.

It was hard to be sure exactly what happened next. He had just announced Brian's name to thank him for his wonderful accompaniment. The organist started to get to his feet to take a bow, but somehow his chair got tangled up with the wire carrying power to his electronic keyboard. The falling chair thumped him in the back of the legs, and in a tumble of limbs, cables, chair and sheet music, he landed with a sickening thud on the cobblestones of the market square.

Wendy rushed over to help him up, but it was clear from his ashen expression that he was in a bad way.

"Oh my goodness!" breathed Peter Fellowes as his wife Val, a trained nurse, sped over to see if she could help. "Look at his arm! That looks really bad."

* * *

Brian's absence made the mood of the next day's services sombre. He was still in hospital waiting for a surgeon to be found on Christmas Eve to pin his badly broken shoulder back into place. He'd also suffered a break in his elbow and another just above his wrist.

"He's not going to be playing the organ for quite a while," mused Harry the next morning over a cup of coffee at Iris's when Neil popped in to see his mother.

"The thing is," added Iris with every ounce of drama she could muster, "will he *ever* be able to play the organ again?"

Neil knew they were only voicing the thoughts of the whole congregation. The day before Christmas Eve! What a time to lose their organist – *and* his wife who was the choir leader, *and* their daughter who ran the worship group as they were both looking after him. It was a disaster.

Into the breach had stepped the man who understood his duty and his excellent qualifications for the job. Once he'd offered, no one dared to raise any objection. James Molyneux wasn't everyone's favourite person after his domineering behaviour as producer of the pageant. In addition, he liked to play all hymns *very* slowly, or at the pace of a quick march! Many of the congregation members asked whether Clifford, well known as the flamboyant accompanist at the local crematorium, might be able to stand in, and Clifford himself was more than willing to help. In fact, he was absolutely delighted at the suggestion. But no one dared argue with James. He told them he would be taking over the role of organist for the foreseeable future, and that was that.

Neil was run ragged that day. This was partly because, for all ministers, Christmas Eve was traditionally the busiest day of the year – but for him that was truer than ever as he worked his way through the implications of suddenly losing the complete music team of St Stephen's at such a difficult time. By six o'clock he realized he hadn't eaten all day, so he switched off his phone and left the church, pleased that Claire had promised to cook a meal for everyone that evening. With all the drama of the previous day, he hadn't seen her for more than a few minutes after the pageant. He longed to hold her and tell her how much he adored her.

The door to Harry and Claire's house was slightly ajar when he reached there, and he pushed it open silently, charmed by the sound of Sam's giggles and laughter coming from the lounge. As he walked into the room, he was practically knocked off his feet by Sam whooping and squealing as he rode on Ben's back as if he were a horse. Claire was standing to one side by her mother, Felicity, both of them laughing out loud at the spectacle. The delight on Claire's face instantly changed when she spotted Neil. She seemed flustered, caught on the hop. Neil smiled warmly at her, and went straight over to put his arms around her and kiss her soundly.

"How's my darling girl? I've missed you so much!"

Claire returned his embrace for just a few seconds before she stepped back, seeming embarrassed at the show of affection with so many people watching. *With Ben watching*, Neil thought. *She's concerned because Ben is watching.*

"Dad's brought me a present. Look, Neil! He knew just what I wanted."

Sam tugged Neil's sleeve to guide him over to the conservatory at the back of the dining room. There, gleaming beside the twinkling Christmas tree, was a brand new bike, complete with an impressive set of gears, lights, alloy wheels and go-faster stripes.

"It's great, Sam. You'll go like lightning on that."

"Dad's going to take me out 'cos he's got a bike too. I want to go out with him tomorrow, but Mum says I can't, not on Christmas Day. What do you think, Neil? Can I go out with Dad?"

"Ah, that's your mum's call, I'm afraid. She's the boss."

Sam turned back to look longingly in Ben's direction. "But Dad'll be on his own. Can't he come here with us? He won't eat much, and we've got lots."

"Tell you what, Sam," interrupted Felicity tactfully. "I've got a secret I want to show you upstairs. Come with me a minute."

Sam could never resist secrets, so he disappeared upstairs with his grandmother without a backward glance. There was an awkward silence in the room before Ben spoke.

"Thanks, then, Claire. Thank your mum and Harry, too, for letting me see Sam tonight. Of course I won't disturb you tomorrow. You and Neil will want to spend Christmas Day together with the family."

"What will you be doing?" Claire couldn't resist asking.

"Wendy and I were going round to her parents' house for Christmas dinner, but obviously that's all changed now. They'll be spending most of the day at the hospital with Brian. I've offered to rustle up a meal for Sylvia and Wendy when they come back in the evening. That's the least I can do."

"Well, give them all our best wishes," said Neil, "and Merry Christmas to you, Ben. Can I show you out?"

≫ CHAPTER 6 ≪

For Neil, the weeks after Christmas felt a bit like the lull after a storm. Once the Christmas morning services were over in both St Stephen's and St Gabriel's, and he'd made calls to a few parishioners who couldn't get to the service themselves, it was after three before he finally arrived to join Claire and the family for a late lunch. Iris had been planning the meal for weeks, and Neil remembered with nostalgic affection how her Christmas offerings had always been a great treat at the end of the year. At last, replete with turkey, plum pudding and far too much festive punch, he collapsed in a heap against Claire's shoulder as the others all sat round trying to follow the James Bond movie on television over the sound of his snores.

The days that followed demanded much less from him in terms of work. Peter Fellowes had offered to take phone calls and generally keep an eye on things for the holiday period so the exhausted young curate could have a well-earned rest.

On the day after Boxing Day, Felicity and David insisted that Claire and Neil should get away from everything, and take themselves off somewhere nice. Feeling like naughty children skipping school for the day, the couple couldn't wait to bundle their walking boots and anoraks into the car and head off towards the Suffolk coast. It was a favourite area for them, because it seemed as if the march of time had passed it by. Hand in hand, they put their heads down against the biting east wind, their boots scrunching on the shingle beach. Then, making themselves comfortable on an old wooden bench in a shelter at the end of the deserted beach, they dug out their picnic and sipped cups of steaming coffee.

They sat there for some time, mesmerized by the waves as they battered the shore, peering at the seabirds squawking above them, and warmed by the thought that the cold wind whistling around the walls couldn't reach them as they cuddled together inside, Claire's head on Neil's shoulder.

"I have to ask you," Neil started carefully, "about Ben. He seems very pushy."

"Nothing I can't handle."

"Don't you feel he's crowding you a bit?"

"He's just impatient to establish a good relationship with Sam," she replied, keeping her eyes down as she gazed at their intertwined hands.

"Just Sam? Or is it really you he'd like a closer relationship with?"

"I'm Sam's mother. He will only ever be close to Sam if I allow it. Is it really surprising that he's working on me too?"

"You used to love him…"

"That was a long time ago."

"He's a good-looking guy, obviously fun to be with…"

"You used to love Wendy – and she's sticking her nose in far too much for my liking as well."

"We're friends. That's all."

"For you, maybe, but she's still after you. Whether that's because she loves you and wants you back, or because she hates you and wants to see you suffer, I really don't know – but don't be naïve about her, Neil."

"Nothing I can't handle."

"Inviting Ben over to stay with her, as if she had no idea of the trouble it would cause? Bringing him along to our engagement party?"

"Ben played his part in that too…"

"Yes, he did," retorted Claire, sitting up to look directly at him. "So what we have to do is to spell it out to both of them that we're a couple. They need to get the message loud and clear that we're strong together and committed to our love for each other."

"And let them handle that!" laughed Neil, hugging her tightly. "Oh, I do love you, Claire – but lately I know I've not told you enough, or shown you how much you mean to me. Nothing's more important than that. I adore you – and I can't bear the thought of anything coming between us. You do know that, don't you?"

Claire leaned forward until her lips met his in a kiss that was soft and lingering.

"I do, and you mustn't doubt even for a moment that I love you too, very much."

"But we've had so little time together. I'm really sorry…"

"You're busy. It's your job. I understand."

"It's only now, with Margaret gone. When we get a new rector…"

"… things will be different, I know. It's not your fault."

"And my curacy ends in July, so I can start applying now for a parish of my own, somewhere that we really want to be. We'll be married. We can settle into a house you choose…"

"… with a big garden?"

Neil grinned. "A *huge* garden, to keep your green fingers busy!"

"Not too busy for you, though…" Claire brushed her lips

across his again. "It has been hard, you know, with you being so distant recently. I've felt a bit adrift at times."

"And that's my fault, because I've let other things get in the way of what's most important. I spoke to Bishop Paul a few days ago. He said I should start applying now for any vacancy that looks interesting, especially if we want to be settled somewhere by the end of this summer."

"That sounds wonderful," sighed Claire.

"And he asked whether we'd set a date for the wedding yet."

"Did you tell him I've seen so little of you that I can hardly remember what you look like, let alone get round to planning a wedding with you?"

"I'm not going to let that happen any more. We need time just for us, time to be close, to share, to talk, to plan, to love one another…"

"You say that now, but is it possible? You *are* the only minister here. How *can* you stop? How *can* you take more time for yourself – for us?"

"I'll have to call on Hugh and Rosemary and any other retired or non-stipendiary ministers around who might be able to help me out a bit more. And I'll talk to both the bishop and the parish council to tell them in no uncertain terms that I need more help. They know it, really, but because I've seemed to manage so far, they're inclined to let me get on with it – and that's got to stop. I accept that this is my vocation rather than just a job, but I must get things into proper perspective. You're my priority: you, Sam and our life together. I'm better at anything I try to do as long as I have you by my side."

"Even if I can't sign up completely to the Christian God thing?"

"Faith is a journey, Claire. It was for me. I think it is for you too; one that started when Harry was so ill. Your journey may take you down a different path from mine. I understand that. I also recognize that you are the most sincere, warm-hearted, caring person I've ever known. What better qualities could a minister ask for in a wife?"

"That I'm also your idea of sex on legs, and you fancy me madly?"

Neil laughed. "That too. That's top of my list."

And caught up in passion and longing, it was a very long time before they emerged from the shelter, their arms wrapped tightly round each other as they walked. They were in love, they were together and, as a couple, they would face whatever the future brought their way.

* * *

"It's probably the wrong time to suggest this," Clifford began, when Neil arrived for a service at the crematorium a fortnight later.

"But you're going to mention it anyway," replied Neil.

"Seeing as the pageant was such a success at Christmas, apart from the very unfortunate and dramatic ending, of course…"

"And apart from the fact that you and James very nearly came to blows during rehearsals?"

"We're both artistic! True artistes will always have different opinions."

"Artistic? James Molyneux? He's a stiff-backed military man through and through – a trained killer!"

"Hardly," chuckled Clifford. "He conducted the band. He may have murdered a few melodies by playing them either at quick march or deathly slow, but unless the enemy had very sensitive ears, I think they were safe enough."

"Hmm." Neil was plainly not convinced where James was concerned. "What's your suggestion, then?"

"Well, I wondered if we might try something a bit more challenging? A variety show – you know, funny sketches, music-hall songs, dancing girls, speciality acts…?"

"Really?" asked Neil doubtfully. "Is there anyone at St Stephen's who can do stuff like that?"

"Of course, with the right direction and staging!"

"And that's you, is it?"

Clifford looked suitably offended. "Thirty years working in show business, from musical director to costume designer with everything in between – choreography, stage sets, lighting, sound systems. For heaven's sake, I can even do a mean time-step! Look!"

He leapt to his feet to glide and twirl around the back of the crematorium, his feet tapping with all the style of Fred Astaire. Neil couldn't help but laugh and finally applaud.

"Oh, I don't know, Cliff. Things are so unsettled at the church right now, what with Margaret gone, Brian out of action, me rushed off my feet and James trying to run everything. I think we've got enough on our hands at the moment."

"Precisely. The church is stuck in a rut of depression, just getting on with the bare minimum, when what's actually needed is something to stir up a bit of enthusiasm and galvanize people into action."

"And how's James going to react to that?"

"Who cares? It doesn't have to involve him. In fact, I hope he chooses to wash his hands of the whole idea and wait for us to fail – which we won't, of course…"

When Neil still looked extremely uncertain, Clifford went in for the kill.

"And it will be for a good cause: to go towards a new set of bells at St Stephen's. We've needed them for ages. That appeal's been going for as long as I can remember, and we've still only got a couple of hundred pounds in the coffers. Just think: we'll not only put more money in the kitty, but we'll get some fantastic publicity for the appeal too."

Clifford's face was as earnest and excited as that of a small boy trying to persuade his mum to let him have a bar of his favourite chocolate, and Neil couldn't help but laugh.

"Look," he said at last, "I'm not saying yes, but I'm not saying no either. When have you got in mind for this extravaganza?"

"We'll need a long run-up, and I'm not interested in doing it unless it ends up looking really professional. I was wondering about something like the end of May, perhaps over the bank holiday weekend?"

"Well, get the details down on paper and let the churchwardens and the other parish council members see it. If they agree, I've no objection. I just can't be involved myself – not with rehearsals or tickets or publicity – nothing! Claire and I will just come along and cheer loudly on the night."

"You two OK?"

Neil looked at him sharply. "Why do you ask?"

"No reason. Just not seen you together much recently."

"Well, we're just as concerned about that as you seem to be. That's why I've promised not to take on anything else when I'm supposed to be making more time for us."

Clifford's expression was touchingly serious. "Good idea. She's a great girl, Claire, perfect for you. You've not always had such good taste in women, as I recall."

Neil knew that Clifford had had a couple of musical tussles with Wendy in the past, and chose to change the subject.

"So write up your ideas for a variety show, and if everyone else agrees – and I have to do nothing more than buy a ticket – you're on!"

With a pirouette of delight, Clifford placed an imaginary top hat on his head and launched himself into his best time-step routine with all the dashing style of Fred and Ginger.

* * *

Audrey Baker always did her shopping on Wednesdays – she liked routine. Not that she particularly needed a routine these days. She had a great deal more time on her hands without the flowers at St Stephen's to worry about, but old habits die hard. She'd shopped on a Wednesday for all the years she'd been married to Barry. That day had suited her because, like most of the local high street retailers in north-west England at that time, she shut up shop at one o'clock sharp every Wednesday afternoon, and didn't put the key in the door again until eight o'clock the following morning. Barry was long gone now, of course. He'd been dead for fifteen years.

So, as usual, on Wednesday morning Audrey arrived at the supermarket behind the market square in Dunbridge, thankful to find it quiet as she hung her shopping bag on the hook at the back of her trolley. She always headed off in the same direction. She started at the far end so that she could follow her usual route down each and every aisle, taking her time to touch and compare, inspect and smell whatever took her fancy.

After she'd worked her way through Gardening, Clothes and Shoes, Kitchen, Bathrooms and Bedding, she turned her trolley down the Electrical aisle, thinking as she walked that it was unusually warm in the shop that day. By the time she'd reached Fresh Fruit and Veg, she had unwound the thick woollen scarf she had wrapped round her neck to keep out the January chill. It was as she walked past a display of make-up mirrors in the Pharmacy aisle that she caught sight of her own face; it seemed unnaturally flushed and shiny. Time to take off her outdoor coat, she decided. She unbuttoned her cardigan in the Pet Supplies area, and resolved as she turned into Cleaning Products to call in at Customer Services on the way out to suggest in the strongest possible terms that they stop wasting energy by keeping their heating at such a ridiculously high level. By the time she'd got to the Bakery section, the sweet aroma of freshly cooked bread and cakes suddenly made her feel slightly sick. Grabbing the steel support at the end of one of the shelf displays, she clung on tightly as the scene around her started to swim before her eyes.

"She's going down!" a distant voice seemed to say. "That lady over there. I think she's fainting..."

She tried to call out, to tell them she was absolutely fine and just wanted to be left alone, but the voices faded into the distance as she felt herself sinking down and down, the world darkening around her. And then there was nothing – no feeling, no time, no thought – until, out of nowhere, she gradually became aware that her senses were struggling to surface again. When she came to, she blinked uncomfortably at the glaring shop lights around her – and then, as her eyes started to focus, she realized with horror that she was now perched on a chair in the middle of an aisle surrounded by a gawping crowd of onlookers. Worse still, someone had their hand on the back of her neck, trying to force her head down in front of her.

"Come on, madam! Head between your knees! That will get the blood circulating properly again."

The young shop assistant was bending over her as he spoke so that her nose was practically squashed up against his *First Responder* badge. She felt a scream of pure panic bubbling up inside her.

"Stop that!" commanded a new voice with such authority that it made the ridiculously young first aider stand back abruptly. "Can everyone just move away so that the lady can have some air? Let her get her breath back."

"I'm sorry, madam, we have procedures..."

"And if we have any further need of those procedures, I will call on you. In the meantime, I will stay with my friend until she is fully recovered."

Audrey wanted to cheer with relief that at last someone had shown a bit of good sense. Bringing her head up as slowly as she dared, she turned to look gratefully at her rescuer.

"Don't worry, Audrey," said Pauline Walters. "You've got more colour already. Here, have a sip of this water. Take your time – and when you're feeling stronger, I'll sort out your shopping and get you home."

* * *

"All I'm saying, James," said Sue Molyneux, her voice rising in volume to make absolutely sure he had to listen, "is that Danny is not *you*. He's not been in the army for years – like you. He's not remotely interested in military music or playing the organ, because he's tone deaf – like me. He's not confident enough to be able to stand out in a crowd and feel comfortable – like you. He's a gentle, sensitive soul..."

"Like you?" snapped James. "Have you heard yourself lately?"

Sue grabbed her husband's arm with frustration as he strode down the church aisle away from her. "Oh no you don't! If you're any sort of man, or even a half-decent father, you'll listen to what I'm saying."

"I've got to sort out the music for tomorrow's choir practice."

"That takes you minutes, so do it later. You say you care about Danny, so prove it. Listen to what's happening to him before you drive him away completely."

"It's me who's being driven away by your constant whingeing and snivelling – just like your son!"

"*Our* son. He's *your* son, James, and he's falling apart under your endless rules and criticism. He's not one of your soldiers."

"Too bad. He'd have a bit of backbone if he were. But Daniel's too much of a mummy's boy for that. You've ruined him, Susan! He's a lazy, good-for-nothing wimp."

"He's bright and caring and artistic."

"So are most wimps I've ever met. That won't get him on in life. That won't give him a good living or make him a leader of men."

"To be like you, do you mean? A pig-headed, short-sighted, tunnel-visioned bully?"

"Susan, we will not agree on this, but I accept that, as a woman and a mother, your love for Daniel is so blind you simply aren't capable of seeing his faults and failings."

"And you *can*? You arrogant…"

"… which is why I intend to make a stand on this. Daniel is to knuckle down to his school studies in subjects that matter. There is no point whatsoever in him wasting time painting and drawing, or on useless subjects like drama or theatre studies, or whatever it is he's been sulking about. And what's all this rubbish about kitchen craft and catering? That's not a job for a *man*! What he needs is good grades in core subjects. Mathematics, English, history, science – that's what he should concentrate on, and that's what I intend to school him in."

"You can't teach him! It's years since you were at school, and the way things are taught now has changed beyond recognition."

"I shall teach him at home. He will study the subjects I choose. He will work for eight hours every weekday and four hours on Saturday. He will follow a regime of energetic exercise, which I will design for him. A healthy body, a healthy mind – that's what works. There's nothing at all healthy about that son of yours at the moment!"

"And what about *love*, James? What about loving him enough to listen to what *his* plans are for his life? Have you any idea at all what interests him? Do you know that he has an exceptional talent in fine art? Have you read any of his poetry? Do you know what a wonderful and imaginative cook he is?"

"You're turning him into a pansy, Susan, and I refuse to allow any more of this nonsense. That boy needs a firm hand – and he's going to get one."

"What Daniel needs is a father who isn't a blind, self-opinionated idiot."

James looked down at the furious face of his wife with patronizing disdain.

"Get out of my sight!" He spat the words directly into her face, before marching smartly out of the building.

* * *

"How's he doing, Blanche?"

"I can hear you, Neil," muttered Ernie from underneath the bedclothes. "She's the one who's as deaf as a post. I'm the one who's got cancer."

"What you saying, you daft old duffer?" Blanche smacked her husband's arm as if he were a naughty child. "The vicar's come to see you. Shall I get the nurse to use that motor thing on the back so you can sit up a bit?"

"I'll do it," offered Neil, working the handset at the side of the bed. "How are you feeling, Ernie?"

"Like I'm dying – and that's because I am."

"Don't talk like that, you rude old man. He's a man of the cloth. Behave yourself!"

"Are they giving you any treatment? What does the doctor say?"

"Not much. They're not interested in old blokes like me cluttering up the beds in here."

"I was chatting to the sister on this ward just before I came in," said Neil. "She seemed to think you might be moving from here soon."

"To the hospice," replied Ernie. "Best place for me if I'm dying."

"It'll be nicer there, you ungrateful man," grumbled Blanche. "You get your own room with a TV and your own toilet and bath. The food's good too, from what I hear."

"Don't need a telly. No good me watching any of those drama series. I'll have popped my clogs before I ever find out whodunnit!" And Ernie threw his head back and roared with laughter at his own joke.

"You see?" moaned Blanche in Neil's direction. "You see what I have to put up with?"

"Have you ever wondered, Vicar, why my wife never calls me Ernie? It's always *you daft old this*, or *you stupid old that*. That's because she forgot my real name years ago. She's probably forgotten hers too."

Neil held his breath waiting for an indignant reaction from Blanche, but to his surprise her eyes lit up with fun as she started to laugh even louder than her husband.

"You think we've lost the plot, don't you?" said Ernie, once the wheezing fit that followed his laughter had finally subsided. "But look, Neil, you're about to get married, aren't you? Let me tell you, man to man, the secret of a long and happy marriage. You got to laugh. Life's so hard at times, and if you can't laugh together, you'll never get through. Look at us after all these years. We lost our boy when he was ten; our house was flooded; I was made redundant three times. Blanche had to look after her invalid sister for years, and that was a thankless task 'cos she was a dreadful grump. And now I can't walk, she can't hear – but my girl's been bloomin' brilliant, in spite of what my mum said on the day I married her! I chose a good'un, that's for sure."

"Ah, shut up!" said Blanche, but her eyes were suspiciously shiny. Neil suspected her problem wasn't deafness at all, but selective hearing to suit her convenience.

"It was at the registry office, our wedding. Not long after the war. No money for wedding finery."

"I wore my mum's best suit, the one she wore for christenings and funerals," said Blanche, a faraway look in her eyes.

"And she was as pretty as a picture. No photos, because we didn't have a camera, but I can remember how she looked as if it were yesterday."

"So it was a civil ceremony?" asked Neil. "Weren't you both churchgoers, then?"

"Oh, yes," replied Ernie. "We met in the church choir."

"So didn't you want to say your vows in church?"

"We'd have liked that," agreed Blanche, "but that would have been a big affair, and my mum was a widow. We just couldn't run to it."

"Didn't matter though," added Ernie. "We said our prayers together that first night, and we've been saying our prayers together ever since."

At that moment, a bell rang to signify the end of visiting time.

"Take her home for me, will you, Vicar?"

"I'm not going yet," objected Blanche. "You won't eat a thing if I don't help you."

"I'm honestly not hungry, love. I'm tired. I'm going to sleep for a while. Come back in the morning when I'm feeling better."

"He doesn't eat!" Blanche turned her worried face to Neil. "He doesn't look after himself – and those nurses are far too busy to run round after a silly old man who won't accept help when it's offered."

"I'm going to the hospice soon," sighed Ernie, closing his eyes as Neil lowered the back of the bed and let him sink down into the pillow. "I'll be better then. Bye, Neil. Good night, sweetheart. God bless."

"And may the Lord bless you too, Ernie, and keep you in his eternal love," said Neil, laying his hand on Ernie's forehead.

The old man was asleep before Neil and Blanche had picked up their things and tiptoed away from the bed.

* * *

The first few days of her illness were little more than a fog to Audrey. She had a dim memory of coming round in the supermarket, and then, horror of horrors, that busybody Pauline Walters, of all people, being there to gawp at her in all her indignity and embarrassment. She remembered feeling helpless as she was pushed out into the car park in some sort of wheelchair and then helped into a car, but she had no idea whose car it was, or what had happened to her own vehicle. During one of her more lucid moments, she wondered if it was still at the supermarket.

But there were very few of those in those first confusing days. She had a vague recollection of waking up in her own bed with Dr Saunders beside her, leaning her forward so that he could listen to her chest. She had nightmare-like dreams in which she was hot and feverish, desperate to cool her parched throat, and then the impression that her head was being lifted so that she could swallow some cool water, gulp by painful gulp. There were pills slipped into her mouth too, and sticky sweet medicine that seemed to numb her throat a little. And there was the nurse, whose presence she was sometimes aware of, although she didn't see her face clearly. Perhaps there was more than one nurse? Just how ill was she?

Once, the rattle of raindrops on the window pane roused her from her sleep. The room was dark. Stiffly, she turned her neck to try and see the display on the clock radio beside her bed. It was twenty-past three in the morning. Minutes later, when she opened her eyes again, she could hear the familiar sound of children in the school playground just around the corner. Struggling to turn her head again to see the clock, she realized that there was now a note propped up against it.

"I called in about half-past eight this morning, but you were sleeping so peacefully I didn't like to disturb you. I'll pop back at ten. I hope you're feeling better. Regards, Pauline."

Pauline. Not Pauline Walters! Please God, not her!

She lay back against the pillows in exhaustion, but soon realized that she needed to visit the bathroom – something she couldn't remember doing for days. Gingerly, she pushed herself up so that she was sitting on the bed, then slid her feet towards the floor. Taking a deep breath, she pushed with her hands to give her the strength to rise. But as she tried to stand up, her knees buckled beneath her and she fell spreadeagled back on the bed. At that precise moment, she heard a key in the front door and the person she least wanted to see in all the world marched into her bedroom without a by-your-leave.

"Oh, Mrs Baker, let me help you. You've normally needed to hang on to my arm when you've wanted the bathroom. Here you are, now. I'll leave the door ajar in case you need me. Just let me know when you're ready to go back."

Sure enough, when Audrey emerged, Pauline was waiting for her again, supporting her as she made her unsteady way back to bed.

"I've brought you some soup. It's chicken. I made it myself, so I hope you like it. Don't worry if not."

In spite of herself, Audrey's nostrils twitched at the savoury aroma of the soup Pauline had put on a small fold-out table beside her bed. It must have been days since she'd eaten anything.

"And you've got to have your pills, of course. One of the red ones, and two of the little white ones. I've put them in a seven-day pill dispenser for you, over here on your cabinet where you can reach it easily. The medicine is three times a day after meals. This'll be the first proper food you've had, though."

Her hand trembling as she grasped the spoon, Audrey was loving every mouthful of the creamy soup.

"You look like you could do with a refill."

Audrey tried to speak, but there seemed to be something wrong with her throat.

"Your voice will come back, Dr Saunders says, but this awful flu bug seems to attack the throat and chest very severely. You've been really ill."

Audrey nodded wearily, knowing that was true.

"Look, I don't want to crowd you, but I do want to help. Tell me if I'm driving you mad and getting everything wrong – but if it's all right with you, I'll pop in again early this afternoon."

Audrey was too exhausted to argue, and shortly afterwards she heard the front door being shut. It must have been some time later, but the next thing she heard was the sound of her bedroom door being pushed open again. Pauline walked in with a tray bearing a china mug of tea, a flowery plate on which she'd arranged a boiled egg and soft bread soldiers, and a cheerful display of daffodils in a small porcelain jug. Smiling at Audrey, she put everything on the table while she helped the patient sit up, before gently leaning her back against the newly plumped pillows. Then she placed the tray carefully on Audrey's knees. Audrey gazed down at the array in amazement, her eyes drawn especially to the glorious golden petals bursting out of their tight green buds.

"I wanted to find something to cheer you up," said Pauline quietly. "It had to be flowers, didn't it? And I remember you saying once that these are your favourites."

Audrey felt something shift deep inside her – the unknotting of the tight ball of resentment that was starting to unravel itself.

"Thank you, Pauline," she whispered. "Thank you for everything."

❧ CHAPTER 7 ❧

"So where exactly do you want to live, then?" Iris's voice was tinged with impatience as she asked Neil about his plans for the umpteenth time.

"I keep saying, Mum. I'm not sure. It might be nice to stay in the diocese, because that's only fair. After all, they've gone to the trouble and expense of training me to the point where I can take over a parish myself. And we like this area. Claire's lived here for years. Her friends are here. You and Harry are here."

"What a sensible idea. Do that, then!"

"But…" Neil raised his voice a little in order to continue. "*But* after all the pressure of being responsible for the whole parish on my own over the last few months, I also quite like the thought of moving away somewhere completely different."

"Where? Somewhere near Bristol where you grew up?"

"Perhaps."

"But you've got no family there now. I moved over here to be where you are."

"Your choice, Mum, as I said at the time. It's lovely having you here, and great to see how well your back-to-back houses work between you and Harry, but I always said I'd have to move on from Dunbridge eventually."

"I'm not an idiot," retorted Iris. "I know you're not likely to stay in this town, but there are plenty of others nearby. The sensible thing would be for you to find something conveniently *near* Dunbridge."

"Well, I'm keeping my eye on that, and it does seem there might be an opening or two in the diocese. I'll talk to Bishop Paul about it."

"You do that."

"But I'm keeping an open mind at the moment, Mum. There are other places Claire and I might like to consider too."

"Well, at least Claire has a sensible head on her shoulders," snapped Iris, gazing out of the kitchen window in her customary habit of keeping an eye on the neighbours. Her scan of the scene stopped abruptly when it reached Neil's car. "Your car needs a wash!"

"You may not have noticed, Mum, but it's been snowing. Snow on the ground and grit on the roads make cars dirty. When it stops snowing, so I'm not completely wasting the small amount of spare time I have, I'll wash the car. Will that meet with your approval?"

She shrugged her shoulders dismissively. "Do you want a sandwich before you go?"

"I'm going to the Mayflower. They always feed me tea and cakes there."

"And you'll choose to eat that when you know sugar always goes straight to your waistline. For heaven's sake, have a proper ham sandwich with some decent salad!"

"I'm fine, thanks."

"It's no trouble. I've already made it, just in case you were hungry."

There was an uncharacteristic note of uncertainty in her voice. Neil realized suddenly that it really mattered to Iris that she still had a part, however small, to play in his life.

"Tell you what," he replied, putting an arm round her shoulder. "Would you mind wrapping it for me and I'll eat en route?"

"Well, don't blame me if you get indigestion," she said, opening the drawer to get out a sandwich bag. "Chew every mouthful *slowly*!"

* * *

Although Claire had steadily built up a list of private customers, her biggest garden maintenance contract was still for St Stephen's. She had been looking after the churchyard for three years now, and her programme of pruning and planting was beginning to make a real difference. In spite of the cold February weather, bright patches of snowdrops and crocuses were already starting to appear along the pathways, and she knew that the beds would soon be bursting with colour from daffodils and tulips.

She was cutting back one of the shrubs behind the church hall when a movement caught her eye, somewhere in the middle of a group of gravestones to her left. She carefully laid down the blade she was using, and peered over to see a wisp of smoke rising from behind one of the large raised family tombs. Silently, she crept over to investigate.

"Danny!"

The teenager jumped at the sound of her voice, visibly relaxing when he saw it was only Claire.

"I thought you were Mum."

"And I thought you were a tramp. Aren't you frozen, sitting there?"

"Yes."

"So…?"

"It's still better than home."

With a nod of understanding, Claire pulled down her anorak so that she could sit on it, then lowered herself to perch beside him.

"Dad?"

"He's a monster."

"Hard to live with, eh?"

"Impossible."

"And Mum? Do you get on with her?"

"She tries. I know she sticks up for me, but he won't listen. He never listens."

"Anything in particular – or are you just generally unhappy?"

"He's only been down to the school and told them I'm leaving. He reckons what I need is home teaching."

"From him?"

"Just because he likes the sound of his own voice, he reckons everyone else needs to hear it too. But the best thing about a good teacher is that they know how to *listen* as well."

Claire nodded with understanding. "And your dad isn't known for that."

"It's the subjects too. I know I've not put much effort into maths and English lately, but I will before my GCSEs – of course I will. What Dad doesn't get is that I'll do best in the subjects that really interest me."

"Like?"

"You won't laugh?"

"Listen, I'm a gardener. Can you imagine what happened when I told my careers officer at school that was what I wanted to do? No, whatever it is, I definitely won't laugh."

"I like cooking. I want to be a chef."

"Well, there are some great chefs on television nowadays. They've made a real success out of that profession. And as long as people get hungry, there'll always be a need for professionals who can cook well."

"Exactly!"

"Your dad doesn't agree?"

"He doesn't listen long enough to let me tell him that's what I want to do."

"And now he's taken you out of the school system completely?"

"No chance of getting a GCSE in catering now, is there!"

"Have you spoken to the staff at school; told them how you feel?"

"Yes, and my form tutor tried to talk to Dad, but he just told her she was a disgrace because she obviously had no idea what was needed to get jobs in the real world."

"Oh, for heaven's sake…"

Danny fell silent as he took another drag on his cigarette.

"So if you're not going home, where are you living?"

"Anywhere except with him. I'm going over to my mate's for a bit. He's at school now, though, so I can't go there till later."

"And your parents don't actually know where you are?"

"I bet all hell let loose when he found out I wasn't sitting at the table waiting for him to give me my first maths lesson this morning."

"Would you like me at least to ring your mum? I've got her mobile number on my phone, I think."

"If she knows and doesn't tell him, it'll only cause more trouble for her. And if she does tell him, he'll be right over here, won't he! No. Thanks for the offer, but I'd rather you didn't ring her, even though I don't like the thought of her worrying."

"Well, how about you waiting in the church hall for a while, then? The playgroup kids have all gone now, so it should be empty till it's time for you to go round to your mate's house. I'm pretty sure there's a nice full biscuit tin in the kitchen cupboard, and milk in the fridge if you fancy making yourself a hot drink."

"You don't think Neil'll mind?"

"Not at all. He'd be pleased to know you're not freezing your socks off on this icy ground. Come on. I've got the key in my work bag over there."

And with what could almost have been a smile, Danny got stiffly to his feet and followed her over to the gate that led towards the hall.

* * *

At that moment, Neil was on his way to visit the son of an elderly lady who had died a couple of days earlier. He found the house quite easily, in the middle of a large council estate not far from the centre of Dunbridge.

"Mr Jones?" he asked as the door was opened by a stocky, forty-something man, casually dressed in track-suit bottoms and what was obviously a favourite old T-shirt.

"That's right, Vicar. Come on in."

Mr Jones padded ahead in his socks towards the living room. Every seat and surface was covered with papers, children's toys and dirty crockery. He picked up armloads of children's clothes which might have been destined for the washing machine, or perhaps had just been rescued from it, before gesturing to Neil to take a seat.

"Cup of tea?"

Eying the row of grubby mugs abandoned on the coffee table, Neil decided to decline.

"So, Mr Jones…"

"Call me Alan, please."

"I have a copy of the service plan you drew up with the undertaker, and that all seems perfectly in order. I gather that you'd prefer me to give the eulogy, rather than a member of the family. It would be helpful to know more about your mother, so I know what you'd like me to say."

Alan got to his feet and started to rummage among the papers in one of the sideboard drawers.

"Hold on! I've already written something. Ah, here it is."

The text was hard to decipher because of the spindly, uneven handwriting but, making a few notes in the margin, Neil finally reached the end.

"That looks fine. All the details about her early life, meeting your dad, and the family are really useful. You've put some humour in it too, which is good. It sounds as if she was a really lovely lady."

Alan's eyes filled. "Oh, she was. Always there for us, ready with everything from a cooked meal to a cuddle. Had a heart of gold, did our mum."

"And your sister, Delia? Will she want to add anything to this?"

"I don't think so. She seemed happy enough to leave all the arrangements to me."

"Does she live in the area?"

"Next door to Mum. Very handy for keeping an eye on her all those years when she was ill."

"And no one else in the family wants to say anything at all – a poem or a reading perhaps?"

"I don't think so. We're not that type of family really."

"Fair enough."

"She's a bit cold, my sister. Not emotional like me. That's why I wanted to make sure I told you what to say in the tribute. You've got to mention what a lovely, kind-hearted lady she always was. Say about her being a good mum and how she looked after my dad. Would never harm a fly. Great with the grandchildren. Always got a good word for everyone – that sort of thing. You know the score."

"I think so," agreed Neil. "The service is at the crematorium next Wednesday, isn't it? I'll take a proper look at these notes and get something finished for you to check by the end of the week, if that's OK."

On the way back to the church, he had to drive past Blanche and Ernie's house, so decided to pop in on the off-chance that Blanche might be in. She was. She bustled to the door in her carpet slippers, insisting on putting the kettle on and placing a large slab of fruit cake on a plate before him.

"Ernie's going to the hospice any time, they told me," she said. "They're not sure when. I suppose they've got to wait for someone to die before they've got a bed to give him."

"Not necessarily, Blanche. Lots of people go into the hospice just to get a bit of rest and specialist care before they go home again. It doesn't always mean the worst."

"It does for Ernie, though. I'm going to lose him, aren't I?" Tears welled up in the rheumy old eyes. "After all these years. It'll be our sixty-third anniversary on the twentieth of next month. We won't be having any more."

"Ernie said the other day that your son died when he was very young. Did you go on to have other children?"

"We'd have liked to. It never happened, though."

"So are there any other family members nearby?"

"None. We've outlived them all. There was only my sister, who was an invalid most of her life. She died about twenty-five years ago. Ernie had a brother who lived up north somewhere, but they were never close, so we didn't really know his children and never kept in touch after he passed away."

"So we need to be thinking about your future, too, Blanche, if Ernie's too ill to be at home with you."

"You mean Ernie's going to die, so how am I going to manage here on my own? Well, the answer is that I won't manage at all. It's not just that he's always done so much around the place. The thing is I couldn't live in this house if he wasn't in it, laughing, throwing things at the telly, making a mess everywhere. I always told him what an awful man he was to live with, but we both knew I didn't mean it."

"Would you like me to have a word with a social worker to see if they have any suggestions about where your home might be after this?"

"No need."

"Really?"

"All our lives, wherever Ernie and I go, it's together. When he dies, I don't intend hanging around a day longer than I have to. Oh, don't look so shocked, Neil. I'm not going to do anything stupid. I'm just going to stop wanting to live. I'm ready to die anyway. I'm old. I ache. I'm well past my sell-by date. When my Ernie goes, I'll just go too."

* * *

They sat on the bench at the side of the playground watching Sam, who was totally engrossed in the challenges of the large, intricate climbing frame. Claire didn't quite know why she was there. After the cinema trip, she'd made a point of turning down any offers Ben made for her to join him in his time with Sam. But then today she'd not been able to get out to work because of constant rain from early in the morning, and he happened to ask her just as the first shaft of sunlight broke through the clouds. She was stir-crazy. A bit of fresh air would do her good. What harm could it possibly do if she went along to the playground with her son, and his father happened to be there too?

"This is the first time you and I have been alone in years," said Ben.

"You being on the other side of the world would be the main reason for that."

"Have you ever wondered – if you hadn't got pregnant, if everything had stayed less complicated – what would have happened to us? Would we have stayed together, do you think, or would we have broken up anyway?"

Claire thought about the question for a while before replying.

"I was so much in love with you. I couldn't imagine a future without you in it."

"Even though you knew I was only visiting, and that my home was in Australia?"

"I suppose I just put that out of my mind. You became such a part of my world here in Dunbridge, I couldn't imagine you not belonging here always."

"And if we'd stayed together, do you think you could have left Dunbridge and come over to try living in my world?"

"Yes, I think so. You were my home. Provided you were with me, I'd have gone anywhere."

"I remember feeling the same."

"Hardly. You left, didn't you, without a backward glance?"

"I admit I panicked. I was getting a lot of pressure from the parents – mine and yours, if you remember. Mine had been wanting me to go back for ages. They thought I was just swanning around on an extended holiday, and it was time I got back and sorted my life out. And yours were obviously very supportive of you. They were trying to be fair, I remember, but they really weren't sure if they thought I should stay and do my duty as a father, or if they just wanted to get rid of me because I came across as too much of an idiot to be any real help to you. And from the start, you made it clear that an abortion was out of the question. At the time, the thought of the whole problem going away seemed like a good one to me, but now I'm glad you felt that way. It was just a mess – an emotional, frightening mess – and I admit I did just run away and leave you to it. It was an unforgivable thing to do, and I don't blame you for being bitter and angry with me. I deserve it all."

Claire said nothing, her eyes fixed on Sam as he clambered over the climbing frame, her thoughts plainly in turmoil.

"I'm sorry, Claire. I'm very sorry I hurt you, that I betrayed my love for you, and abandoned you and Sam. From the bottom of my heart, I'm so sorry."

Still Claire was silent.

"If all I achieve on this trip is to convince you how much I mean that, that'll be worthwhile in itself. There's much more I could say, though."

"Don't!" Claire turned to look at him then. "Please don't."

"I love you, Claire. You're the only woman I've ever truly loved – and seeing you with Sam now, getting to know you both, I realize what a treasure I've lost."

"You have lost us, Ben. I'm engaged to Neil. We're already a family."

Ben nodded sadly. "OK. I know that. I just can't accept it without letting you know you also have another option. We could be a family too, the family we always should have been. Sam is *our* son. Nothing will ever change that."

"Neil's a good man."

"I can see that, but I still can't really see you with him. He's a vicar! That's not you at all. How's that going to work, Claire?"

"It works. That's all you need to know."

"No, it isn't. If he's going to take on the role of being a father to my son, then I need to know your relationship with him will work and that being with him will make you truly happy. It wouldn't be right to build a life for Sam with Neil in it unless you're absolutely sure you're going to stay together. You owe Sam that."

"Don't you dare tell me what I *owe* Sam! And you have no business questioning what Neil and I feel for each other. We're engaged. We feel enough to know we want to spend our lives together. Neither of us is capable of making such an important decision lightly. It's a measure of the depth of our love that we want to be partners for the rest of our lives."

"And do you feel passion for him, Claire? The passion we felt when we couldn't keep our hands off each other? When all we wanted was to be together every moment of the day? The urgency we felt to show love and feel love and make love? Have you ever felt anything to compare with that? I haven't. And if you don't feel that for Neil, you've no business marrying him, because once you've known that sort of passion, you'll always long for it. Have you got that with him, Claire? Have you?"

Claire turned away, unable to speak. Ben, too, fell silent. So many thoughts, not enough words to express them.

"Would you prefer me just to go home?"

"I don't know. I don't know what I want."

"Then there's something I need to ask you, but only if you promise to give me a completely honest answer."

She sighed heavily.

"Now we've met again, don't you find yourself remembering what it used to be like between us? All the love and passion we felt? Could you ever feel that again?"

Claire didn't answer. Her head drooped, and clasping her hands in her lap she slowly leaned over as if she were in pain.

When Ben reached across to take her hand in his, she didn't resist. And when he laid his head against hers, she did nothing to stop that either. They just sat there, the two of them, watching their son as the pale winter sunshine finally faded and the gloom of evening fell around them.

* * *

Neil arrived at the crematorium in good time for Mrs Jones's service the following Wednesday. Clifford was already there, having played for two other services that morning.

"I've had a good response to my note in the church magazine about volunteers for the variety show. Who would have thought there was so much talent in Dunbridge?"

"Really? You've got your chorus line, have you?" grinned Neil.

"And a harmonica player, and a couple of good comedians, and a magician who says he doubles as an escapologist."

"Have you checked our insurance on that one? What happens if he doesn't escape?"

"This is variety. Maybe, in his act, he's not supposed to. You'll just have to wait and see."

"Vicar!"

Neil looked up with surprise to see Alan Jones striding up towards them, his face stern.

"Hello, Alan. You did get the copy of the tribute I've written for your mum, didn't you? I dropped it through your letterbox on Friday. I assumed it was all OK as I've not heard from you."

Alan's expression was stony. "You can forget anything nice I ever told you about her, Vicar. I just seen the will. My daft old bat of a mother has left the whole lot to that conniving sister of mine. Just tear her tribute up and chuck it in the bin! And as for her funeral, I certainly won't be coming."

* * *

Neil had noticed how quiet Claire had been over the past few days. She seemed distant, preoccupied with her own thoughts. Several times he asked her if she was all right, but she simply smiled and said she was probably a bit tired.

And then, when they were washing up together one evening, she suddenly turned to him and begged him to hold her tight. He put his arms around her, kissing her hair, whispering in her ear how much he loved her.

"We will be all right, won't we?" Her voice sounded almost childlike. "We will make this work? We are sure enough of how we feel?"

Neil gently pushed her away from him then so that he could look into her eyes.

"Of course we are. There is so much love here, my darling, deep and true. No doubt about that. We're a perfect fit, you and me: two parts of a whole."

She smiled at the thought.

"It's all a bit daunting, isn't it, launching out on a new life together," he whispered, his eyes not leaving hers, "but you are my whole world. I adore you. I need you. I want you…"

He kissed her then, deep and satisfying, until they broke away breathless.

"That's all right, then," she said, winding her arms around his neck. "Would you mind doing that again, just so that I'm absolutely sure?"

≈ CHAPTER 8 ≈

*I*t was some weeks before Audrey felt she was anywhere near regaining her usual energy. It had been the worst bout of flu she could ever remember. Pauline had been a constant help throughout, not outstaying her welcome, but popping in whenever she was passing to drop off a flask of home-made soup, some fresh bread and milk and, every now and then, a small bunch of flowers to bring spring into the house, until Audrey felt strong enough to venture out herself.

Neither woman would say that they'd struck up an instant friendship. Pauline was acutely aware of the animosity Audrey had previously felt towards her, and Audrey remembered with some embarrassment the vitriol and bitterness she had shown at a time when she neither knew nor cared about Pauline at all. Getting to know each other, day by day, was a revelation to them both. They discovered that they were both in their early sixties. They were both widows, although Pauline remembered Ken with the deepest love, while any love Audrey had felt for her husband Barry had been eradicated when he betrayed her by leaving his half of the flower shop to two sons he'd never bothered to mention. Perhaps the most hurtful part of that betrayal was that although she'd always longed for children of her own, Barry had made it clear that he had no interest in being a father. No wonder! He already was a dad – one who had apparently walked out on his young family and then had a fit of conscience years later, with devastating implications for her, his loyal wife of almost thirty years.

"No wonder you were so angry," said Pauline when Audrey told her the whole story. "Something like that would make it difficult to trust anyone ever again."

"You're right," agreed Audrey. "I loved Barry. I worked hard at that shop because it was a future for both of us. He didn't get involved with it, really. It was all mine in terms of building up the business, but in my mind it was for the two of us, so we could retire comfortably together some day."

"He must have been quite young when he died."

"Only fifty; two years older than me. He was as fit as a fiddle, an engineer in a local tool company. Then one morning I woke up – and he didn't. He'd died lying in the bed beside me, and I never even realized."

"What a terrible thing for you to go through."

"Yes, it was terrible, coming out of the blue like that. But the real shock came when his will was read, and I realized the man I'd woken up beside for all those years was someone I didn't really know at all."

"And then to lose the shop…"

"I'll never forget turning the key in the door for the last time. That place had been my dream, my life's work."

"What made you come down here?"

"The only family I had was a much older sister living in Bedford, so I decided to head down this way and get as far away from my life with Barry as I possibly could. When this bungalow came up in Dunbridge, I'd never even heard of the place. It's been my salvation, though. I've found peace here over the years."

"And purpose too, at St Stephen's?"

"I hadn't been a churchgoer since I was young. Life got busy, and I just drifted away, as you do. But down here, with no job and no friends, I found myself wanting to go to church again. It felt familiar and reassuring after all the change I'd been through."

"What about your faith over the years? Was that still important to you?"

"At the time, I'd have said no. But that first Sunday morning when I sat at the back in St Stephen's, it felt like coming home. I couldn't wait to go again the following week. I might have drifted away from God over the years, but it seems he never let go of me."

"And then you owned up to your amazing talent with flowers?"

"We're talking about more than fifteen years ago now. It was all a bit hit and miss when it came to flowers in St Stephen's then. If there was a wedding, they'd organize a display or two. Sometimes there'd be floral arrangements left after a funeral too, but generally we didn't have flowers in the church much at all."

"So you decided to do something about it?"

"I had a word with the vicar – it was Victor Brooks then, the minister who retired before Margaret came here – and he just said that if it interested me, I should get on with it!"

"And you've been getting on with it ever since?"

"With occasional help from a few others – but yes, mostly I've done it on my own."

"Then I come along, the little upstart that I am, and disrupt everything!"

"You didn't really. Actually your displays were very good." Audrey gave a slightly embarrassed smile. "That's probably why I was so hard on you. I could see you snapping at my heels wanting to take over."

"Honestly," laughed Pauline, "that really was never my intention."

"I know. I can see that now. I'm sorry, Pauline. I behaved very selfishly towards you, and all you've done is repay me with kindness."

Pauline stretched out her hand to place it over Audrey's.

"We're both Christians. We're taught to turn the other cheek, to treat others as we would like to be treated ourselves..."

"To love our enemy!" finished Audrey. "That's what I must have seemed to you. It was unforgivable of me."

"Not just forgiven but forgotten," replied Pauline. "And actually, I want to ask you a favour."

"Ask away!"

"You were absolutely right when you said I'm nothing but an amateur when it comes to flowers. I've worked in the business, but not like you. I was head of admin in the back office of a wholesale flower warehouse. We sold all the stock that shops like yours ordered, but it was boring. What I really wanted was the chance to learn about flowers and how to arrange them, as you were probably doing every day. I envy you – you've spent your life being artistic, creating displays that really move people. I've been trying to pluck up courage to ask you whether you would teach me a little. I know I'll never have flair and talent like yours, but I'd like to learn the basics properly from someone who really knows and understands flowers. Would you help me – please?"

The small smile on Audrey's face became a warm, welcoming beam. "Let's start right now! March is a wonderful month for gardens. Everything's springing into life. Let's take a look and see what we can find to work with."

* * *

"Neil! Great news!" Cyn's voice shrieked from the telephone handset. "Jeannie had her baby late last night – a boy!"

"Oh, thank God! And he's well? Jeannie too?"

"He arrived in the world bawling his head off and he's done nothing but eat and sleep ever since. He's perfect, Neil. Perfect in every way."

"Has he got a name yet?"

"Jamie. Officially it's James after my Jim, but he'll be Jamie from the start."

"Please give Colin and Jeannie my very fondest love, and tell them the whole congregation's looking forward to meeting the newest member of the St Stephen's family."

"Thanks, Neil. I'm heading back to the hospital now, so would you mind mentioning the news to a few well-placed gossips – like Beryl, Clifford, Boy George and your mother? That'll save me an awful lot of phone calls!"

Still chuckling as he replaced the phone, Neil was surprised when it immediately rang again.

"Hello, Neil," said a voice he instantly recognized as belonging to Mike Heald, the head of nursing at the local hospice. "I'm glad I've caught you."

"Is everything OK?"

"Not for Ernie Perkins, I'm afraid. He's going downhill faster than we anticipated. I know how close you are to him and Blanche, so I thought you'd like to know. She could do with a bit of support."

"Right, I'll come straight away. Actually, I've been meaning to ring you. I'd like to make a suggestion to Ernie and Blanche, but want to talk it over with you first."

* * *

As a result of that conversation between Neil and Mike, and a subsequent discussion with Blanche and Ernie, a very special group of people gathered around Ernie's bedside a day and a half later. Peter and Val Fellowes were there, as well as Cyn Clarkson and her husband Jim. Some of their oldest friends were there too – Boy George, Harry, who'd been brought along by Claire, and Iris, who was never one to miss a drama.

Ernie was propped up against the pillows, very smart in a new set of pyjamas, although his face was pale and drawn, exhausted by the ravages of the cancer that would shortly claim his life. True to character, though, he was smiling – not only to welcome his friends, but also at Blanche, who looked very sweet in a pale pink suit. On her lapel was pinned a deep red rose to match the buttonhole attached to Ernie's pyjama jacket.

Clearing his throat, Neil began.

"As we all know, Ernie and Blanche were married sixty-three years ago. Back then they weren't able to have a church wedding, because the whole celebration would have cost more than they could afford. However, they are both lifelong Christians who, every day of their marriage, have lived out their faith together. And so today, surrounded by friends who love them and in the presence of God, they are going to renew their vows using the Christian words they were not able to say all those years ago."

Iris reached up her jacket sleeve for her hankie and daintily dabbed her nose.

"We have come together," continued Neil, "in the presence of God to give thanks with Ernie and Blanche for sixty-three years of married life, to rejoice together and to ask for God's blessing. As our Lord Jesus Christ was himself a guest at the wedding in Cana of Galilee, so through his Spirit he is with us now. Marriage is a gift of God in creation and a means of his grace; it is given that a husband and wife may comfort and help each other, living faithfully together in times of need as well as in plenty, in sadness and in joy, in sickness and in health. In marriage a couple belong together and live life in the community; it is a way of life created and hallowed by God, that all should honour. Therefore we pray with them that, strengthened and guided by God, they may continue to fulfil his purpose for their life together."

Neil gestured then to Ernie and Blanche to read from the card he'd prepared in extra-large print and laid where they could both read it on the bed in front of them.

Ernie began, taking Blanche's small hand in his as he spoke. "I, Ernie, took you, Blanche, to be my wife."

Shaking with emotion, Blanche looked straight into Ernie's eyes as she replied, "I, Blanche, took you, Ernie, to be my husband."

And hardly glancing at the card, they said together the familiar words they knew so well:

> *"To have and to hold from that day forward,*
> *For better, for worse, for richer, for poorer,*
> *In sickness and in health, to love and to cherish,*
> *Till death do us part.*
> *This is our solemn vow."*

No one spoke or moved, all held in the private moment shared by the old couple as they looked at each other with love, joy and infinite sadness reflected in their eyes.

"Will we," asked Neil, "the family and friends of Ernie and Blanche, continue to support and uphold them in their marriage now and in the years to come?"

"We will," was the assembled response.

"Heavenly Father," said Neil, "may Ernie and Blanche know the risen Christ with them now, as they celebrate this covenant together. We ask for your blessing on them both as they face the challenge of Ernie's illness. Comfort them. Protect them. Love them. We pray that you will make them strong in faith and love, defend them on every side, and guide them in truth and peace. And may the blessing of God almighty, the Father, the Son, and the Holy Spirit, be with you, Ernie and Blanche, now and always. Amen."

In the emotion-charged silence that followed, Neil felt Claire's hand slip into his, and he turned to draw her to him.

Then, slowly and painfully, Ernie leaned across to place the softest of kisses on his wife's lips – and as her tears fell across his cheek, someone started clapping, until the round of applause and cheers became deafening.

* * *

Later the next day, Ernie died with Blanche's hand still clasping his. She was surprisingly calm at the end, and having touched his face and stroked his hair one last time, she asked Neil to take her home. Cyn stayed with her that evening, making sure she was comfortably tucked up in bed before she left. The following morning, she popped in again.

Blanche was still lying in bed, her long silver hair spread out across the pillow. She was smiling. At least it seemed that way – even though, somewhere in the night, life had seeped away from her. She was with her beloved Ernie. She had said they always went everywhere together. And she was right.

* * *

The joint service for Blanche and Ernie was one of the saddest and also one of the most joyful funerals Neil had ever conducted. Although it was held on a weekday afternoon, St Stephen's was packed – a measure of the popularity of the elderly couple who had endeared themselves to so many.

"Blanche and Ernie were an example to us all," said Neil during his sermon. "They showed us what love should really be: a reflection of the love of God himself. From the moment they met, they lived out their Christian faith. They read the Bible together every day. They prayed together morning and night. Whatever happened, happened to them both – the good times and the bad, and they certainly had their share of tough times. But they saw the positive in every experience, the best in each other, the best in the people they met, and God in everything around them. And one of the most wonderful of their many blessings was their love of laughter. They laughed *at* and *with* each other every day of their lives. And now, just as they were together in life, they are also together in death; exactly as they wanted."

Mr Whalley, the undertaker, was in tears by this point, although he certainly wasn't alone. Hankies were out to dab damp eyes in every corner of the building.

Finally the crowd followed the two coffins out to the corner of the graveyard that the couple had chosen many years before as their final resting place. Ernie always said that he and Blanche had been part of the congregation at St Stephen's for nearly six decades, and they really didn't fancy leaving. It had been their spiritual home on earth, so they wanted it to be a worldly home for their bodies once their spirits had gone to heaven.

A dull greyness filled the sky as Ernie and Blanche were lowered into the ground in the shadow of an oak tree that

Blanche had once said looked like Ernie's face because it was so old and battered. And as Neil said the prayer of committal, he didn't know whether what he felt most was sadness to be losing them, or happiness that Ernie was no longer in pain and was reunited with the love of his life.

As soon as Neil was finally free to leave, Claire and he walked hand in hand down Vicarage Gardens, warmed and inspired by the events of the previous few days. In Ernie and Blanche they had seen the love they prayed would be theirs throughout their marriage, and that vision made everything seem more urgent. They couldn't stop talking about their plans: when they would marry, who would be there, what they wanted to say in their vows to each other. They talked about the home they would build together, the family they'd have, the lifelong commitment and devotion they promised to each other.

As they turned into the gate of Harry's house, Sam came running out to greet them.

"Oh, you're holding hands! You like holding hands, don't you, Mummy? You were holding hands with Daddy when he took us to the playground the other day, and you put your heads together like you were having a cuddle. Were you having a cuddle with Daddy? I think you were because he's always saying he loves you. And you love him too, don't you! I can tell."

Claire immediately looked at Neil, her eyes full of pleading. "Neil, let me explain. It isn't what it sounds."

Neil gazed at her blankly before pulling his hand away from hers. "I have a feeling," he said sadly, "that's exactly what it is."

* * *

Neil knew that Wendy always arrived early for the Thursday night worship group rehearsal: she liked to arrange the church hall, sort out the music stands and think through what items they needed to rehearse. He glanced in through the window and was glad to see that she was alone.

"Are you busy? Got time for a quick chat?"

If seeing him was a surprise, it was clear from Wendy's expression that it was a pleasant one.

"Of course. No one'll be here for another quarter of an hour. Shall I make coffee?"

"Not for me. I'm fine."

She eyed him carefully. "You don't look fine."

"A bit tired, I expect. It's a pretty relentless schedule at the moment."

"No news about someone to replace Margaret as rector, then?" she asked as she pulled up a couple of chairs and gestured for him to take a seat.

"Bishop Paul says these things take time. I'm not sure they've even advertised the post yet."

"That's probably because you're making such a good job of holding the fort."

"I'm not, though, am I? I'm a curate. I'm still training. There's so much I don't know. Most of the time I feel completely out of my depth."

"If you are, you hide it well," she smiled. "But I've shared so much with you in the past. I know having confidence in yourself has always been difficult for you."

"For good reason. I'm very aware of my shortcomings. I still hate giving sermons, although I've worked out that the trick is to do my homework and have everything prepared in advance so I know exactly what I'm doing. And I'm still not good at thinking on my feet. I wonder if I ever will be."

She leaned in towards him. "Of course you will. You're doing really well. Everyone says so."

He gave a wry grin. "Hardly!"

"No, really they are. In fact, lots of people in the congregation are very worried about what'll happen when you take up a new parish. You can do that later this year, can't you, when your three years are up?"

"Yes, I've been thinking quite a bit about that."

"What does Claire think? Is she happy to move to a new area?"

When Neil didn't immediately answer, Wendy looked at him quizzically.

"Trouble in paradise?"

"Not really. At least, I hope not."

"I'm a good listener, Neil, if that helps. All part of my teacher training."

"There's probably nothing to say. It's just Ben."

"Ah," she said. "I understand."

"Do you? I mean, what's he doing here? He's still living at your place, isn't he? Does he talk to you? What exactly is he up to?"

"He says he wants to get to know his son, do the decent thing and be a proper father to him at last."

"And, of course, that's the right thing for him to do. I accept that. I don't like it – or him – but I can see that's what he should be doing."

"And he's happy in Dunbridge. He's got a job at that big garage now, so he's settling in quite well."

"For how long, though? He is planning to go back to wherever he came from, isn't he? Preferably very soon?"

"He hasn't said much about that lately."

"But surely his life is there! His work prospects must

be better in a big city in Australia than here in sleepy old Dunbridge."

"If work was all he cared about, you're right. But he knows his heart wouldn't be in it."

Neil nodded. "Because his heart is here with Sam…"

Wendy finished the sentence for him: "… and with Claire."

When Neil didn't reply, she picked her words carefully before continuing.

"But Claire loves you. She's your fiancée. Why should what Ben wants matter to her? Or to you?"

Neil shook his head, his expression troubled.

"It matters to you," she went on, "because something's making you question her loyalty. Am I right?"

"I don't know. I really don't know what to think. She behaves differently when he's around. I can see they must have been good together in the past. I mean, just look at him. He's handsome, he's good with Sam, he charms the socks off Harry and Claire's mum. What is there *not* to like? Why wouldn't she find herself falling under the spell of a man like him? After all, he was obviously the great love of her life last time he was here. Why shouldn't he be again?"

Wendy didn't bother to contradict him, but Neil was too full of his own thoughts to notice.

"And look at me," continued Neil. "I'm hardly God's gift to women, am I?"

"I always thought so."

"Put Ben and me up together, and who would you choose?"

Wendy said nothing.

"Of course she'll choose him. He's the father of her son. For Sam's sake, they *should* be a family. And Claire is the most honourable person I've ever met. She would want to do the right thing. I know she would."

"Even if it hurts the man she's promised to marry? That doesn't sound very honourable to me."

"She says nothing's happened, and I believe her, but that's not the point, is it? It's not always about what you do, but how you feel that matters."

"And you think she has feelings for Ben?"

"Perhaps, yes."

"Then she is being very disloyal to you, Neil, and that's not good enough. You're a kind, sincere, decent man. You've given your heart to her. You've offered her everything you are, to share with her for the rest of your lives as her husband. She's accepted that offer. Now, if she's got feelings for someone else, a man with whom she has such a complicated and emotional history, she really should be doing the honourable thing – she should break off your engagement. And if she won't, then you must. Anything less would be completely unacceptable."

For just a moment, Wendy's heart lurched at the forlorn sadness in Neil's eyes as he stared at her.

"You think so?"

"I do."

His head drooped and she wondered if he was crying.

"I'm here, Neil. I'm always here for you. There are plenty of people at St Stephen's who are concerned about the way Claire's treating you. We're worried you're losing your way. Please remember you're not alone in this. Whatever happens, you have friends; good and caring friends."

"Thank you."

She looked at her watch, then started to push back her chair. "They'll be here soon."

"Of course. I'll clear out of your way."

"Actually, if there's anyone you might like to clear out of my way, it's James Molyneux. That man is so difficult to get on with. He's actually an excellent musician, but he's so full of his own importance that he's impossible to work with. He thinks he's still in the army, standing out in front shouting out orders to everyone. I don't think he's ever heard of the word *teamwork*."

"You don't need to tell me! It must be difficult for you. You've been involved in the music in this church for most of your life. He should recognize what an asset you are instead of trying to lord it over everyone. We need your dad. How is he? Any news about when he might be well enough to play for us again?"

"Well, it can't come soon enough for him. He's going stir-crazy, having to take a back seat for so long."

"What does he think of James and his musical style?"

"Do you really want to know? Suffice it to say that my dad is not James's biggest fan!"

"Just tell him to get well soon, because we can't wait to welcome him back where he belongs."

The door opened to reveal a group of young people from the St Stephen's youth group carrying a variety of instruments from guitar to violin.

"Have a good rehearsal, then," said Neil as he got to his feet. "And thank you, Wendy. Thanks for everything."

* * *

When Neil got back to his house in Vicarage Gardens later that night, a note had been pushed through his letterbox. The moment Neil saw the green ink Claire always chose to write in, he tore open the envelope.

My darling Neil,

My heart is breaking at your silence when there's so much for us to talk about. This has all been such an awful misunderstanding. You are my love. After all we've been through, especially over the past few days, how could you doubt that for a second?

Please call me. Better still, come and put your arms around me so that I can show you how much I want and need you.

I love you.

Claire x

Neil read the note three times before he carefully refolded it and slipped it back into the envelope. Then he reached up to place it on the mantelpiece, where he gazed at it for some time before he finally walked away.

* * *

It was still dark the next morning when the bedside phone rang. Dragging himself from sleep, Neil fumbled for the receiver.

"Reverend Fisher?" The man's voice sounded alarmingly official.

"Yes?"

"I'm ringing from Dunbridge police station, sir. I'm the staff sergeant on duty."

"Has something happened?"

"We pulled a young man off the track at the railway station about half an hour ago."

"Oh no. Is he…?"

"Thankfully not, sir. Apparently he was trying to jump in front of the passenger train that stops here, but it turned out to have only four carriages instead of the eight he was probably expecting. That meant that by the time the train was near enough for him to jump, it had slowed down so much that the driver was able to make an emergency stop before it hit him."

"Was he hurt?"

"Well, he's been taken to hospital because he was quite badly bruised from the way he landed, but that isn't what worries us most. My guess is that this was a suicide attempt. When he realized it had all gone wrong, he was in a bad way, very emotional and distressed."

"How can I help?"

"His mother has asked if you would join her and his father at the hospital as soon as you can, sir."

"Of course. What's his name?"

"Hold on a minute," said the sergeant as Neil heard him searching through his papers.

"He's a Daniel Molyneux of 39 Selwyn Avenue in Dunbridge. Do you know him, sir?"

"I most certainly do. Thank you for letting me know. I'm on my way."

* * *

James and Sue had been asked to wait in a side room at the back of the Accident and Emergency department. As Neil walked in, Sue got up immediately, relief written all over her tear-stained face. Neil glanced over to where James was sitting, stiff-backed and silent. He made no attempt to greet Neil. He was too deep in his own thoughts, his face so gaunt and ashen that he looked about twenty years older than the immaculately dressed, forceful character Neil was used to.

"How is Danny?"

"We don't really know. They've not let us in. They said he doesn't want to see us."

Sue was trembling as she spoke, so Neil gently led her over to the brown sofa opposite the high-backed chair where James was sitting.

"Do you know what happened?"

"My son tried to take his own life," said James, his face expressionless.

"We don't know that for sure, do we?" said Sue. "Perhaps it was an accident. He might have slipped or fainted. No one really knows yet."

"Was he going somewhere?" asked Neil. "Why was he at the station at that time in the morning? It was probably quite busy, because a lot of commuters head into London on those very early trains."

"He intended to kill himself. That was his only reason for being there."

"James, please…"

Her husband looked towards her, his eyes almost lifeless. "Deal with facts, Susan. Daniel doesn't want to live any more. Not with us, not with anyone, not at all."

She sobbed then: gasping sobs that shuddered through her body.

"Was he injured by the fall?"

"Severe bruising, so the doctor said," answered Sue through her tears.

"It's just as well," added James, "that there are overhead cables there. At other stations, he might have fallen onto an electrified rail, which would have achieved his aim with a lot less mess than being hit by a train."

"Stop it, James, please. Don't say that as if you don't care. You do. I know you do."

"But our son doesn't, does he, Susan? Today's events have made that very clear. He doesn't care about us, or anyone else who might have been traumatized if he'd succeeded this morning. That's because he doesn't care about himself. But then that's been obvious for a long time."

"You've never understood him. You've never tried to find out what he's *really* like. You never listened."

"Apparently not, but then he never listened either. I'm his father. I only ever wanted the best for him. A wise person would realize they could save themselves a lot of trouble by observing the lessons their parents learned before them."

"I don't think we ever really learn from other people's experience, though," said Neil. "We all have to make our own mistakes, painful as that might be for those who love us."

"Well, there you are," replied James. "That's another one of my mistakes in what is fast becoming a very long list."

"So if Danny only has bruising, are they talking about him coming home?" asked Neil.

"I think the psychiatrist is with him now." Sue scraped her hands across her cheeks, not succeeding in rubbing away the streaks left by the many tears she'd shed that morning. "I suppose he'll find out what really happened; whether it was all just a terrible accident…"

"It was no accident, Susan. Danny made a deliberate decision to kill himself."

"You don't know that."

"Yes, I do."

"How? How can you possibly know when no one has managed to speak to him properly yet?"

"Because he told me."

"What! What do you mean?"

"He sent me a message."

"What message? Where?"

"On my mobile. He sent it at four thirty-five this morning. He must have spent all night thinking about it."

Susan snatched up the phone, frantically punching the buttons as she searched for the message list.

"Don't worry about finding it," continued James calmly. "I remember every word he wrote. 'You did this, Dad. You'll have to live with that because I can't live with you. You've made my life hell. I hope that what I do today makes your life hell too.'"

Suddenly James, that dignified, uncompromising man, began to shake uncontrollably. His face crumpled and his body folded in on itself as he began to rock violently backwards and forwards. And from the depths of him came a wail, the cry of an animal in agony, that went on and on as if he could never stop.

≫ CHAPTER 9 ≪

"Guess what, Neil! She said yes!" Cyn was bursting with excitement when she found Neil ploughing through paperwork in the church office. "Margaret will be coming back for Jamie's christening next Sunday. How wonderful is that?"

"Great news. I don't suppose it was an easy decision for her. The last time she was in this church was the day of Frank's funeral. And the day she left the vicarage for good."

"That's true," agreed Cyn. "The house has become a bit of a sorry sight with no one living in it. I hope seeing it won't upset her."

"Do you know, I think I'll be quite nervous taking that ceremony with her in the congregation instead of leading it herself."

"Well, don't be. I speak to her quite often, and she's always really interested in what you've been doing and how you're getting on. She's well aware that she left you with a huge workload which you've had to carry alone."

"I've really missed her. I do know that."

"She'll be very glad to see you."

"Is she going to stay for a while?"

"No. She couldn't cope with that. Too many memories here. Losing Frank so unexpectedly is still very raw for her."

"And her ministry? Is she thinking about resuming that?"

"Early days yet, I think. I keep praying, though."

"Neil!" Brenda pushed open the door and came to join them. "You've remembered about Sonia's housewarming this afternoon, haven't you?"

"Yes, I've got the address on a bit of paper somewhere on this desk. I know I have."

Brenda grabbed a pen and a post-it note. "Here it is again. Don't lose it! Three o'clock for tea and cakes, OK?"

"Your cakes?"

"Of course."

"Then I'll definitely be there."

Once they'd both gone, Neil looked at the clock. He glanced out of the window to see Claire in wellie boots completely engrossed in digging out one of the large flower beds towards the back of the church. Grabbing his jacket, he let himself out by the side door while she worked on, unaware she was being watched.

The recent weeks hadn't been easy for either of them. Sam's revelation had set in motion a lot of soul-searching for them both. At first, she had vehemently denied that she'd been holding hands with Ben in the way Sam explained it, and had been angry with Neil for even thinking that she might. She said that must mean he didn't trust her. He said he wondered if he could. They both went away to lick their wounded feelings for a while, during which time Wendy's words kept circling round Neil's mind. Was she right? While there was even the slightest suggestion that Claire was not wholeheartedly and exclusively committed to their relationship, shouldn't they call off the engagement? When, with great sadness, he sought Claire out and suggested it, she had burst into uncontrollable tears, which meant that he simply threw his arms around her, kissing her and reassuring her that he could never seriously consider doing such a thing.

In the days that followed, though, Claire did open up to tell Neil about her muddled emotions where Ben was concerned. She admitted feeling a twinge of the old attraction that had been so powerful when they'd first met. She talked about how moved she was to see Sam's happiness in his dad's company, and how much of a jolt it gave her to see how alike they were, not just physically, but in their mannerisms and sense of humour too.

"Do you still love him?" Neil had asked, dreading her reply.

"Yes, I have to admit that in a way I do. I wish him well. I'd like to see him happy and settled. I know now that he genuinely cares about Sam. I have a sort of family feeling about Ben, if you can understand that – as if he's part of our family, Sam's and mine, and his welfare matters to us because of that."

"And if he asked you to marry him so that you could be that family, as I think you may have always wanted, what would you say?"

"I would say," said Claire slowly, her eyes fixed on Neil's, "that I'm in love with a wonderful man who fills my mind and claims my heart – and that I'm going to marry *him*."

She leaned forward to kiss him with a tenderness that deepened into passion as they left the world and its problems behind them.

We're going to be OK, Neil had thought, as his senses reeled. *Thank God, I think we're going to be OK.*

The memory of that conversation came to mind now as Claire caught sight of him coming towards her, and her face lit up with pleasure. She stuck the fork hard down into the soil and walked into his arms, kissing him without caring who might see them.

"I bring news," he said finally. "I've heard from that parish up in Derbyshire. It sounds really nice. A small country town, a bit like this, but with a couple of small village churches I'd have responsibility for too."

"Do they say what the house is like that goes with it?"

"I've printed out a picture," he replied, rummaging in his back pocket.

"Wow!" she whistled under her breath. "That's absolutely gorgeous. It's huge – and just look at that garden!"

"I can imagine Sam running around there. Can't you?" he asked.

"Definitely. Do they want you to go up to see them?"

"Not just me; they'd like to meet my wife too."

"And that will be me."

"That *will* be you as soon as I can get you up the aisle."

"Have they given you a date? When can we go up and take a look?"

"As soon as possible, they say. They've not had a minister for nearly a year now."

She chuckled. "So they're desperate!"

"I hope so. I might not have much competition then."

"How about next Monday? It's your official day off, after all, even if it rarely works out that way."

"I'll give them a ring. You're up for this, then, are you, Mrs Fisher-to-be?"

"Come here," she said, leaving him in no doubt that she most certainly was.

* * *

"Guess what?" enthused Pauline when she popped in for what had become her regular morning coffee with Audrey. "I've had a call from Greg – you know, my son in Canada. He's coming over."

"How wonderful! When did you last see him?"

"I went over with my daughter Pattie about five years ago, before she had the children, but Greg's been in Ontario for about fifteen years now. He just went over for a gap year after he'd taken his degree, but romance got in the way. He met Tina, his wife, and that was it. He didn't want to come home any more. He's in chemical engineering, got a very good job. And, of course, they've got Zoe now. She looks quite the young lady these days when I see her on Skype."

"How old is she?"

"Thirteen at Christmas."

"And are they all coming?"

"No, just Greg, apparently. His company's sending him for some international conference or other. It's in London, so it'll be very convenient for him to stay here." Looking like an excited child, Pauline clapped her hands with glee.

"And when's this all going to happen?" asked Audrey, catching her friend's mood.

"Three weeks' time: the first week in May. I can't wait."

For just an instant, Audrey was aware of her old self, bitter and jealous at someone else's happiness. Why should Pauline have it all? Why did she have the joy of a visit from a loving son when Barry had denied Audrey the only chance she'd ever had to become a mother herself?

Not for long, though. As Pauline scooped her friend up into her arms in a hug of delight and excitement, Audrey found herself doing something very unexpected... She hugged Pauline back.

* * *

"Come on in!" said the burly fireman at the front door of Sonia's new home. On three sides it was surrounded by a decent-sized corner garden, which already contained a swing, a sandpit and a selection of bikes and buggies, all bought from the proceeds of the highly successful *Undercover Firemen* calendar.

Neil fought his way through the small hallway where what seemed like the entire team from Dunbridge fire station were sipping tea, coffee or the occasional can of beer. Through the crowd in the dining room he could see Matt, with his arm around Maria's shoulders, chatting to Sonia. Nearby was the buffet table. Anyone in the know could see it was Beryl's handiwork, because the magnificent and mouthwatering spread was a far cry from the "tea and cakes" she'd told Neil to expect.

"Psst!"

Neil looked towards the stairway to see two little faces grinning cheekily at him. Jake, who considered himself very grown up since his recent fourth birthday, and his little brother Charlie, had got to know Neil quite well: they often saw him when he visited the church playgroup.

"Our new room's cool. Want a look?"

The boys' room was definitely "cool", freshly decorated in shades of blue, with cupboards, shelves and table all built in around bunk beds that had been made to look like a space ship.

"This one's mine," puffed Jake as he sat bouncing up and down on the top bunk. "That means I'm the captain of this ship!"

In the best words a two-year-old could muster, Charlie made it clear that he wanted the top bunk too.

"No, Charlie," explained Jake firmly, "you're the youngest, so you sleep on the bottom bunk. I'm the eldest. I'm in charge!"

Mayhem broke out as the two boys argued, but before Neil could wade in as referee, he felt a slight tug on his jacket. Rosie was standing there, grinning broadly to reveal the gap where four teeth were currently missing.

"The boys aren't allowed in my room, Neil. Come and see!"

Rosie had been allocated what his mother would have called "the box room", but it had been transformed by clever design into a small girl's paradise in which every inch of space was put to good use. There was a mirror on the wall surrounded with coloured stones, a cot for her dolls, and shelves for her books and puzzles. Rosie beamed with pride as he commented on everything he saw. Below the window was a desk where she kept a pile of drawing paper and crayons. Suddenly, Neil stopped in his tracks as he looked down at the picture on the top of the pile.

"I've done a lot like that," lisped Rosie through her gappy teeth. "Look!"

She pointed to the large display board covering the top half of the opposite wall. The board had almost completely disappeared beneath rows of pictures, all of them on the same subject.

"It's my angel," she explained patiently, in case he wasn't clever enough to work that out for himself. "I haven't got a white crayon, so I've mostly coloured him yellow, and I've put sparkles all round him like you do when you draw a star. That's so you know he's shiny, see? And there's his hair, and there's his face and these are his wings. I'm not sure I've made them big enough," she finished, gazing thoughtfully at her handiwork.

"And this is what you saw on the night of the fire?" asked Neil, moving closer to inspect the pictures.

"Well, I'm not very good at drawing, but I don't think he'd mind. He was nice."

"Did he talk to you, then?"

"Umm…" Rosie frowned as she tried to remember. "No, I don't think so. I knew what he meant, though."

"How – if he didn't say anything?"

Rosie shrugged her shoulders dismissively. "Don't know. I didn't talk to him and he didn't talk to me, but we got along all right."

"Did you know there was a fire downstairs?"

"No, but he sort of let me know. And I knew I didn't have to worry because he was there to look after me."

"And when your mummy came in, did she see your angel too?"

"I don't think so. She didn't say she did."

"I wonder why that was."

"I don't think she believes in angels, really."

"Oh?"

"When I told her about him, she said I must have been dreaming."

"Maybe you were?"

"No," she said simply. "I was awake. Anyway, you know all about angels because you talk about them. You remember when you came into school and we made those cards for our mums and you said Baby Jesus' mummy had an angel come to see her. I wonder..." she paused to think. "I wonder if that was *my* angel?"

"That's exactly what I'm wondering too," murmured Neil.

"I'm starving!" announced Rosie. "We've got lots of cakes downstairs. Want one?"

And putting her small hand firmly in his, she dragged him downstairs in the direction of the fairy cakes.

* * *

Danny was in the psychiatric hospital for two weeks before his case worker asked to see his parents. James wouldn't go. Since the day of Danny's suicide attempt, he had become a shell, a pale shadow of the overbearing, pedantic, neat and tidy man he'd always been. Sue was struggling with her own emotions, recognizing that her feelings towards him see-sawed between furious anger – because she believed him to be the real cause of Danny's problems – and an overwhelming sense of compassion for her principled, basically caring husband who was crushed by regret and guilt.

The man who greeted her looked scarcely older than Danny, and Sue wondered how someone so young could take on the responsibilities of a case worker, making life-changing decisions affecting the fate of others. That impression was soon dispelled once Kevin started speaking: it became clear that he had spent a lot of time in deep conversation with Danny in the weeks he'd been in hospital.

"We have come to the conclusion, Mrs Molyneux, that Danny is not suffering from any ongoing mental condition. He rarely takes any form of drugs. He admits to the odd puff of cannabis, but that's not enough to be relevant here. He does drink, occasionally too much, but he hadn't been drinking at all that night, so alcohol isn't likely to have been an influence on that occasion. It seems that what drove Danny to such despair – what made him feel he would rather take his own life than try and carry on – were the circumstances he found himself having to cope with."

"And by *circumstances* you mean his father?"

"It certainly seems that way, but that's probably only part of the explanation. Usually the reasons are much more complex than just a single source of concern. Taking Danny out of school for home schooling was one of those triggers, but it seems that he hadn't felt he fitted in particularly well at school for some time. He'd been skipping classes, not doing homework, and he was ostracized by some elements in his social circle for preferring artistic subjects like cooking and art, rather than sciences and the football field. He also has some issues about his sexuality. Were you aware of that?"

Sue was shocked. "No, not at all."

"He suspects he might be homosexual. Nothing more than a suspicion at this stage, because he says he's not done anything about it, but he speaks of being drawn to images of men rather than women."

"He's gay!" she breathed in disbelief.

"Would it be a problem at home if he were?"

"Certainly not to me. I'm not sure about his father."

Kevin nodded without comment, then looked down at his notes before he continued. "So our recommendation is that he doesn't come home to live. Certainly not for the foreseeable future."

"But he's our son. We're his parents. We love him. I know there've been problems in the past, but we can change. We just want him home."

"We recommend," continued Kevin, "that Danny has a place in one of our sheltered houses in Bedford. It's a proper home in a normal street, except that there will be four or five young people there. They all face their own challenges, but they'll be similar in many ways to Danny. They're supervised twenty-four hours a day by trained youth workers. The aim is to help each young person to understand themselves, their situation, their limitations and their goals. We encourage them to study. Mostly they go to Bedford College. They have a wide range of courses there, both academic and vocational, at every level. The aim, though, is that they come out with a clear vision of themselves, their hopes and their potential."

"But that might take months, years even. Surely Danny can come home before that?"

Kevin smiled. "Very likely, but that'll depend on Danny himself and on the two of you as his parents. Danny won't be put back into the situation that led him to such despair until we're sure he has the emotional, intellectual and practical tools he needs to protect himself. However, we also recommend that you and your husband undertake a course of counselling, which will give you a chance to talk over what's happened with an expert in family relationships. You said you could change. Perhaps you won't have to change too much, but you need to develop a very clear understanding of what's gone wrong in the past, and how the atmosphere and chemistry between family members can be either a positive or a negative influence."

"Would we be able to see him?"

"If Danny's willing, then I think that would be an excellent idea. I know he's been missing you."

Sue fought back the tears choking her throat.

"How is your husband?" asked Kevin when she'd composed herself.

"Not good. He blames himself, and that's not easy for a man who's always considered himself to be in the right. He never usually acknowledges blame for anything."

Kevin reached for a file, searched for a particular page, then scribbled a name and number down on a small slip of paper.

"Here," he said, offering it to Sue. "You might like to give this lady a call. She's a very skilled and experienced counsellor. Perhaps your husband should meet her."

"Thank you," she replied. "I'll see what he says."

"In the meantime, would you like to see Danny now? He told me this morning he could think of nothing better than a hug from his mum."

Sue didn't need a second bidding. In an instant, she was on her feet and following Kevin out of the room.

* * *

"Artie!" called Neil. He had spotted the lively octogenarian within minutes of his arrival at the Mayflower. "You were up in your room last time I came. Had a cold, they said. Are you better now?"

Artie's beaming smile lit up the room. "Not a cold, a *chill* – that's what I had. These nurses say there ain't no such thing as a chill these days, but my ma had chills, my pa had chills, and I've had 'em all my life. Don't know much, these nurses with all their new-fangled qualifications!"

"Are you being rude about me again, Artie?" Sylvie, who had been a care worker in various residential homes for more years than she could remember, bustled in, clucking at Artie as if he were a naughty schoolboy.

"Here's my girl!" said Artie, reaching out to touch her arm. "She's the woman of my dreams, is Sylvie. I'm going to leave her all my worldly goods, providing she looks after my bodily needs while I'm here."

"Steady, Tiger!" grinned Sylvie. "I'll put your teeth in a jar for you, brush your hair and, if you're extra nice to me, I might even cut your toenails – but that's about it."

"But you're my pin-up girl! Look at you, you're gorgeous."

Sylvie leaned over to place a fond kiss on top of Artie's almost bald head. "I love it when you've forgotten to put your specs on, Artie. You can't see a thing, you dopey darling! Just as well, though, because if you could, you'd see I'm not gorgeous at all. I must have been at the back of the queue when they were giving out boobs. In fact, if you turned me upside down so I could swap the measurements of my hips and my boobs round the other way, I'd have the body of Dolly Parton!"

"Anyway, Artie," laughed Neil, "aren't you going to leave all your worldly goods to your family?"

"Got no family left." It was almost as if a light had gone out in the old man's face as he answered.

"Yes, you have," said Sylvie. "You've got a boy. There's a picture of him with your wife on your chest of drawers."

"I used to. Not any more."

"What do you mean?" demanded Sylvie. "Your son's your son. You can't *used to* have a son. He's your only one, isn't he?"

Artie was picking at a loose end of wool on the sleeve of his cardigan, pretending he hadn't heard the question.

"What's wrong, love?" asked Sylvie, drawing up a chair to sit down beside him. "That *is* your son, isn't it? I'm sure you told me he was."

"Haven't seen him for years."

"Oh," sighed Sylvie, "that's a shame. Have you any idea where he is?"

"Bit of a wild fella, he was, when he was a youngster. Got into trouble with the law and all. He really upset his mother, and Hetty was always sensitive. I didn't like to see her hurt. Made me angry, it did."

"When did you last see him?" asked Neil.

Artie shrugged. "Thirty-odd years ago. He was in his twenties then, a right tearaway. Never worked, always sponging off his mum. He had her in tears time after time. While he was out one night, I bundled up all his stuff and threw it in the street, locked all the doors and went to bed. Hetty bawled her eyes out, but I wouldn't give in. The more we spoiled that boy, the more he wanted. Enough was enough."

"What happened?"

"He thumped on the door for hours, then went off shouting abuse at us. He came back every day after that for a couple of weeks. I told Hetty if she let him in, I'd be out the door – and she knew I meant it. It broke her, though. Broke us as a couple too. Our marriage was never the same after that. She blamed me, you see. In the end, he didn't come back at all. Broke her heart."

"He didn't come even when his mum died?"

"Nothing."

"Does anyone know where he is?" asked Sylvie. With five children and eleven grandchildren of her own, she couldn't imagine being estranged from any member of her family.

"Doubt it."

"Aren't you curious, though, Artie?" asked Neil. "Time changes everything, doesn't it? He'd be in his fifties now, probably with kids of his own. You might have grandchildren. It'd be nice to know, wouldn't it?"

"Perhaps," agreed Artie. "But I don't suppose he'd want to know me."

"What's his name?" demanded Sylvie, grabbing a pen and notebook from her pocket. "Come on, give me his full name and details about when and where he was born."

"You won't find him."

"Try me," retorted Sylvie. "God may not have blessed me with Dolly Parton's body, but I do a good impression of Inspector Clouseau."

Artie looked uncertain.

"Let's just see, love, shall we?" said Sylvie kindly, placing her hand over his. "If we get nowhere, we'll have lost nothing, will we?"

* * *

On the day of Jamie's christening, Neil was invited over to Cyn and Jim's farmhouse early, so that he'd arrive before Margaret. She was being driven over from Beaconsfield by her daughter

174

Sarah. He joined the Clarkson family as they crowded round the car to welcome the rector they had loved so dearly. There were hugs all round, with Neil waiting patiently at the end of the queue to greet his old friend and mentor. Margaret had been unconventional as a teacher in many ways. She came across as disorganized and spontaneous, but she'd been supported so wonderfully by her long-suffering husband, Frank, that most of the congregation never noticed her complete lack of interest in any form of paperwork. All they could see was her compassion, her sense of fun and her completely unconventional approach to just about everything. They simply loved her.

Margaret gazed fondly at Neil as she finally reached him. As they hugged he could feel how thin she was compared to the strapping, handsome woman she'd once been. She was paler too, with dark circles under her eyes that had never been there before. Those eyes were smiling at him now.

"I'm hearing great things of you, young Neil," she said as they went indoors and settled down for a chat in Cyn's living room.

"Trial by fire, I'm afraid," he grimaced. "I can't tell you how much I've missed you. I had no idea how little I knew until you weren't there to show me the ropes."

"I'm sorry about that, really I am," she replied, her expression darkening with regret. "When you're thrown in the deep end, as you undoubtedly were, you either sink or swim."

"Glug, glug!" chuckled Neil.

"Not from what I've heard," retorted Margaret. "Bishop Paul rings me quite frequently, and he often mentions how competently you've stepped up into the role."

"Really? He never tells me that!"

"He probably wants you to keep on doing what you're doing, then. If it ain't broke, don't fix it – that's Bishop Paul's motto. Have you thought about where you'd like to have your own parish after this?"

"Claire and I have been discussing it. We quite like the idea of going somewhere completely different. Derbyshire's an option we rather fancy at the moment. But then, my mother..."

"Ah, Iris: the mother who must be obeyed!"

Neil grinned. "Not so much these days, believe it or not. Did you know she's left Bristol and now has a house which backs on to Harry's? He's been a wonderful friend to her..."

"... heaven help him!" laughed Margaret.

"Yes, but it's a relief to know she has good friends here in Dunbridge. She's got involved with quite a lot of activities at St Stephen's. And she's joined a bridge club. She did say when she came that even if I did have to move on, Dunbridge was going to be her home – and it seems it is."

"Good. That's one of your challenges settled. What about the other? How *is* Wendy?"

"Very supportive, actually."

"She invited Sam's father over from Australia, I understand – and he's still staying with her now?"

It was clear to Neil that Margaret really had been keeping up with everything that went on at St Stephen's. "Yes, that has been difficult."

"Not that supportive, then. How are her family?"

"I suppose you heard about Brian being out of action? He broke his shoulder and arm badly at the Christmas pageant, of all places."

"So who's tinkling the ivories in his place?"

"Well, it *was* James Molyneux. Do you remember him?"

"Army type? An authority on absolutely everything?"

"Got it in one. James was our regular organist until the upset with his son Danny."

Margaret nodded. "Cyn mentioned that. How's he doing? And, just as important, how is his dad coping with what happened?"

"He's in a bad way. I pop round to see him regularly, but it's like the life has been sucked out of him."

"Guilt, do you think?"

"Definitely – and getting things wrong would be a hard pill to swallow for a man who prided himself on always being right."

"So that leaves no one at all to play the organ for services at the moment – is that right?"

"Except for our wonderful Clifford Davies. You remember Cliff from the crematorium? He's a very talented pianist, as you know."

"For singalongs, yes, there'd be no one to match him – but with hymns? Does he want to play them all at dance tempo with a soft-shoe-shuffle chorus?"

"Probably, but he does behave himself most of the time. Actually, he's been a godsend. We've all become very fond of him. And he's planning a variety show Extravaganza for the end of next month, which I'm looking forward to and dreading in equal measure."

"You'll cope, I've no doubt."

"What about you, Margaret? Ministry was your life. Your work here inspired so many people. Can you see yourself coming back and taking up that role again, if not here then somewhere else a bit less hectic?"

"No."

"No, not now – or no, not ever?"

"Not *yet*. It's getting better, I do realize that. I can't begin to put into words, Neil, the bleakness, the despair, the darkness I felt when Frank died – as if God had died to me too. I'd spent years telling people that the way through bereavement and loss was to cling to God; to know the security of being held in his loving hands. But when I had to put it into practice myself, everything I thought I believed seemed to fall away from me. My darling Frank was gone – and God had taken him. I didn't want God any more. I didn't even know if I believed there *was* a God, because the God I thought I knew was one of compassion and love."

"A God of suffering and death too," whispered Neil.

"Yes. Yes, he is – and I'm beginning to recognize that. Prayers were hopeless at the start. I didn't feel like praying anyway. Why should I pray to a God who either wasn't there or who was so cruel that I couldn't trust him? And I know it's a bit of a cliché, but time does heal. It hasn't healed my broken heart or my life. That feels like nothing at all with Frank no longer in it. But it has brought some healing in my relationship with God. We've got a long way to go, but we're back on speaking terms now."

"Margaret," called Cyn, "we should get going soon. There's a lot of people waiting to meet you."

Margaret turned back to Neil, taking both his hands in hers as she spoke. "God is real. I know that. It's just the situation I went through that seems so unreal. Frank was my whole world, you see. I wish that for you too. I wish you a marriage that is filled with passion, fun and deep, deep love. I hope you've found that in Claire."

"Ours'll certainly never be a quiet life," smiled Neil.

"Then God bless you in your life together, whatever you make of it – and God bless you in your ministry, Neil. He chose well in you."

An hour later, standing in front of the gathered friends and family at the special service to welcome James Colin Clarkson into the world and into the church, Neil felt a wave of love sweep through him as he caught sight of Claire standing next to Harry and Iris, with Sam at her side.

Father, dear God in heaven, he prayed silently, *please pour your blessing on Claire and me as we plan our life together. Help us to be tolerant and understanding, supportive and caring. Be with us as we work through the tough times, and allow us to know the joy of laughing together every day of our lives. Bless our family – Mum, Harry, Sam, Felicity and David – and if it is your will, one day I pray we might add to our family circle with children of our own. Help us to find the depth of love and partnership we've seen in Ernie and Blanche and in Margaret and Frank. We pray that your love, which passes all understanding, will support our love now and always. Amen.*

❧ CHAPTER 10 ❧

*I*t was the first day of May, and Dunbridge was looking glorious. Its gardens were full of late spring flowers, and trees, bushes and shrubs were shooting out lime-green leaves that warmed into darker colours in the sunshine. Neil walked down the garden path on his way to the church office knowing that he had a day's worth of paperwork to get through. He needed the car for meetings later that afternoon, so he threw his briefcase onto the back seat and pulled away.

Afterwards, he couldn't put into words why his plans had changed so dramatically. Without any warning, an image of Pauline Walters came into his mind. He smiled at the thought. The blossoming friendship between Pauline and Audrey was nothing less than a miracle to members of the congregation, who could remember the bitterness Audrey had always shown towards anyone who dared to muscle in on the flower-arranging at St Stephen's, with Pauline being a particular target for her vitriol. The pair now worked happily together, creating a result that was better than anything the church had ever known. Somehow, Pauline's warm, caring personality had worked its magic on the hardness in Audrey's heart, and the pleasure it had brought to both women was a joy to see.

Neil had no idea why he found himself suddenly turning

the car in the direction of Pauline's house. He had nothing in particular to say, no special reason to seek her out, and when he had parked the car outside her home, he sat for a while wondering why on earth he'd thought to drive there. Should he just go?

At that moment, Pauline opened the front door and called out to him. "Neil? I thought that was you. Come on in, the kettle's hot!"

Minutes later, with a cup of steaming tea in one hand and some ginger cake in the other, Neil thought that he needn't have worried about having a reason to visit Pauline. She was so open and naturally chatty that their conversation flowed as if they were old friends.

"So I'll be driving down to Heathrow to collect him tomorrow evening," she was saying. "I haven't seen Greg for more than five years now. I can't wait to give him the biggest hug in the world!"

"That's lovely, Pauline. It may be a short visit, but I'm sure you'll have lots of time to catch up properly."

"We always have got on well, Greg and I. He reminds me a lot of his father. He's solid and decent – a good man, and a great father if Zoe is anything to judge by."

Just then, the telephone rang. Pauline got up to answer it, reeling off her number as she picked up the receiver. Neil couldn't help but overhear, and found himself becoming curious as he listened to her end of the conversation. Suddenly, she held the receiver out to him, her face unusually pale.

"It's not Greg. I thought it might be because it's come up as his home number. It's another man with a Canadian accent. He's rung me – but he wants to speak to whoever's with me."

"Hello?" said Neil.

"Hello, sir, my name is Robert Dodd. My daughter Tina's married to Pauline's son Greg."

"Yes?" Neil replied, glancing over at Pauline.

"Would you mind telling me who you are, sir?"

"I'm the Reverend Neil Fisher. Pauline's a member of my congregation."

Neil sensed rather than heard a sigh of relief at the other end of the line. "Then it's very opportune that you're there, Reverend, because I need to ask you to pass on some bad news. I just didn't want to do it directly to her over the phone."

"Go on." Neil felt he could hardly breathe.

"Greg was picked up by a taxi taking him to the airport this morning. He's been so excited at the prospect of coming over to England to see his mother."

"And?"

"We don't know the exact details yet, but from what we understand there was a devastating pile-up on the motorway just after his car joined it. Several cars were involved. One of them was the taxi Greg was travelling in."

"Oh no!"

"What? What is it?" cried Pauline. "Give me the phone! What's he saying?"

Neil gently put up his hand in a way that seemed to stop her in her tracks.

"The driver was hurt – not badly – but Greg wasn't wearing a seat belt, which is not unusual for passengers in the back of taxis here. He went straight through the front window. He was thrown at speed onto the road surface. He didn't stand a chance."

There was an unmistakable sob in the man's voice as he tried to speak.

"I think," said Neil slowly, "you've told me enough. I need to speak to Pauline now. She says you're ringing on the family's home phone. Is that right?"

"It is."

"Then can we ring you back a little later? Let me speak to Pauline first."

"I understand – and Reverend? Take care of her. Tell her we feel her grief. Tell her we share it."

"I will. Thank you. Goodbye."

"Tell me!" Pauline's eyes were wide and glassy. "It's Greg, isn't it? Oh, God, it's Greg. I know it."

Putting his arms around her, Neil guided her over to the kitchen table, pulling out chairs for them both to sit down.

"There was an accident, Pauline."

Her hand flew to her mouth in horror.

"He was going to the airport in a taxi that got caught up in an accident on the motorway."

She let out a long, deep moan, closing her eyes tightly as if she could shut out the news, block out the image. "He's dead, isn't he?" she wailed. "My boy's dead…"

All Neil could do was hold her helplessly as she rocked backwards and forwards, until her scream subsided into shuddering sobs.

* * *

Audrey simply took over when she arrived. Tenderly, as if Pauline was an injured child, she made her comfortable on the sofa in the living room, stroking her head and listening to her outpouring of sorrow with great patience and care. Eventually she signalled to Neil that she thought she had everything under control, and she would take care of whatever was needed.

And so she did. Two days later, Audrey was at Pauline's side when the two women boarded a plane for Ontario. Audrey knew her friend would never be able to manage either the physical or the emotional journey on her own, and so there was never any discussion needed as they planned the trip together.

While Neil was driving back from delivering them to the airport that morning, he found himself wondering at the coincidence that he just happened to be there at the exact time the awful news had come through.

No coincidence at all, he thought. *Blessed be your name, O Lord. Blessed be your name.*

* * *

"Reverend Fisher!" Lady Romily strode towards him as he waited to greet the worshippers at the end of the Sunday morning service. "It is now mid-May. Sir Andrew's civic service here in Dunbridge takes place on the last Thursday in June in six weeks' time. You have everything prepared?"

"Well, not completely, but I've been talking to Sir Andrew's private secretary, who seems to have most of the arrangements in hand."

"There can be no mistakes on this, Reverend Fisher. This is vital to Dunbridge and very important for St Stephen's too. This event will put both very firmly on the social and cultural map of Bedfordshire."

"I understand, Lady Romily. How involved would you like to be yourself? I would certainly appreciate your input on the plans so far. Perhaps I could bring the paperwork up to the Hall?"

Lady Romily's expression was stony. "There is little point in that if the event itself is here. I will come here to the church tomorrow morning at ten to discuss every aspect of the service and its arrangement in minute detail."

"Of course," agreed Neil, his mind racing as he thought about what other meetings he'd have to move in order to accommodate her visit.

With the slightest nod of her head, the lady of the manor walked on past him as if he were no longer there.

Coffee in the hall was the normal mix of clinking cups, biscuits, cake and chatter. Neil hadn't even made it to the serving hatch before he felt a pair of hands grab his elbows firmly.

"Got you. Need to talk to you. Now!"

He swung round to see Clifford, hot-foot from his organ-playing duties, pushing him through the crowd with great determination, refusing to allow anyone else to distract him before the two of them were able to sit down on empty seats in the furthest corner of the hall.

"It's chaos!" Clifford's expression was tragic and full of drama. "We're on in three weeks – and it's chaos! Dee – she's the local dancing school teacher who's *supposed* to be doing the choreography – has gone down with some awful bug or other, so the dancers can't rehearse. Bob promised he'd have our sets painted in plenty of time – and for heaven's sake, he's had them in that barn of his for *months*. Now he says he's too busy on the farm to do anything for a while, and he may not be able to get them done at all! The escapologist seems to have difficulty escaping from his wife on any evening he's supposed to be at rehearsals. The jazz band from Dunbridge Upper School have been told by their parents that they've got to knuckle down to their A-level studies, so it's touch and go whether they can get to practices. The only things going really well are the tickets – and they're practically sold out. So we've got an audience – but no Extravaganza, if people don't get their acts together and do what they said they'd do."

"Oh dear," replied Neil, attempting to digest the flood of information he'd just been given, but Clifford was on a roll, scarcely drawing breath before he started again.

"I can't take on everyone's responsibility myself. I just can't.

I can't be producer, director, wardrobe, sound, lighting, musical director *and* odd-job boy. What sort of Extravaganza is it going to be if it's just me running round doing everything? Why do people volunteer to help if they're not prepared to put in the commitment to see it through? For pity's sake, I'm a *professional*. Why did I ever think it would be a good idea to work with amateurs like them? Whatever happened to 'the show must go on'?"

"Well, it must," agreed Neil. "Now let me think. Didn't I hear that Kyle's mum – you know, Kyle who sings in the choir – used to be a dancer? Couldn't she help with choreography? I know Bob Trueman's always busy at this time of year, but he's chairman of the Friends of St Stephen's. I wonder if some of the Friends could give a hand with set painting? And if the escapologist's too tied up to make rehearsals, what about John Harris? He does magic at children's parties. Perhaps he could perform something suitable for the show. And talk to Wendy about the jazz band. She teaches at a different school, but these music teachers meet up at festivals and concerts all the time. She'll probably be able to put in a word to get that sorted. What else was there? Costumes – well, Richard Barnes runs the Dunbridge Amateur Dramatic and Operatic Society. He keeps a lot of costumes in a shed in his garden. From what I gather, he's always willing to lend them out in return for a small contribution to the society's coffers. I'm sure St Stephen's could stretch to that. Anything else?"

Clifford looked at Neil in amazement. "Music! I need a rehearsal pianist. I can't direct the performers and play the piano myself. I thought I could, but I can't."

"Hmm, that's a tough one," agreed Neil. "The only person I can think of is James, and he's hardly in a fit state to help, is he?"

"Excuse me, Neil," interrupted Peter Fellowes. "I've got those papers for you to sign before you head off to St Gabriel's."

"Sorry, Cliff, got to go!"

As Neil got up to leave, he remembered how his dad always used to say that if you want something done, you need to ask a busy man. These days his schedule was relentlessly busy and he always had a lot on his mind, but it seemed he was developing the skill of coming up with instant solutions to the many problems that constantly came his way. A busy man, that was what he'd become – but apparently one who, once in a while, could come up with answers that might just be helpful. He smiled at the thought of his dad's reaction to that, then grabbed his robes and rushed towards the car and St Gabriel's.

* * *

It was only a fortnight into the month of May, and Neil was already about to conduct his fourth wedding service. Ann-Marie had been planning her wedding to Steve for nearly two years, and for months Neil had been receiving frequent phone calls from both the bride and her formidable mother, checking one detail after another.

The couple's big day dawned dry and bright, although a keen wind was whipping the trees around the church into a frenzy. It was doing much the same to the Disney Princess dresses worn by the eight bridesmaids, as they lined up with Neil to greet the sleek white limousine that swept up to the porch gate.

The bride beamed with excitement through the window of the limo, waving at the bridesmaids as she waited for the driver to come round and help her out. Neil wondered how on earth Ann-Marie had ever managed to squeeze herself, her father *and* her enormous Big Gypsy Wedding dress into the car, because there seemed a great deal of doubt that they would be able to get her out again. Her father pushed, Ann-Marie squealed, the driver tugged, the bridesmaids shrieked and Neil shifted from foot to foot, uncertain how to help. Five minutes later, the manoeuvre was complete, but the bride was thumping her father's arm in fury as her chief bridesmaid repinned her tiara, fixed her hairpiece back into place and dabbed under her eyes with a tissue in a fruitless attempt to remove smudges of mascara.

At last the gathered bridesmaids were able to reassure the tearful Ann-Marie that she'd never looked lovelier, and the contrite father of the bride took his place on her arm. At once the official photographer went into artistic mode to capture the moment forever, with what must have been about fifty different stylish shots. Neil took a quick look at his watch. There was another wedding scheduled for later that afternoon. If they didn't get cracking soon, he might not make it.

Finally the photos were done, and the parade of bridesmaids, the bride and her father formed up. Neil walked to the front of the church to announce Ann-Marie's arrival and give Clifford the cue to start the familiar strains of "Here Comes the Bride". Everyone in the packed church got to their feet as the procession made its way up the aisle with some difficulty. The main problem was the width of the bride's dress: it swept flower heads off the arrangements at the ends of pews on one side, and pushed her father aside on the other, so that several times he actually stumbled into the pews as he tried to stay on his feet. The bridesmaids in their wide, hooped skirts also decided halfway along that they simply couldn't walk side by side, so reached the front of the pews in an unseemly crocodile instead – with the exception of the smallest flower girl, who suddenly spotted her mummy standing in the side aisle, recording every special moment on a video camera. With a squeal of delight, the toddler broke ranks to make a beeline for her, clambering inelegantly over the guests before she reached her target.

"Welcome, everyone," began Neil, once Ann-Marie and Steve had taken their places and everyone had settled. "In the presence of God, Father, Son and Holy Spirit, we have come together to witness the marriage of Ann-Marie and Steven, to pray for God's blessing on them, to share their joy and to celebrate their love."

Ann-Marie giggled girlishly, and Steve looked very hot as he nervously tried to loosen the collar on his dress shirt. Neither of them seemed to be paying much attention to what Neil was saying, so he just soldiered on, eventually asking the traditional question.

"The vows you are about to take are to be made in the presence of God, who is the judge of all and knows all the secrets of our hearts; therefore, if either of you knows a reason why you may not lawfully marry, you must declare it now." Neil looked questioningly at the couple standing before him.

"What?" asked Steve.

"Are you married to anyone else – or a convict or a basket case, anything like that?" whispered Ann-Marie.

"No," replied her groom, obviously confused by the question.

When Neil repeated the enquiry to the whole congregation, there were several seconds of silence before someone towards the back shouted, "That's it, then, Steve! No one's going to save you!" at which the whole congregation burst out laughing.

Neil caught sight of Peter Fellowes frowning with disapproval near the door at the back of the church.

"Who gives this woman to be married to this man?" continued Neil.

No one responded.

"Dad!" hissed Ann-Marie. "Dad, that's you!"

"Oh, I'm sorry," stuttered her father, before finding a clear voice to announce, "That's me."

Neil then asked the couple to turn to each other so that the groom could take his bride's hand and repeat the vows after him line by line. Steve looked nervous and uncertain, struggling with the unfamiliar language.

"I, Steven Norman, take you, Ann-Marie Louise Tracey, to be my wife, to have and to hold, from this day forward; for better, for worse, for richer, for poorer, in sickness and in health, to love and to cherish, till death us do part; according to God's holy law. In the presence of God I make this vow."

At last it was over, and he sighed with relief as he watched Ann-Marie say her version of the vow in a voice which echoed around the building, performing more for the crowd than her husband to be.

Neil then asked for the rings from the best man, who looked even more nervous than Steve as he fumbled frantically in his right-hand suit pocket for several heart-stopping moments, before he finally found the rings in the corresponding pocket on the left-hand side. Steve was invited to take the ring he'd chosen for Ann-Marie and place it on the fourth finger of her left hand. Keeping his eyes firmly on the ring as he held it in place, Steve mumbled after Neil: "Ann-Marie, I give you this ring as a sign of our marriage. With my body I honour you, all that I am I give to you, and all that I have I share with you, within the love of God, Father, Son and Holy Spirit. Amen."

At that point Ann-Marie's mascara, which seemed to be playing a leading role in the day's proceedings, began to form two pools under her heavily made-up eyes. Picking up the ring that she was giving Steve, she turned her tear-stained face towards him, reciting the same promise in a voice that was filled with pathos and drama. Sighs could be heard all round the church from the rapt congregation, especially when

Neil stepped in to place the couple's right hands together and proclaim them husband and wife.

Ann-Marie sniffed with emotion, her chin trembling, eyes streaming, as Neil smiled at the groom. "Steven, you may kiss your wife."

There was delighted applause as Ann-Marie grabbed Steve to pull his face down towards hers so that she could plant a passionate kiss on his lips. Then she whispered urgently in his ear, gesturing to something behind her. Not certain what was happening, Neil realized that Steve had slipped his hand down Ann-Marie's back, then suddenly the bodice of her dress burst into brilliant colour as dozens of tiny lights sewn into the material flashed and sparkled. A gasp of admiring astonishment resounded around the church before the congregation got to their feet stamping and cheering. Glancing up again in Peter's direction, Neil wasn't surprised to see that the churchwarden was looking very disapprovingly at the theatricals.

Finally, Neil called for silence so that he could carry on with the service. Speaking quietly to the couple, he invited them to kneel on the step below him so that he could ask for God's blessing on their marriage. He soon realized this was easier said than done, as Ann-Marie struggled to get down on her knees beneath the folds of her huge flashing wedding gown. Steve looked on helplessly as the chief bridesmaid crept forward and shoved her hands up the bride's dress so that she could guide her knees safely onto the step.

Waiting patiently for the bridesmaid to move back to her seat, Neil raised his hand to bless the couple before inviting the congregation to stand for the hymn, a rousing if perhaps slightly inappropriate choice: "The Battle Hymn of the Republic".

As Clifford struck up the opening chords, Neil bent down to speak quietly so that only the bride and groom could hear him.

"I'm going up to the altar where we will have more prayers. Could you two please follow me up there during this hymn?"

"Mine eyes have seen the glory of the coming of the Lord..." sang the congregation as Neil turned to make his way up to the altar, reaching it just as they were getting to the chorus they all knew:

> *Glory, glory, hallelujah!*
> *Glory, glory, hallelujah!*
> *Glory, glory, hallelujah!*
> *His truth is marching on.*

At this point Neil became aware that, apart from singing, he could also hear the sound of laughter. He turned round to see Ann-Marie and Steve, both still on their knees, crawling up past the choir stalls to reach him at the altar.

"Oh, my goodness!" cried Neil. "You don't need to stay on your knees. Just get up and walk."

"I can't," replied Ann-Marie firmly.

"I'll help you, babe," offered Steve.

She turned to him sharply. "I can't, all right! In this dress, once I'm down, I'm down. When he says we've finished all the bits where we've got to be *down*, I'll get *up*. Understood?"

"OK, babe," agreed a decidedly sheepish Steve.

"So, Vicar, is it OK for me to stop here for the *down* bit?" Ann-Marie asked Neil the question in a tone that defied him to suggest she had to move an inch further.

"That will be fine," replied Neil, who'd got to the point where he didn't care if the two of them did a jig while he said the prayers, as long as they got on with it.

Once the prayers were over, both Steve and Neil bent down to offer supporting arms to Ann-Marie as she got triumphantly to her feet, and returned with her husband to the seats waiting for them at the front of the church. Neil began his sermon, aware that the bride was constantly nudging her groom, pointing out guests in the crowd and blowing kisses at them.

After that, the service went relatively smoothly. Three of the bride's friends stepped out to sing while the register was being signed. Looking at each other for encouragement, they sang to a backing track: "Here I am, baby: signed, sealed, delivered, I'm yours!"

The congregation loved them, whispering to each other how good they were as they waited for the new Mr and Mrs Green to emerge from the vestry. With a nod from Neil, Cliff burst into an enthusiastic rendition of Mendelssohn's "Wedding March" as the couple made their way down the aisle. The bride's flashing dress once again swept along the flower displays at the end of each pew, while Steve struggled to hang on to his wife, although there was no space for him to walk by her side.

Following behind them, the guests filed out of the pews as Peter came across to Neil, whistling under his breath. "Well!" he exclaimed. "I'm relieved that those lights on her dress worked properly. I'm not sure our insurance would have been much good if they'd burst into flames."

"Oh, don't worry, Vicar," said the bride's mother as she came towards them, digging deep into the voluminous bag she was carrying. "I came prepared!"

Like a magician, she produced a small red fire extinguisher from the bag, waving it in the air cheerily before pushing her way through the crowd to greet her newly married daughter.

* * *

"Come in," said Sue, rather surprised to find Clifford Davies, of all people, at their door asking to see James. "He's in the living room."

The room was dim when Clifford walked inside: the curtains were closed, although it was mid-afternoon. A small table lamp shed light on the hunched figure in an armchair that looked far too big for him.

"Good gracious!" cried Cliff, who had never been known for his tact and diplomacy. "Look at the state of you. Oh, I know about Danny going through a tough time. But you? You look dreadful!"

There was a sharp intake of breath from Sue, who was standing behind him.

James looked up at Cliff with eyes that were almost lifeless.

"Go away." His voice was so low, he could hardly be heard. "Get out of my house."

"Why? So you can sit here and wallow in self-pity? If anyone should be getting out of this house, it's you."

"Get him out, Susan. I don't want him here."

"Don't you move a muscle, Sue," said Cliff, drawing up a chair in front of James.

"Now, look here, James. In all the time I've known you, you were always a smart, clever man who took pride in his behaviour and appearance. You've been through a terrible time, no one's denying that. But can you explain to me how you sitting here in the dark, stubble all over your face, looking like you haven't had a decent meal for weeks, can possibly help the situation in any way?"

"You don't understand…"

"Well, let's just see about that. You've got a son who's sensitive, but he's actually very capable and talented, and you've been far too hard on him for years. Everyone but you could see that. He couldn't cope with it, and was finally driven to the point where he tried to take his own life. He didn't manage it, though – so now, thank God, you've got another chance to be the dad he needs you to be. And how are you facing up to that chance? You're just sitting here feeling sorry for yourself, when it's your son who really needs sympathy. And what about your wife? She's Danny's mother. She's watched you bullying him – and probably her too – for years. But she's still here caring for you, when it's you who should be caring for her. After all, most of what's happened is your fault."

"Don't you think I know that?" snapped James. "Of course it's my fault! Of course it is! But can you imagine for just one minute how it feels, to know your own son would rather die than live one more day in your company? It destroys you. It destroys you." James's whole body shuddered with despair and anguish.

Clifford moved his chair forward, placing both his hands on James's knees as he spoke. "But you can't let that happen. That won't help Danny. It won't help Sue. And it's certainly not helping you."

"He thinks he might be gay," sobbed James.

"That's OK. So am I. Nothing wrong with that. Besides, he's still young. His feelings may change. They may not. Either way, he'll still be Danny."

"I don't know him. What good can I be to him if I don't know anything about my own son?"

"Well, that's up to you, isn't it? You can either keep on wailing about what you *can't* do, or you can stop sitting here sniffling like a big girl's blouse, and start doing something useful. I bet Danny's feeling pretty lonely right now. I bet he's full of guilt because he thinks he's let you down again. But you've let him down too, haven't you? Isn't it time you started working out what you can do to build bridges with your own son? What about reassuring him that you're proud of him and you love him – no matter what? What about telling him you'll be there for him, on his terms, whenever he needs you? That you're prepared to listen to him rather than just talk at him? Those are the questions you need to find answers to. And to do that, you've got to get out of that chair, smarten yourself up – and get on with life!"

The silence in the room was deafening. James looked intently at Clifford, who steadily held his gaze. Then, very slowly, James turned to look at Sue, who was cowering in the doorway. "I think I could do with a shower," he said, "and a change of clothes. My razor's still in the bathroom, isn't it?"

"And when you come down," said Clifford, "how about you try eating a proper meal? It looks like you need it."

With great effort, James pushed himself up onto his feet, walking a few steps before he turned to look back at Clifford. "Thank you," he said simply, and started to make his way up the stairs.

Sue watched him go, open-mouthed with astonishment. "I can't believe you just did that," she said.

"Neither can I," replied Clifford. "I'd never make a counsellor, would I?"

She laughed. "No, but I think everyone's been pussyfooting around James, afraid to say anything that might upset him even more, when actually what he needed was some plain talking."

"He certainly got that – with both barrels," grinned Clifford.

A thought suddenly struck Sue.

"I forgot to ask you – what made you come tonight?"

"Well," said Clifford, "I do have an ulterior motive. I need James's help. The St Stephen's Extravaganza is in a fortnight's time and I need a pianist. He's the best I know."

Sue threw her head back and laughed. "So you didn't have

time to hang around. You need him fit, well and up to speed, and you need him now!"

"Got it in one," chuckled Clifford. "Let's go and see how our boy's doing, shall we?"

* * *

If someone were to ask Claire where she felt happiest of all, she would say in her vegetable plot at the bottom of Harry's garden. That evening as she dug her fork with a satisfying thud into the dark soil, she felt the sunshine warming her back. She loved this time of year, when the spring bulbs had faded, and the clusters of pale blossom on the trees were gradually drifting to the ground. The heavy scent of hawthorn hung in the air now, along with the delicate sweetness of the elderflowers which suddenly appeared on normally insignificant-looking trees along the roadsides and on almost every piece of waste ground. It was a time of change and promise. Change and promise? That sounded a bit like her life right now.

Change was most definitely on the way and, on the whole, she welcomed it. She knew that in time she would love Derbyshire. She and Neil had been charmed by the small town as soon as they drove into the High Street. There were solid-looking houses, slightly old-fashioned shops with window displays full of bits and pieces you'd never find in a supermarket, and homely signs of the rural community who lived and worked there.

Neil's face had lit up with enthusiasm the moment they walked through the porch gate of St Jude's. Together they wandered through the graveyard with its mixture of ancient and recent plots, lovingly cared for by family members who could trace their surnames back for generations. They loved the shadowy warmth inside the church, punctuated by the pools of light shining through the Victorian stained glass. Neil touched each pew on his way up the aisle, climbing into the pulpit and gripping the dark wood as he leaned forward to look at an imaginary congregation. Then he moved back to sit in the stately old chair that could well become his. As Claire watched, she could see he was instantly drawn to the place. Meeting key members of the parish council had cemented his feeling that he could happily work here. He was sure this could be his spiritual home and that his ministry could have meaning and purpose in this warm-hearted Christian family.

When they were shown around the vicarage, with its rambling rooms that seemed to echo with the sound of children's laughter, and its views from every upstairs window that drew the eye over miles of Derbyshire countryside, she felt the place wrapping itself around her heart. They could settle here. They could create a home they loved for themselves and for Sam – and perhaps one day for other children they might be blessed with too. They had driven back down the motorway in an excited haze of hope and adventure, certain that they had glimpsed their future and loving what they had seen.

But now she was digging in her favourite place in all the world and the sun was shining and the air was sweet. Around her she could see the first shoots of all the vegetables she'd planted and nurtured in the plot she had worked on for years. She loved this garden. She would miss it.

She stopped to get her breath for a while, looking around at this patch of land in which she knew every twig, branch, weed and insect. What would happen when she wasn't here to care for it? She glanced across the fence where Iris's garden backed on to Harry's. How would the two of them manage if she and Neil were no longer on call for them? Neither of them was getting any younger.

She sighed. They'd be OK. They had friends here. The crowd at St Stephen's would keep a watchful eye on them, and there'd be a new minister to look after them and all the people in Dunbridge who had become so dear to her. Besides, she would be the wife of the man she loved – and she did love him, didn't she? She would be moving to Derbyshire not because she had to, but because she wanted to be at his side, sharing his life for ever. Two become one, forsaking all others.

Unbidden, an image of Ben swam into her head. With a determined shrug of her shoulders she lifted the fork. Yes, she thought, there were many things she would miss in the life ahead of her. She'd miss this garden. She'd miss the town.

Wedging her heel in place, she thrust the fork and the rest of her thoughts firmly into the ground.

* * *

"You're here!" Clifford's face lit up with relief as James walked into the church hall, Sue at his side. Several of those gathered for the rehearsal looked surprised and called out a greeting, but James kept his eyes on Clifford as he marched across to the keyboard.

"Where's the music?"

"Right here, maestro!" replied Clifford. "This is the first number. Keep the pace up. Don't let it get stodgy. OK: places, everyone! From the top, after my count. Huh-one, two, three, four!"

* * *

Ben arrived home from work that evening to find Wendy sitting on the floor leaning against the sofa, the carpet around her covered in photographs. She seemed unusually preoccupied, picking up first one photo and then another, gazing at them all.

Ben quietly lowered himself to sit beside her. As he studied two or three of the pictures, he realized how many of them were of Neil: Neil at the church, Neil at some sort of gathering in the market square, Neil with a pint of beer in his hand, Neil smiling at the camera with his arm round Wendy's shoulders.

"You still love him?" he asked gently.

She nodded. "Stupid, isn't it? I don't know what it is about him. He's not particularly good-looking. He's not especially bright. He's awkward and clumsy and often gets himself in a mess."

Ben smiled. "So that's why you're drawn to him. You want to save him from himself."

"He needs it!" She thought for a moment. "Well, he used to need it. He seems to be doing rather well at the church these days. He's grown into it – grown up, I suppose."

"And that makes you want him even more?"

"Stupid, eh?"

He reached over to take her hand. "We can't always choose who we love – and we can't always have who we choose, not if they don't choose us."

She looked at him with what could almost be a smile. "A couple of rejects. That's us, isn't it?"

"Are we? Do you think there's no chance for either of us, then?"

"Perhaps for you. You're Sam's dad. You'll always have a place in Claire's life because of that."

"It's not just about Sam, though, for me. Seeing Claire again – well, it's hit me harder than I thought."

"You love her."

"I realize now that I never stopped. When we were together, it was just magical. From the moment we met, there was such a spark between us. I've never felt anything like it. I don't think I ever will again."

"Do you think she feels the same?"

"She remembers. I know she does. Although she's fighting it."

"And she's marrying Neil."

"I left it just too late, didn't I? The night of their engagement? If only I'd come across a few weeks earlier."

"Do you honestly think it would have made a difference?"

"I don't know. I'd like to think so. There's still a powerful attraction between us, but she's honourable and decent. She's promised to Neil and I don't think she'd break that promise."

"Even if she knows she's still drawn to you?"

"She's never said that. She wouldn't. It's just a feeling I get."

"So are you going to act on that feeling?"

"I don't know. I might."

Wendy eyed him thoughtfully. "You know, there's an old saying. What you don't tell people, they won't know. Maybe Claire doesn't know how much you feel. Maybe she thinks it's all about Sam, whereas it's really about her, isn't it? Tell her. Tell her straight."

"All or nothing?"

"Why not?"

"And you? Does Neil really know how deeply you feel for him?"

"Probably not. I've played games with him; I know that. I thought he needed me so much, he wouldn't be able to resist coming back. He probably would have done if Claire hadn't turned up when she did."

"Will they be happy, do you think?"

"I hope not."

He laughed. "You don't mean that."

"No, I don't, really. I'd like him to be happy. I just wish it was with me."

"Well, you said it yourself: what you don't say, people won't know. You're pretending your feelings are casual, and you're simply his friend, but you're not being honest with him, are you?"

"You think I should tell him?"

"What have you got to lose?"

"Exactly the same as you, I guess."

"So what do you think? We both make our last stand, declare our feelings and see where it gets us?"

"I will if you will."

"Whatever happens, you'll be OK, Wendy. You're a beautiful, resourceful woman. Any man would be glad to have you on his arm."

"It's got to be the right man, though, hasn't it?"

"Or the *next* right man – and there will be one, I know." And Ben lifted her hand to his lips and kissed it.

⋙ Chapter 11 ⋘

Tickets for the Extravaganza sold so well that eventually the decision was taken to put on two performances on the Saturday of the late May bank holiday, one in the afternoon and one in the evening. The week leading up to "Show Day", as Clifford called it, was manic, and try as he might to stay out of the nitty-gritty of the organization, Neil found himself dragged in on every level. It was fortunate that Brian Lambert had recovered sufficiently to be able to take over most of the music duties in the church itself, as James seemed to be constantly tied up playing for rehearsals with one group or another. Clifford was described by Peter Fellowes as "always around but never there": he seemed to be constantly rushing between meetings about set design, costume making, props collection, the sound system, lighting, ticket sales, whether the dancing girls should be allowed to use pointe shoes or not, how to stop the stage in the church hall from being too slippery, who was authorized to use the smoke machine, the layout of seating in the afternoon when there would be lots of wheelchairs as opposed to the evening when there would not – and even what flavour ice-cream should be served in the interval!

Calling in to the dress rehearsal the night before the performance, Neil went to sit next to Sue, who was keeping out of the way in a seat at the back.

"How's James doing?" he asked, looking over to what Clifford euphemistically called "the orchestra pit", where the piano had been placed alongside an electric keyboard (to be manned at certain times in the programme by Wendy), with a drummer and two guitarists from the worship group to swell the sound.

"Unbelievable really, when you think how shattered he was after that day – and even more remarkable when you consider what sort of person he was all the years leading up to it. It's as if he's decided to wipe the slate clean of everything he was before, and start again. That sharp temper of his, his assumption that he was always right, always in charge, always the centre of the universe – that's not something I see these days. In some ways I miss it: I feel as if I'm living with a completely different man after all these years."

"Do you trust it? Do you think he'll revert to type?"

"I'm not sure. Funnily enough, the way he is now reminds me of what he was like when I first met him back in the sixth form. That was before he joined the army and worked his way up the ranks, until it was his job to boss everyone about if they didn't come up to the regulation high standards."

"So perhaps he *is* reverting to type?"

"I hope so. The James I fell in love with was a really lovely man. Who knows? Perhaps both of us are going to find him again."

"And Danny? How's he?"

"He's good. The place he's living in is really very nice. The staff are great: supportive and encouraging, always got time for a chat with the lads – or me when I pop in."

"Do you go often?"

"Just once a week at the moment, but they're happy to loosen the rules on that if Danny himself wants it, and especially if it's seen as part of his journey back to his own life. He could choose to live at home again in the future."

"What does he do there?"

"He's at college doing GCSEs. He's chosen a good range of subjects – a lot his old dad would approve of, and several I'm glad to see him have a chance to study, like art and music, and something called food technology. I think it used to be domestic science in my day."

"Has James seen him yet?"

"Just once. The case worker organized it but stayed in the background. I went in as well, but I stood back so the two of them could take things at their own speed."

"Was it difficult?"

"I don't think Danny expected to see his dad so changed, not just physically but in character too. James was more nervous than he was, I think. They made small talk for a bit, and then out of the blue Danny suddenly burst into tears and blurted out how sorry he was. Well, that was it because then James was in tears too, hugging Dan as if his life depended on it."

"All of you have been through so much," said Neil gently.

"Yes," agreed Sue, looking down at her hands. "Yes, we have."

"One more time with the lifeboat sketch, please!" shouted Clifford at the other end of the hall. "And girls, please don't screech. You're supposed to be gentle Victorian ladies..."

"Actually," said Sue, smiling now at the goings-on at the front, "I have a bit of a surprise in mind for James."

"You do?"

"I do – so say a prayer for me, Neil. I think I might need it."

* * *

Just before two o'clock on Saturday afternoon, Neil took his seat in the hall alongside Claire, Sam, Harry and Iris. There was a buzz of excitement as the audience trooped in, many of them waving to greet him. When the minibus from the Mayflower arrived, a simple wave wasn't enough for Artie, who whistled and shouted from the side aisle where space had been left for all their wheelchairs.

At last the hall lights dimmed and one single spotlight illuminated a gold-backed chair and a round table covered in a deep red cloth, placed at one side of the stage. Through the closed curtains stepped Clifford, moving to take up his place at the table in a resplendent outfit that looked as if it belonged to the ringmaster at a circus.

"Ladies and gentlemen!" he announced. "Welcome to the St Stephen's Extravaganza, which our company has prepared for your delectation and delight. We wish to make it clear, though, that the most important ingredient for enjoyment this afternoon is chiefly yourselves. So feel free to laugh out loud, stamp your feet, clap your hands, sing along…"

"Heckle?" asked a voice from the back.

"Er, no, sir, heckling may be frowned upon unless it is totally appreciative! So please would you put your hands together to welcome the whole company on stage for their opening number 'Tonight's the Night'."

James and the band struck up, and the curtains were pulled back to reveal a chorus line of familiar faces all dressed in bright red and gold costumes. One song flowed neatly into another as toes tapped, hands clapped, men swayed, ladies twirled, occasionally in time with the music, but always with smiles and gusto.

The programme was a masterpiece of variety. There were two other big production numbers in the first half. One was entitled "Cockney Sparrow", with all the performers dressed like pearly kings and queens singing old favourites like "My Old Man", "Maybe it's Because I'm a Londoner" and "Underneath the Arches", finishing with an energetic rendition of "Knees up, Mother Brown". The other was a vision of red, white and blue, which Clifford introduced as "Yankee Doodle Dandy", where the company had everyone singing along to "Polly Wolly Doodle", "When the Saints Go Marching in", "Red, Red Robin", "Sonny Boy" and "Swanee", which brought the house down. In between the big production pieces came individual acts: John Harris with a deft display of magic; a high-kicking chorus line from the local dancing school; and ten-year-old Kyle from the church choir, singing "Bless this House" in a sweet treble voice that brought a tear to many an eye in the hall. The popular singing duo Ken and Elizabeth Hanson had a starring role too, and Neil glanced over with interest to see that once again Artie remained doggedly silent during their spirited "All Together Now" of old wartime songs.

Sylvie had come along with the Mayflower group, and in the interval she managed to grab Neil and draw him into a quiet corner.

"I think I've found him."

"Artie's son?"

"Yes, your contact at the Salvation Army Missing Persons Bureau was really helpful. He told me how to access public records and exactly where to look, and I might just have tracked him down. Believe it or not, if I've got the right man, he's still living in Burnley, where Artie lived with his wife until she died."

"So he lived round the corner but chose never to get back in touch with his mum and dad? Makes you wonder if he'd want anything to do with Artie now."

"Well, we can but try. I've written him a letter asking if he could be the right Ian Stuart Simpson and explaining about Artie's situation. Just have to wait and see if he replies."

"Thanks for doing that, Sylvie. Let's hope it works out."

At that moment, the lights started to dim again, so Neil hurried back to his seat as the curtains opened on yet another production number, this time a country and western scene with everyone dressed up as cowboys, singing numbers like "I've Got Spurs that Jingle, Jangle, Jingle", "Home on the Range" and "I'm a Bow-legged Chicken". The jazz band from Dunbridge Upper School brought cheers from the crowd – and then it was the turn of The Amazing Houdini. The escapologist's wife was sternly watching his every move from the front row, so he plainly hadn't managed to escape from her even for the big day! His act produced gasps and cheers, though, bringing the show to its grand finale.

"And now, ladies and gentlemen," announced Clifford, "I ask you this. While you sleep soundly in your beds, do you ever spare a thought for our country's seamen, who sail the high seas to bring food to our table and clothes to our backs? And when the wind roars and the waves roll, think for a while about the hardy sailor, tossed and battered in the storms of life, adrift at sea with no one to save him. That's when the call goes out to our noble lifeboat men. We pay tribute to them now with 'Who Will Man the Lifeboat?'."

The curtains opened to show stretched across the back of the stage a deep band of blue paper, cut and painted to look like high waves on a stormy sea. In dramatic silent movie style, James played some jaunty seafaring music as a brightly coloured boat appeared to bob its way across the sea. Suddenly, the boat turned ninety degrees onto its end and sank slowly out of sight.

At that moment, a group of Victorian ladies stepped onto the left of the stage, primly singing as if they had a plum in their mouths. The words of the old hymn brought a smile to the older members of the audience who remembered it from their childhood. The dramatic music and the overacting had everyone in fits of laughter, especially when, while the ladies were singing, a seaman in an old-fashioned long-legged stripy swimsuit could be seen bobbing up and down in the sea behind them, desperately trying to attract their attention as he drowned.

> *Who will man the lifeboat?*
> *Who the storm will brave?*
> *Many souls are drifting*
> *Helpless on the wave;*
> *See their hands uplifted,*
> *Hear their bitter cry;*
> *"Save us ere we perish,*
> *Save us ere we die!"*

With the poor seaman still waving and getting ever more desperate behind them, the ladies were joined on the other side of the stage by a group of courageous lifeboat men, complete with handlebar moustaches, galoshes and sou'westers, who took up various poses to show their manly strength and prowess. With deep, gruff voices, they reassured the ladies in suitably dramatic terms:

> *We will man the lifeboat,*
> *We the storm will brave,*
> *We will help to rescue*
> *Dying souls today.*

We will man the lifeboat,
We will breast the wave,
All its dangers braving,
Precious souls to save.

After several more verses from both the ladies and lifeboat men, the poor sailor was seen to give up the ghost as he plunged backwards, arms akimbo, heading for Davy Jones's locker. At that moment, the music became dramatically patriotic as the lifeboat men finally turned to notice what was happening. In bold movements, they reached into the sea to drag out the hapless seaman and set him upright so that he could regain his composure and stand smartly to attention to salute the plucky lifeboat men. The music rose as the assembled chorus sang "Rule Britannia", and the place erupted with applause and laughter as Elizabeth Hanson was reverently pushed onto the stage in a huge chariot, looking every inch the image of Britannia, complete with shield and tin helmet.

Clifford shouted over the clamour to ask the crowd to thank everyone, with special mention being made of James Molyneux and the "orchestra", who had done such a wonderful job. And as James stood to acknowledge the applause, he noticed the two people who were first to get to their feet, clapping more enthusiastically than anyone else in the hall. At Sue's side was his son Danny, looking at him with such pride and love that James had to sit down suddenly as the emotion of the moment swept over him.

He's here. My boy is here!

And with the cheers of the crowd still ringing around him, he put his head in his hands with sheer happiness.

* * *

"But where are we going?" Pauline was filled with curiosity as Audrey walked purposefully along, urging her friend to keep up.

"You'll see. At least, I *hope* you'll see the same as me."

"I've never known you as excited as this. I can't think what on earth would make you react this way."

"Stop talking and walk faster. Then you'll know."

Audrey led her up the side street and into the market square, where she kept walking until they stopped on the pavement right in the middle of the main row of shops.

"Look!" said Audrey, pointing across the road to the other side.

"At what?" asked Pauline, scanning the scene in front of her.

"At that empty shop." Audrey was gesturing towards a shop front with a pretty wooden surround, standing in a prime position next door to the town's main bank.

"Where Martin's the jewellers used to be?"

"Yes. What do you think of it?"

Pauline turned sharply to Audrey. "Stop talking in riddles and tell me what's on your mind!"

"I think that would make the perfect location for a really *good* flower shop."

"You're thinking of opening a flower shop?"

"I'm thinking we might *both* open a flower shop: you and me, as partners!"

"Heavens!" Pauline looked across at the shop, her mind reeling. "Well, I know you've run a shop before," she said at last, "but I've only ever done the accounts in the back office. What on earth could I bring to something like this?"

"You could bring your financial experience. And you could manage the record keeping and stock control – I was always hopeless at that. You could contribute a lot to the floral arrangements – your skills are really good now. We both drive, so we could both do deliveries. We'll be imaginative when it comes to special promotions. Just think how we always come up with something different for the flowers at St Stephen's to match every event in the Christian calendar! We've both got a bit of money put by which we've talked about wanting to invest in a constructive way. We've both been through tough times – but we know we've still got a lot of life left in us. Why not? Why not pool our resources and work together on this? I just know we could make a go of it!"

"Do you think there's enough profit to be made in something like this? After all, everywhere from the supermarket to the garage sells flowers nowadays."

"But we'll do arrangements that are stylish and thoughtful and imaginative and pretty and homely and striking – and cheap! That'll be our main selling factor. We'll always come up with something different at an affordable price."

"Will that work, d'you think? Would we be able to get the flowers cheaply enough to do it?"

"I've done my sums on this. I have the paperwork at home. Are you game at least to have a look at it?"

Pauline smiled, taking Audrey's arm as she took one last look at the shop.

"What are we waiting for, then?"

* * *

Neil had had a hard day. It wasn't usual for him to have a christening on a weekday, but he'd been asked to organize a private service for a couple he hadn't met before, whose daughter Emily had just celebrated her third birthday. Emily's mother's parents were visiting from their home in the Far East. It was their dearest wish that they should be able to share in the joy of their granddaughter's baptism, and Neil was very happy to oblige.

Charles and Delia Ford arrived with Emily, who looked charming in an embroidered silk dress that was both dainty and demure. A small group of family and friends soon gathered to join them, including the two women and one man who had been asked to become Emily's godparents. Neil invited them to sit for a while in the church office so that he could talk with the godparents and make sure they fully understood the commitment they were undertaking on behalf of the little girl's spiritual welfare.

Neil was the first to admit that he had little experience with young children, except for Sam, who was easy company compared to young Emily. It became clear very early on in the proceedings that she had her parents firmly wrapped around her little finger.

When the party headed towards the church, she tugged at her mother's arm because she wanted to stay in the church office. When the grown-ups started walking towards the Victorian font in which generations of children had been christened, she spotted the toy corner, and bellowed her objection as she was taken away so that the service could start. As Neil recited the ancient words of the baptismal service, Emily refused point blank to be held by either her grandparents or her godparents-to-be, insisting instead that only Mummy would do.

This is going to be fun, thought Neil – and he was right.

In the end, it was decided that it would be safer to let Delia carry on holding Emily, with Neil standing at her side so that he could pray over her and make the sign of the cross on her forehead. With an expression in her eyes to match the indignation of any bolshy teenager, the little girl first looked at the water in the font and then stared menacingly at Neil. Carefully propping up the service book where he could read it if necessary, Neil scooped up some water and aimed for the child's head. She was much quicker than he was. In an instant, she'd grabbed his fingers, bitten down on them viciously with her sharp little teeth, and in the chaos that followed, slipped out of her mother's grasp and started hot-footing it down the aisle. With Mum, Dad, three godparents, two grandparents and Neil in hot pursuit, the little girl ducked and dived her way around the church – up and down the pews, over the top of the choir stalls, underneath the altar cloth, in and out of the vestry – before she disappeared completely.

Panic-stricken minutes later, with Delia sobbing and Charles snapping at her to stop snivelling and pull herself together, their little angel was found sitting demurely in a corner behind the organ, where she was completely hidden. Her father picked her up, brooking no argument as he carried her back down to the font. There, with Charles practically pinning her to him, and Neil trying all angles before he eventually managed to paint the semblance of a cross on her forehead, the deed was done. After that, Emily wriggled away, sobbing dramatically, as Neil hastily handed out the lit baptismal candle and drew the proceedings to an end. There was relief all round when the family left the church as soon as they could, with one of the godmothers clutching Emily's baptismal certificate tightly in her hand.

Questioning whether fatherhood could ever be a good thing, Neil had just collapsed exhausted into his chair in the church office when he heard a knock on the door.

"Am I disturbing you?" asked Wendy.

"Never! Come on in."

"I wanted to have a quiet word with you."

"Of course; take a seat."

She laughed nervously as she perched on the side of his desk. "This is embarrassing, really."

"For heaven's sake, we know each other better than that."

"OK. Well, someone said to me recently that what you don't tell people, they may never know – so there's something I need to tell you."

"Yes?"

"I need to tell you…" She hesitated, clearly uncertain whether to continue.

Curious and concerned, Neil moved over to sit on the desk beside her, surprised to find that she was trembling.

"Wendy, what on earth's the matter? Whatever it is, you can tell me."

She turned to look him straight in the eye. "I'm in love with you. That's what's the matter. I've loved you from the moment I first saw you. I've tried hard to fight how I feel – to go out with other people, fill my time with different things so that I think about you less – but none of it alters the fact that every second of every day, you are on my mind. I love the way you look. I love the way you think. I love how you smell and feel and move. I love how you care about everything and everybody. I love the way you've grown into the role of minister here with all the ability and promise I recognized in you from the very start."

Neil looked at her wordlessly.

"I've never really understood what went wrong between us. There you were, just about to go off for your ordination as a priest, and we seemed closer than ever. We'd shared so much of what you'd gone through during that first year. We prayed together. We talked endlessly about the Bible and what our faith meant to us. And we loved each other, didn't we? I didn't get that wrong, did I, Neil?"

"No, you didn't."

"And there was an attraction between us too?"

"Definitely."

"Then what did I do wrong, Neil? Why did it change so suddenly? Why did you come back from your holiday after your ordination certain that we had no future? Was it all about Claire – or was it me? Is there something wrong with me? Because if there is, I do need to know if I'm ever going to find true and lasting happiness with someone as wonderful as you."

"No, Wendy, you did nothing wrong. You showed me nothing but loving kindness and loyalty."

"So why?"

"Because it wasn't until I found myself being drawn to Claire that I began to realize what love really is. You can't predict it or force it or deny it. And I can see that to you, and to just about everyone at St Stephen's in the beginning, Claire must have seemed an unlikely choice for me – but she touches my heart and soul in a way that has my senses reeling."

"And you're sure of your future with her? Even though Ben still loves her and most likely she still loves him?"

"Ben is Sam's father. Claire's only interested in him as far as their son is concerned…"

"You're burying your head in the sand if you believe that. Whatever she says, or even thinks she feels, I can tell you there's still a deep bond between them. Ben's told me so. She knows it and so does he. Once you've shared a love as passionate as theirs, the possibility of rekindling that passion is only ever a heartbeat away."

"Claire's always been very open about her feelings for Ben. She's made her choice and that choice is me."

"So when Ben asks her to marry him, which is what he's doing right now, and tells her about the home and the life he can provide for his wife and son in Australia, you're confident she won't be tempted?"

Neil didn't answer. He stared at Wendy, his mind racing with questions.

"He's asking her right now?" he mumbled at last.

"Sam wanted Ben to have tea at their house this evening."

"I know. Claire mentioned she'd agreed to that."

"Ben plans to propose to Claire tonight. He's going to lay it all out before her: the way he feels about her, his understanding of how he let her down in the past, reassurances about the sort of man he's become since then and what he hopes to offer her and their son. He wants them to be a family, because that's what they should be – Mum, Dad and their little boy."

"She'll say no."

"Are you sure?"

"If she has any uncertainty about it, she'll talk to me."

"Well," said Wendy, running her finger down Neil's face, "if she does take up Ben's offer, if her love for you isn't strong enough in comparison with what he has to offer, then I need you to know, my darling Neil, that I'll be here for you. I'm always here, always concerned for your happiness and welfare, putting you first, loving you with every fibre of my body."

Neil caught her hand and pulled it back from his face. "Wendy, don't. Whatever happens between Claire and me, you need to understand that I don't and can't feel for you as you want me to. I know now that I never will. Claire's the one I want to spend my life with. She's the only woman I could ever love."

Wendy smiled. "Let's hope she feels the same way, then, Neil. Let's just wait and see, shall we?"

* * *

Shaken by Wendy's visit, Neil stared at the clock on the wall after she'd gone. He was due in the church shortly to say Evening Prayers, and then he had to get ready for the confirmation course he was taking later that night. He had urgent phone calls to make, paperwork to catch up on – and none of that mattered at all if, right at this moment down the road in Vicarage Gardens, the woman he loved was making a decision to exclude him from her life. Should he go down there? Should he arrive like a knight in shining armour to claim his lady? Or did she need this time to hear what Ben had to say? Time to think, time to make the decision that really was what she wanted for herself and her son.

He felt cold suddenly, chilled to the bone at the thought of losing her. Images of her danced into his mind – her green eyes flashing furiously at him on the first day he met her; her cheeks flushed and glowing when she came in from the garden triumphantly clutching an armful of vegetables she'd grown herself; the sweetness of her voice as she rocked Sam to sleep; the wind in her hair as they chased each other on the deserted beach they found on the coast; the way her body moulded into his when she made sure he caught her...

She had to be certain. There was no way forward for them unless she was. She needed time and space to make the right decision for them all.

Neil breathed in deeply and slowly, releasing his breath in a long, agonized sigh. Then he picked up his pen, opened his diary and started to punch out the first number on the list of calls he needed to make.

* * *

"You all right, Neil? You don't seem yourself tonight."

Peter glanced at Neil curiously during Prayers later that day when, as so often, they were the only two people to attend. The young curate plainly loved the familiar words of the Office, and always recited them by heart. It was so unlike him to stumble over the text as he had today.

"I'm fine."

"Not going down with anything?"

"I hope not."

"You haven't got time to be ill, have you?"

"Hardly."

Peter laid down his prayer book to look properly at Neil. "It is appreciated, you know, all the work you put in to keeping this church running smoothly. We do realize how much you have on your shoulders."

"I don't mind. It's my choice, my ministry."

"It shouldn't have been like this, though. If Margaret hadn't left so suddenly…"

"But she did, and it's probably been a good thing for me, being thrown in the deep end."

"Well, you won't be a curate for much longer. Your training's nearly up. Have you made any decisions about what you'd like to do next?"

"There are a few options – a parish in Derbyshire that looks really interesting."

"Have they offered you the post?"

"Yes, they have."

"And have you replied?"

"Not yet."

"No chance you might like to stay around in this area, then?"

"Well, that's certainly something to think seriously about. Harry's here, and my mum. It's difficult to uproot from somewhere I feel settled."

"I have no idea how we'll manage in this parish if you leave."

"That's been worrying me too. I've put a lot of work into St Stephen's, and know every single member of the congregation as a personal friend. It's really upsetting to think of the church being left unsupported. It'll be such a wrench to leave, but I have to, don't I? I don't want to be a curate for ever. I want to get on with the job of being the priest of a parish in my own right."

Peter nodded.

"I must get home, Peter. I've got a lot on my plate tonight."

Peter looked at him thoughtfully. "I can see that. And Neil, whatever it is that's worrying you, I ask God to bless you through it."

Caught unawares by Peter's perception and sensitivity, Neil caught his breath.

"Thank you, my friend. I'm going to need it."

* * *

Claire was in the kitchen when he arrived at Harry's house. She was wiping up the tea-time dishes, and though she smiled a greeting over her shoulder, she didn't stop what she was doing. Neil glanced at the draining board. Three plates, three sets of cutlery, three glasses. Ben, Claire and Sam – a family of three.

"OK?" he asked.

"Yes," she replied, as if the question surprised her.

"How's Sam?"

"Exhausted. All day at school wears him out."

"And his dad was here for tea tonight?"

"Yes."

"Did that go all right?"

"Hmm." Claire nodded absent-mindedly, apparently concentrating on some invisible stain she needed to rub off one of the glasses. "I think we should buy some new glasses. Uncle Harry got these free from the garage years ago, when we bought petrol."

"Did Ben stay long?"

"He read Sam a bedtime story."

"And after that, did he stay much longer?"

"A bit, yes."

"Did he have something on his mind, then?"

"What is this, Neil?"

"I just wondered what you talked about."

"Why? Why do you want to know?"

"What did you two talk about, Claire?"

"Nothing much." Her face was flushed. Neil knew she hated the way she blushed whenever she was flustered. She was plainly very flustered right now.

"Tell me, Claire. What did Ben want to talk to you about?"

"Oh, just leave it, Neil. There's nothing to say. What do you want to eat? How long have you got before you go out again?"

Neil leaned back against the kitchen work surface, his heart thumping. "So you're not going to tell me. You don't think there's anything to say about the fact that you've just been offered the chance to be a family by your son's father, the man you loved so much in the past?"

Claire looked shocked, unable to answer.

"You told me yourself that you still love him – like a family member, you said. Well, here he is, offering you the chance to become that family. How wonderful for Sam to be brought up by both his mother and his father! It's perfect. Even I can see that. And you weren't going to tell me, were you? What does that mean? You can't have refused him if you still need time to think about it. Or perhaps you didn't need to think at all. Perhaps you've already accepted his offer?"

Claire was staring at him, an unfathomable mix of fear and sadness in her eyes.

"So, are you going back to Australia with him? He's got a nice house, I hear. A good job, too. Australia's the land of opportunity – isn't that what they say on the telly? It'll be a great place for Sam to grow up. Lots of gardens for you to work your magic on too!"

"Don't, Neil."

"Or have you asked him to stay here? He seems to be very settled. He's obviously a good mechanic. Probably have his own business up and running here in Dunbridge before you know it!"

"Neil, stop! Please stop!"

"Stop what? Stop believing the dream that someone as wonderful as you could ever be mine? Stop trusting you? You weren't going to tell me about this, were you? I really believed you would. Aren't we supposed to share everything? Why wouldn't you tell me unless you're seriously considering his offer? Unless you dread what you know you should be telling me – that the decision that's right for you, the one that provides the best future for you and Sam, will be the decision that breaks me apart?"

* * *

The next morning, sitting at a small table outside the café, Claire put her face up to the June sunshine, welcoming its healing rays as they filtered down through her body. She was tired, so tired. Her body started to sway as she felt herself drifting off in the warmth, away from this seat, away from the square, shutting out for a while the bustle of the weekly market that surrounded her.

"Hello!"

She felt a tug on her sleeve. In front of her stood a young man, his face beaming as bright as the sunshine.

"Hello," she said, coming back to earth with a bump.

"I'm called William. I'm named after one of the two princes, but I'm not sure which one."

"Oh," she replied, trying to hide her smile. "How nice to meet you, William."

"You're pretty."

"Well, thank you!"

"I'm going to buy something for my girlfriend."

"That's nice. What do you think she'd like?"

"Girls like flowers." He suddenly looked worried. "I don't know where to buy flowers."

Claire glanced at the large flower stall directly behind him. "How about that stall over there? They've got lots of nice flowers."

"Oh!" said William, his face breaking into another broad grin as he looked around. "What flowers do girlfriends like?"

"She might like some roses. They're the flower of love."

"Which ones are they?"

"There are some small roses with lots of little buds at the end there. They're nice."

William stared at the roses, then allowed his gaze to wander along the length of the stall. "What flowers do you like?"

"I like really simple flowers, like those bunches of white daisies. They'd be my favourites."

"She'll like them, then," said William, wandering over to the stall without a backward glance.

Raising her face to the sun again, Claire drifted off into her own thoughts.

"Here you are!"

She opened her eyes to see William standing in front of her holding out a small bunch of white daisies.

"They're for you. You're my girlfriend."

"How very kind you are, William," smiled Claire, looking up towards Neil, who was just walking towards their table with two cups of coffee on a tray. "But I'm afraid I can't be your girlfriend, because this is my husband. At least, he will be my husband husband as soon as we can possibly arrange it. We love each other, you see. We've been through a lot. We've had quite a journey to get this far – but we both know now, with absolute certainty, that we belong together."

"OK," said William happily. "I'll find another girlfriend, then. Bye."

And Claire lifted her face once again as Neil blocked out the sun to plant a loving kiss on her willing lips.

⇒ CHAPTER 12 ⇐

*B*en handed in his notice at the garage the day after Claire turned down his marriage proposal. She'd listened carefully as he told her about the area of Australia where he lived, about the climate and the countryside and beautiful beaches nearby. He'd told her about the garage business he was building up, and about the spacious family home and large garden he had his eye on. He spoke of the excellence of the school system, and of his parents who were longing to welcome both her and their grandson into their lives. He spoke of his delight in getting to know Sam, who was everything and more than he'd ever imagined he would be. Then he declared his devotion to her and his longing to rekindle the love that had changed their lives with its intensity and promise when they first met.

She had listened to it all with such sincerity and warmth that he actually hoped her answer would be what he was longing to hear. And then she simply said no. Thank you – but no.

He'd pleaded and argued and cajoled, but her answer didn't change.

"It has to be no, Ben," she said at last, "because my home is here in England, along with Sam and Neil."

"But he's not Sam's father!"

"Neil was here when you weren't. Sam loves him. Over the last few months, I'm glad to say he's learned to love you too, and that's right and good. We have Skype and emails and texts. You can speak to Sam whenever you like. He's too young now, of course, but in time perhaps he can visit you in Australia. Or maybe you'll come back to England again to see him, and bring your own wife and family with you."

He left her that evening knowing it was over. It was time for him to go home. So he handed in his notice straight away and started packing.

Later that evening as he searched his laptop for possible flights at the right price, Wendy came in from school. Without comment, she kicked off her shoes and went into the kitchen to make herself an Earl Grey tea and him a strong, sweet coffee. Taking the cup from her, he noticed the dark circles under her eyes, as if she hadn't slept for days.

"How are you feeling?"

"Honestly? Absolutely dreadful. Hopeless, second choice, overlooked, inadequate, worthless. Take your pick!"

"You haven't been to the church this week, have you?"

"No. I really don't want to go there again."

"But it's your life. You grew up there. Surely you're not going to let that man run you out of your own church?"

"He didn't run me out. He's a really nice person. He would want me to be there. He's probably hoping I'll get over my silly infatuation, pull myself together, organize the worship group to sing something delightful at their wedding, and be the same old reliable Wendy I always have been."

"Stuff that!"

"My feelings entirely."

"So what are you going to do?"

"I don't know. I'm at a bit of a crossroads really."

"Well, why don't you come with me, then?"

"What?"

"Come back to Australia with me. Just for a holiday. You can take a look around and see if you like what's there."

"You can't be serious!"

"Why not? They're always looking for good teachers, and you're the head of a music department in an excellent school. They'll snap you up!"

"But my family are here."

"And they'll still be here if you decide to come back – or they can always visit if you find you like it enough to want to make a go of things there. It's a small world now, you know. Just a day of travel to get there and the same to get home."

"I'd have to give in my notice at school."

"Or you could say you're facing a family emergency and have to leave immediately."

She looked doubtful. "That would be untrue, reckless, irresponsible, totally out of character…"

"… and the start of a great adventure! Come on, Wendy, loosen up. You're an attractive, capable young woman and life's passing you by. Grab it! Come to Australia with me. Just come."

A smile spread slowly, so slowly, across her face until at last she grabbed a chair and came to sit beside him at the computer.

"Right! Where are we going and how do we get there?"

* * *

"I just wanted to check, Neil, that you received the copy of my sermon for Lady Romily's civic service tomorrow," said Bishop Paul when he rang.

"I saw your email, but haven't had chance to open it yet."

"That doesn't surprise me. These summer months are busy for a church like St Stephen's."

"Seven weddings, three baptisms, and six funerals so far this month. We have eleven candidates for confirmation, too, when you come to take that service in a few weeks' time."

"That's good. Are they all young people?"

"Mostly – but we also have a couple in their forties who've decided to be confirmed together after years of sharing their spiritual journey. Oh, and then there's Mr Roberts. He's been coming to services at St Stephen's for longer than anyone can remember. Well, he is nearly eighty, and he's just remembered that he never got round to being confirmed when he was a boy. He's suddenly got very worried that he might not be welcome in heaven if he's not got the certificate to say he was confirmed. He didn't want to come along to any of the classes, and honestly he doesn't need to – his knowledge of the gospel is probably better than mine. He wanted me to tell you, though, that when it comes to the questions you're going to ask him in the service, the answers are all 'yeses' and no 'nos'!"

Bishop Paul laughed. "And you, Neil? How are your plans for the future shaping up?"

"That parish in Derbyshire is very appealing."

"Have you given proper consideration to the idea of staying in this diocese? I'm very reluctant to lose a talented young minister like you. You're the future of our church."

"I'd like to, honestly I would, and so would Claire. It's a matter of finding the right church, though. We're really attached to the community here in Dunbridge. I'm not sure we'd be happy being *in* the area, but not actually *here*. You know that song about leaving your heart in San Francisco? Well, we'd be leaving our hearts here in Dunbridge. Not quite as musical, but you know what I mean."

There was silence while the bishop considered what Neil had said. "Anyway," he said at last, "I would like you to cast your eye over my sermon for tomorrow. I want to stress the importance of community, of people working together for the common good. And then I thought I'd talk about age-old Christian principles, and how they're as relevant today as they ever were. What do you think?"

Slightly surprised that a bishop should be seeking the opinion of a humble curate, Neil considered what he'd just heard. "That sounds good. You might include something about the future too – how important it is for us to pass on those Christian principles to our young people, who'll be carrying the flame of faith long after we've gone."

"An excellent idea. Got to get it right for Lady Romily!"

Neil groaned. "She's certainly a very exacting taskmaster."

"Driving you mad, is she?"

"I can't begin to tell you how relieved I'll be once this civic service is over."

"And by this time tomorrow, it will be. You do know I'm tied up with that conference for a good part of the day, don't you? I'm chairing the panel, so I won't be able to leave until two-thirty at the very earliest."

"You'll be cutting it quite tight. The service starts at three."

"My driver will be standing by. I'll be there."

"Promise? You won't abandon me to the wrath of Lady Romily, will you?"

"Of course not, dear boy. The very thought!"

* * *

Those words raced around Neil's mind the next day as he glanced nervously at his wrist watch. Ten to three, and there was still no sign of the bishop. Lady Romily was hosting a reception in the church hall for visiting dignitaries. They had arrived in their chauffeur-driven cars from all over the county, practically bringing traffic in the centre of Dunbridge to a standstill. She didn't seem to have noticed yet that her bishop, the main speaker of the day, was still missing.

Neil wasn't sure where to wait: on the church steps, where he could catch the first reassuring glimpse of the bishop's car as it arrived, or in the hall, welcoming Sir Andrew Bartlett's VIP guests to St Stephen's.

"Still no sign of him?" asked Peter, coming out of the packed church to join Neil on the steps.

Neil shook his head with frustration. "He promised he'd be here! He knew he would be cutting it fine with the conference in Bedford, but he said he'd definitely be here on time."

"Then he will," agreed Peter. "Look, you go over to the hall and line everyone up so that they can process into the church in the right order. I'll wait here."

Organizing a chattering crowd of dignitaries into some semblance of a line was far from easy. Most had a glass of wine in their hand, and they were reluctant to leave either their beverage or their conversation to be herded like schoolchildren, two by two, into a line led by Sir Andrew and his wife at the front, with Lord and Lady Romily immediately behind them.

As the procession reached the church door, Neil looked anxiously at his watch again. There was still no sign of Bishop Paul! At that moment, precisely three o'clock as previously arranged, Brian Lambert launched into Parry's "I Was Glad", the entrance music specially requested by Sir Andrew. Following the cross at the front of the procession, Sir Andrew took his place behind the choir as they all started a slow march down the aisle.

"Neil!" Peter hissed, grabbing Neil's robe as he too started to move off.

"I've just had a message from the bishop's office. The car's broken down. A flat tyre, apparently. They're working as fast as they can to get it repaired. The bishop asked if you could hold the fort until he gets here."

"What? Of course I can't! This service has been planned for months. He's just *got* to be here."

"And he will be, Neil. Just keep things going. I'm sure he'll arrive soon."

Neil felt like screaming with frustration, but instead he pinned what he hoped was a suitably sombre expression on his face and walked slowly down the aisle. As the special guests fanned out into the three front pews, shown to the places reserved for them by Cyn and her husband Jim, Neil remained centre front, where he bowed deeply to the crucifix, praying desperately that the bishop would be following him up the aisle at any moment. His heart sank when he turned round to see there was still no sign of him. He was on his own!

"Good afternoon and welcome to St Stephen's," he began. "It is a particular honour to welcome the Lord Lieutenant Sir Andrew Bartlett and his wife; Lord and Lady Romily; Mrs Hubert-Brown, the High Sheriff of Bedfordshire; the mayors and mayoresses of twelve different towns and communities across our county; distinguished members of the clergy and other honoured guests here this afternoon. We will start this civic service with a hymn based on the inspirational words of St Francis of Assisi, 'All Creatures that on Earth do Dwell'."

Brian took his cue, and the church was filled with the glorious full-throttle sound of the organ as the congregation opened their programmes to find the words. Once the hymn was safely under way, Neil walked as inconspicuously as possible across to Lady Romily. Her eyes narrowed as she looked at him.

"Ma'am, the bishop has been held up. Apparently his car has broken down."

She turned away from him to look ahead, briefly glancing down at the words of the hymn. "Reverend Fisher, this service will continue as planned."

Neil crept back to his seat confused and slightly irritated. What did she mean by that? How could she possibly consider that answer helpful? This service was *her* baby. What were *her* suggestions if the bishop simply didn't arrive?

Several minutes later, when the majestic hymn had come to an end, Sir Andrew moved into the centre aisle, bowed respectfully toward the cross, and took his place at the lectern, flattening out his notes before him. His speech was too long for most of the listeners, who began to lose interest somewhere in the middle of his long list of thanks, monotonously presented with great deliberation, with periods of illogical silence between each sentence.

Neil, however, would have preferred Sir Andrew's speech to last twice as long as it did, if only it would allow time for Bishop Paul to make his smiling, apologetic way down the aisle. However, as Sir Andrew resumed his seat, the bishop was still nowhere to be seen.

Sylvia Lambert got up then, taking her place in front of the choir. With a nod to her husband Brian, she lifted her arms as the introduction to John Rutter's arrangement of "For the Beauty of the Earth" began to echo around the church. The choir sang at their best, which wasn't surprising in view of the extra rehearsals they'd been putting in for weeks to make sure that their contribution to this special service was nothing less than a joy to hear.

Neil peered anxiously towards Peter, who was still standing at the main entrance from where he could keep an eye on the traffic outside. As Neil caught his eye, his heart sank. There was no cheery "thumbs up" to signal all was well; just a shrug and a grimace as Peter returned to watching the road.

There was an awful inevitability to the rest of the service after that, as Neil crossed off his programme each speech, prayer and anthem with increasing desperation. Finally, Lady Romily took her place at the lectern for the last reading of the afternoon. Once she'd come to the end, instead of stepping down as Neil expected her to, she addressed the gathering.

"We will now stand to sing our next hymn, 'Love Divine, all Loves Excelling', with words by the great Charles Wesley. After that, there will be a slight change to our programme. Unfortunately, the Bishop of Bedford has been unavoidably detained. He sends his heartfelt apologies and hopes to be with us later. Meanwhile, because the future of this county and this church is undoubtedly in the hands of the younger generation, I would like to ask our curate here at St Stephen's to provide the sermon."

Open-mouthed with shock, Neil stared pleadingly at Lady Romily, who managed to return to her seat without looking in his direction once. Frantically, he searched his brain to think of something he could say. What was it the bishop had talked about on the phone yesterday? Community and principles and young people? For one heart-stopping moment, he wondered again why a bishop should have wanted to talk through a keynote speech with someone as lowly as a curate. Could he have planned this? Surely not! That was a completely senseless idea…

As the hymn neared its end, Neil took several deep breaths to try and shut out the deafening thud of his own heartbeat, which was thundering in his ears. He had no notes, no ideas, no strength in his legs and no help in view as he slowly climbed the stairs to the pulpit. Then, as Brian brought the final chorus to a triumphant climax, Neil prayed as he'd never prayed before. *God, be in my head and in my heart and in my mouth and in my stupid brain and in my understanding. God, help me, help me, please!*

The audience took their seats, then looked expectantly at him. Choked with fear, Neil was amazed that any voice came out at all as he began to speak.

"In the name of the Father, the Son and the Holy Ghost. Amen."

He looked down on the faces staring back up at him: Lady Romily, Sir Andrew, the High Sheriff, the Mayor of Dunbridge, Harry, Iris and Claire. There was something in Claire's expression – the way she was looking at him with such love, willing him determination and courage – that seemed to calm his muddled thoughts as he desperately tried to think of how to start.

"I remember when I arrived in Dunbridge for the very first time," he began. "It was market day in the square as I drove through on my way to this church. I stopped the car for a while to look around and soak up some of the atmosphere of this town which could well become my home. I watched the stall holders selling their wares, serving people of all ages and backgrounds, neighbours living and working together in a town that I could immediately see was down-to-earth and friendly. The sense of community I felt in our square on that first visit was real and tangible, and it's that community which has surrounded and supported me in my role here ever since. Not everyone is a Christian, and yet I have been welcomed as a Christian minister in every aspect of life here – in the streets, in the pubs and clubs and at social gatherings, in our schools and residential care homes, in the hospice, in our shops and businesses. There is a sense of unity and belonging that draws all those individual elements into one, our town of Dunbridge, which has at its centre this great church that has stood not just at the heart of everyday life, but in the spirit and soul of this town for centuries.

"The principles of the Christian faith have been handed down to us by our Lord himself. They are the principles that made sense of the community in which he lived two thousand years ago – the same principles that make sense of our communities today. How can community life survive unless neighbour cares about neighbour; unless we make a point of trying to learn about and appreciate the different cultures and traditions that have become an integral part of most communities across our county and our country today; unless we have understanding and tolerance enough to allow each of our neighbours to be true to themselves, while at the same time asking for their understanding and tolerance of the beliefs and traditions that are dear to us? How can we expect compassion unless we show compassion to others? How can we teach our young, unless we are also willing to listen to them and learn about how they view the world we are building for them and will eventually relinquish to their care? How can we plan any sort of future unless we have an honest and realistic understanding of our past? How can we know our strengths unless we also accept our weaknesses and failings? And how could we possibly bring all those diverse elements together without having God at the centre of it all?

"Jonathan Sachs, who for many years was Chief Rabbi of the British Isles and the Commonwealth, once said very wisely, 'There is only one God, but he speaks many different languages; as many as there are people on earth.' We all hear God's word in our own individual way, as uniquely as God intended when he created each and every one of us to be different but equal. It is the challenge of the leaders of our communities to embrace and encourage all that makes us different as well as all that makes us equal – one community under God!"

As Neil came to the end of his impassioned speech, the church was filled with a powerful silence. Then Lady Romily was the first to get to her feet and start applauding. To Neil's utter amazement, the applause continued to grow, just as he noticed the lone figure standing at the back of the centre aisle. Bishop Paul was applauding too, a knowing smile on his face, nodding his head in greeting as he saw Neil look in his direction.

By the time Neil had clambered back down from the pulpit, feeling as if his legs were made of jelly, Bishop Paul had made his way to the front of the church, where he turned to address the crowd.

"Ladies and gentlemen, I apologize most profusely for the unavoidable delay that led to my tardy arrival this afternoon. Knowing the months of preparation that have gone into this magnificent gathering in Dunbridge, I was very anxious at the thought that there might be no member of the clergy here who could step into my shoes and say exactly what needed to be said during this special service. I need not have worried, because it seems to me that our young curate here at St Stephen's has come of age. I think the church we love and the communities it serves will be very safe in the hands of inspired and capable ministers like this young man, the Reverend Neil Fisher!"

Waiting for yet another round of applause to die down, the bishop then continued. "And you are all invited now to tea and cakes served next door in St Stephen's church hall. Thank you so much for coming – and may the blessing of God the Father, the Son and the Holy Ghost be with you and remain with you always. Amen."

Neil smiled at the term "tea and cakes", knowing that once again it was a striking understatement for the impressive buffet prepared by Beryl, Maria and the rest of the catering team. It took a few minutes for him to get out of his robes in the vestry, then make his way to the back of the church where Claire was waiting for him, her eyes shining with pride and love.

"I knew you could do it. I just knew it!"

He kissed her gratefully. "Hand on heart, I really didn't. I don't know where that all came from. There was absolutely nothing in my mind when I climbed into the pulpit. I threw up a prayer of complete despair – and all that lot just poured out."

"Well, let's go and have a cuppa. You must be parched. Iris said she'd grab a couple of extra teas for us."

Boy George and the team were still going strong in the bell tower, with a complicated peal that rang out across the town, as the couple made their way out of the church and over to the hall. Neither of them ever got anywhere near a cup of tea, because from the moment they walked in Neil found himself surrounded by well-wishers. Beryl was the first to wrap him in one of her great bear-hugs, followed by Peter, who shook his hand warmly. The two men laughed with relief that the service had ended well in spite of its very shaky start. Maria let go of Matt's hand for just long enough to kiss Neil on both cheeks, while Clifford led an impromptu chorus of "For He's a Jolly Good Fellow", which had Neil turning pink to his earlobes. Finally, Iris made her way to his side to ask him why he'd ever considered any other profession but the ministry when it plainly suited him so well – as she had consistently told him, if he'd only listened...

It was some time later that Cyn came across to whisper in Neil's ear that the bishop would like a word with him in the office. Leaving Claire in the company of Harry and Iris, Neil stepped out of the hubbub of the hall into the peace and quiet of the office, where he found Bishop Paul waiting for him.

"Well done, Neil. I couldn't have done that better myself."

"Is it possible, sir, that you planned it to happen that way? I couldn't understand why you'd sent me that script of your sermon."

"Did you read it?"

Neil grinned. "No, sorry, I ran out of time."

"I thought that would happen. Good job we talked it over on the phone, then."

"But why? That was a terrible risk at an event as prestigious and important as this one."

"It was Lady Romily's idea. She was convinced you would rise to the occasion, and she was right."

"I still don't understand."

"Perhaps you need to look at this to understand fully what's going on here." The bishop held out a soft-covered ring binder, which Neil took over to his desk to look at properly. The front page was a letter printed on Lady Romily's personal headed notepaper.

Dear Bishop Paul,

I attach a list of people from the parish of St Stephen's in Dunbridge who wish to express their great appreciation for the work and presence of the Reverend Neil Fisher. We are aware that the Reverend Fisher will shortly reach the end of his training as a curate and, therefore, be eligible to apply for the role of parish priest in any church of his choice where a post is currently vacant.

*As you know, the post of priest in our own parish is
vacant, and has been for a year now. Reverend Fisher
has nobly and selflessly stepped into the breach and
has done a remarkable job in encouraging Christian
life not just within our own church community, but
throughout this town. We feel he is a gifted and able
young man who has brought much benefit to our
parish, and for that reason we are very reluctant to
let him leave us without making the strongest possible
request that he may be allowed to continue his work
here. We understand that it would be very unusual
for a curate to be allowed to stay in the parish where
he is currently based, but Reverend Fisher is a
very unusual man. We request that he be officially
offered the role of vicar here at St Stephen's, a
request endorsed by the whole Parish Council, whose
members are included within the three hundred people
who have signed their names below.*

I remain yours,

Lady Constance Romily

"Unbelievable!" breathed Neil. "I thought she hated me."

"Far from it," replied Bishop Paul, "as you can see. There's
a great deal of affection for you in this parish, and the diocese
would be foolish to ignore that. Of course, the final decision
about how you continue your ministry from now on is yours
and yours alone – but I have to tell you that, at the highest
possible level, there's a will to bend the rules a little in order to
allow you to take over the role of vicar here, if you'd like it."

"Wow!" said Neil, uncharacteristically lost for words.

"Of course, you'll need to discuss the offer in detail, and any others you're currently considering, with Claire."

"I will."

"Oh, and please will you tell that delightful fiancée of yours that I am indeed free on the 28th of July, and would be delighted to come back to St Stephen's to officiate at your wedding. Nothing would give me greater pleasure."

* * *

It was drizzling as Neil hurried down the church path towards his car, and just as he was fumbling with both his umbrella and his keys, his mobile rang. Sinking into the seat, he managed to get the phone to his ear before it stopped ringing. It was Shirley McCann, the manager of the Mayflower.

"Sylvie's busy at the moment, but she asked me to ring you, Neil. She heard from that Ian Simpson last night, and it turns out he *is* Artie's son. Apparently he was really pleased to hear news of his dad, and he's driving down from Burnley this afternoon."

"Oh, my goodness! Does Artie know?"

"Sylvie's breaking the news to him right now."

"I wonder how he'll take it. I guess it'll be very emotional for him."

"That's why I wondered if you'd like to be here. I know you'd usually do your visits and take the service here tomorrow, but could you swap the day, just for this week?"

"I'll definitely do my very best. What time's Ian due to arrive?"

"About two, I think Sylvie said."

"Well, I'll get there a bit earlier so I can have a chat with Artie first."

Switching the phone off, he drove out of Vicarage Gardens and into the market square. He was on his way to visit a family who were planning a funeral service for the following week. He was a little early, and on impulse he nipped into the parking space in front of the newest shop to open in the town centre. Winding down the window, he smiled at its name, PAUSE, a combination of the names of the shop's owners, Pauline and Audrey. And "pause" described exactly the effect their eye-catching window display was having on passers-by, who were stopping to gaze at the cascade of blooms that stretched across the window from red on one side to violet at the other, with every hue of the rainbow in between.

Suddenly the door opened and Pauline was beckoning him to come in, so he dashed through the rain into the warmth and welcome of the shop. Audrey was in the back room making up bouquets and wreaths that had been ordered for delivery that morning, and Neil was fascinated to observe her skill as she worked choosing each individual bloom, then placing, snipping, mounting and wiring.

"This is wonderful!" he enthused. "You're certainly on to a winner here. How's it going so far?"

The women looked at each other and laughed.

"Manic, terrifying, exhausting, overwhelming…" began Audrey.

"… and we're loving every minute of it," finished Pauline.

The door opened as yet another customer came in.

"You're obviously busy. I'll leave you to it."

"Oh, Neil!" called Audrey, looking up from the intricate basket arrangement she was creating. "I hear you've got a special event of your own coming up at the end of the month?"

"That's right," he smiled. "I hope you'll both be at the

wedding. Claire and I owe so much to the congregation at St Stephen's, and you two are right at the heart of it. We want to share our happiness with everyone."

"Wouldn't miss it for the world. So you tell Claire to pop in and see us. We want your wedding flowers to be the best we've ever done. Our gift to you, for all the gifts you've helped bring our way."

Audrey's warm words were still in his mind as he arrived at the Mayflower shortly after half-past one. Making his way into the lounge, he found Artie sitting by the window, where he had a clear view of the drive up to the house.

"My boy's coming. Did you know?"

"I heard. How do you feel about that?"

The old man said nothing at first, staring down at his hands. It wasn't until he sniffed loudly that Neil realized Artie was struggling to hold back the tears.

"Oh, Artie, won't it be good to see him after all this time!"

"Thirty years or thereabouts." Artie wiped his eyes on his cardigan sleeve, plainly embarrassed.

"I'm going to have a cup of tea," said Neil, getting to his feet. "Would you like one?"

Artie nodded.

"I'll bring it here on a tray, then, and we can wait together."

And that's what they did. They sat side by side while Artie talked. He talked about growing up in Burnley, and his mum who worked wonders caring for their family of three girls and one boy. He spoke of his father working on the roads, out in all weathers from early to late.

"As the only boy in the family, were you specially close to your dad?"

Artie huffed. "He was tough with me. Handy with his belt, locked me in the cupboard in the dark. I had to sleep in the outside toilet one night. He wouldn't let me in because I hadn't finished digging up the potatoes. He was a hard man."

"Did you love him?"

"Yes. Didn't like him, though – and he didn't like me much, either."

"So you hadn't had a very good role model when you became a dad yourself?"

"I knew there had to be rules. No good letting kids think the world owes them a living. You need discipline if you're going to get on in life."

"Is that how you were with Ian? He was your only boy too."

Artie looked unseeingly into the distance, as if picturing his memories. "He was probably a bit too much like me," he said at last. "Stubborn as a mule. Knew it all. A cheeky little git."

"Were you tough on him, too, like your dad was with you?"

"I didn't take the belt to him, if that's what you mean. And his mother always mollycoddled him. That didn't do him a scrap of good. Let him get away with murder, my Hetty did."

His head lifted as a blue saloon car just outside the gate caught his eye. It paused, then slowly made its way up the drive and stopped just opposite the window. The driver climbed out stiffly, stretching his back as if he'd had a tiring journey. Then he reached into the back seat to pull out his jacket, which he put on and smoothed down, anxious to make a good impression. He glanced up towards the house and, at that moment, caught sight of Artie sitting at the window. Time stood still as father and son locked eyes on each other for the first time in thirty years.

"He looks like me," breathed Artie, his hands trembling. "That could be me when I was his age." Suddenly, Artie was pushing himself onto his feet. "Help me up, Neil. I want to meet him eye to eye."

Sylvie was the first to come through the lounge door; Ian hesitated behind her as he saw Artie standing to greet him.

"Hello, Dad," he said.

"Hello, son."

Neither moved, although Neil could feel Artie's hand shaking violently as it gripped his own. And then Ian was at his father's side, wrapping his arms around him, hugging him tightly, burying his face in Artie's shoulder. As they clung together in a world of their own, Neil stepped back and tiptoed over to Sylvie who, with one last smile in Artie's direction, pulled the door closed behind them.

* * *

The 28th July was a glorious summer's day. Claire pulled back the curtain on her wedding day and sighed with relief.

"Up you get!" said Felicity, walking in with a cup of tea. "Your bath's running, there's smoked salmon and scrambled eggs for breakfast, and the hairdresser will be here in half an hour."

"Thanks, Mum. How's Iris? Has she actually collapsed with the stress of it all yet?"

"I'm going to take her down to her own hairdresser in just a minute. She'll feel better once she's looking her best."

"Don't let her go down and bother Neil, will you? I think she's the last thing he needs first thing this morning."

"Well, her brother and his family are arriving from Bristol in a couple of hours. They'll keep her busy after that."

Down the road at number 96, Neil was just coming out of the shower when his friend Rob wandered sleepily out of the spare room.

"How's your speech going?" grinned Neil. "As my best man, I'm expecting great things from you. All that training we went through together about how to wow from the pulpit! It went straight over my head, of course, but you always did have them laughing in the aisles."

"I'm a coiled spring," grinned Rob. "Ready to leap into action when needed."

"What I need first of all are the rings. You have got them?"

"Yes."

"You're sure?"

"Absolutely."

"And the ushers' list, about which guests have got special seats?"

"All safe and correct. Peter says he'll talk me through it all when I get there – everyone else can choose wherever they want to sit behind those front few rows. Fancy inviting your whole congregation! There'll be standing room only."

"Just as long as there's room for Claire to make her way down the aisle to join me, that's all I care about."

Rob laughed as he headed downstairs towards the kettle, stopping on the way to pick up a card that had been dropped through the letterbox. Neil padded down in his bare feet to take a look, recognizing his mother's neat writing immediately. She had written:

My dearest son,

On this special day, I want to express on paper the love and reassurance I feel as you prepare for your wedding. Claire's a wonderful girl, probably far too good for you! She loves you, though; that's plain for all to see. The joy you share in each other's company bodes well for the long and happy marriage I'm sure you have ahead of you.

*I wonder if, like me, you're thinking about your
father this morning? How proud he'd be today. How
pleased he'd be to see the success you've made of
your vocation. And he'd be as thankful as I am that
you've always allowed me to be a part of your life,
welcoming me with open arms into your extended
family here in Dunbridge.*

*Sometimes I worry that I've been too hard on you,
Neil; too hasty to point out your failings in an effort
to guide you in the right direction – always for your
own good, of course. I look at you today and realize
that all my efforts, along with your infinite patience
with me, have been more than worthwhile.*

I love you, Neil, and I'm proud to call you my son.

Mum

Neil read the letter three times before he folded it up and
slipped it back into the envelope.

"Thinking of you today, Dad," he said out loud. "I'm
thinking of you today."

* * *

Members of the worship group – minus Wendy – provided a
delicate accompaniment to Pachabel's "Canon in D Major",
played on the organ, as Claire walked down the aisle on
Harry's arm. She wore a classically simple wedding dress,
with a garland of white daisies in her hair. Her eyes were
fixed on the man standing ahead of her, his expression full

of tenderness and joy. As she took Neil's arm, he whispered, "You look beautiful. You *are* beautiful..." and they turned together towards Bishop Paul, whose smile matched those on every face in the church at that moment.

"Dearly beloved," began the bishop, "we are gathered together in the sight of God and in the face of this congregation, to join together this man and this woman in holy matrimony – and nothing could give me greater pleasure than to share with Neil and Claire, and with all the friends and family here with them today, the moment when they finally become man and wife."

Neil had planned to concentrate on every word of the ceremony so that later he would be able to recall each precious second, but in reality the service became a glorious blur of hymns ("Be Still, for the Presence of the Lord" for him; "Let there be Love Shared among us" for her); and readings (what else could it possibly be for him but 1 Corinthians 13, as so many couples had chosen before them? And for her it was Kahlil Gibran's piece about marriage from *The Prophet*, because she liked the thought of the two of them growing together like tall trees, their roots joined, stretching up in parallel towards the sky.)

And then came the intimacy of their vows, the rest of the world fading away as they clasped hands to recite the words they had both chosen to say straight from the heart. Neil stroked her hand as he spoke, overwhelmed by the sense of moment.

"I, Neil Robert, take you, Claire Elizabeth, to be my wife, to have and to hold, from this day forward; for better, for worse, for richer, for poorer, in sickness and in health, to love and to cherish, till death us do part; according to God's holy law. In the presence of God I make this vow."

Claire's eyes shone with emotion as she too made her promise.

When Rob was invited to step forward in his role as best man, Neil looked down at their rings, which had been made in a new design from the gold wedding band his father had always worn. Filled with warmth at the thought that his dad was also sharing in the joy of their marriage, Neil placed the ring on the fourth finger of Claire's left hand, saying, "Claire, I give you this ring as a sign of our marriage. With my body I honour you, all that I am I give to you, and all that I have I share with you, within the love of God, Father, Son and Holy Spirit. Amen."

The same words were echoed by Claire as she placed the matching ring on Neil's finger, before Bishop Paul looked down kindly at the couple, saying the words they so longed to hear: "In the presence of God and before this congregation, Neil and Claire have given their consent and made their marriage vows to each other. They have declared their marriage by the joining of hands and by the giving and receiving of rings. I therefore proclaim that they are husband and wife."

Then, joining their hands together, Bishop Paul smiled broadly as he proclaimed, "Those whom God has joined together let no man put asunder! Neil, you may kiss your bride."

And kiss her he did. Neil gathered his wife to him in an embrace that spoke of love and joy and longing and commitment, and when they stepped back, breathless and laughing, the stately walls of St Stephen's were ringing with the applause and cheers of all who watched them.

* * *

At the reception in the church hall, extra-long trestle tables had been laid out to accommodate more than a hundred and fifty well-wishers. Harry stole everyone's heart as he stood to make the first speech, which should normally come from the father of the bride.

"I'm not Claire's father," he said, looking down fondly at

her as she sat beside him, "I'm her great-uncle – but from the moment her grandad, my brother, introduced me to this lovely girl, I have been devoted to her. I've been charmed by the way she's grown from toddler to young lady, admiring all her skills and accomplishments, and driven to distraction by some of the mad decisions she's made in the past. But I'm relieved and warmed beyond measure by her decision to marry the man she has at her side today and for the rest of her life.

"They'll be happy, these two; I know it. They'll work together, they'll build together, they'll laugh and cry and occasionally fight together. But there's so much love here, so much love – and above all, that's the vital ingredient they need for a happy marriage. And Neil, never stop telling your wife you love her. Tell her at every opportunity, because I made the mistake of never once saying those words to my Rosie. I thought she would just *know* I adored her. And then one day she was gone, taken home by God, and it was too late for me to put into words how much I loved her. Don't make that mistake, lad – and promise me that you'll always take good care of my girl!"

Neil's best man, Rob, proved conclusively that he didn't need a pulpit to wow an audience, and before long he had the guests in fits of laughter as he regaled them with tales of Neil at theological college, homing in on his dismal failings with members of the fairer sex in the past.

Finally, it was Neil's turn to speak.

"My wife and I...." he began, to cheers all round. "My wife and I would like you to know that this is the most wonderful day of our lives, and we are so excited about the new life we're starting together. Am I the lucky one – not only marrying a great girl, but also taking on a terrific stepson, Sam!

"As I look around at all of you today, I see so many people who've become extremely dear to me over the past three years. We've come a long way together. So many things have happened – some challenging, some immensely sad, others heart-warming and exciting – and I'd like to thank each and every one of you, for the richness you've brought to my life here in Dunbridge. In every way, practically, emotionally and spiritually, you've been wonderful companions on the road, and I'm deeply grateful to you all.

"It's hard to put into words the surprise and honour I felt when I heard about the petition you put together on my behalf. That was the last thing I expected and, apart from marrying Claire today, the most thrilling and encouraging thing that's ever happened to me. So often, I've felt as if I've bumbled along, doing my best for St Stephen's, aware that, on many occasions, my best really wasn't enough. It's been a steep learning curve, and I have to thank all of you for your understanding, your support, your patience and your prayers.

"Dunbridge is our home. We love it. We love all of you. You've become our family as well as our friends. We've put down roots here in this church community. But now, Claire, Sam and I, as a family, have to decide where our future lies. We've put a lot of soul-searching into that, balancing the sense of belonging and commitment we feel here among all of you, with the thought that perhaps, as we start out on our life together, it's time for us to move on. It hasn't been an easy decision to make, but we've finally decided that our new life deserves a new start. That's what we feel we need, what we really want – and we hope we go with your blessing and love.

"So it's with real sadness that I'll shortly be relinquishing my role here at St Stephen's, so that I can take on the post of parish priest at St Jude's in Burntacre, a small country town in Derbyshire."

A sigh went round the room at this piece of news.

"St Stephen's won't be abandoned without a priest, though. Bishop Paul tells me that a recently retired minister is shortly moving into this parish, and he's more than willing to help out almost full-time until a replacement can be found. The bishop assures me that now the situation's become more urgent, a vigorous search is under way to find a minister able to serve this wonderful congregation. I hope and pray that you'll soon have a rector again, someone worthy to follow in Margaret's footsteps – and that St Stephen's will continue to be a beacon of Christian light and fellowship in Dunbridge for many years to come!"

* * *

And so it was that six weeks later, Neil, Claire and Sam climbed into the car in Vicarage Gardens, ready to follow the packed removal van which had left for Derbyshire half an hour earlier.

Several friends had come to wave them off: Peter and Val, a whole Land Rover full of the Clarkson family, Clifford, James and Sue Molyneux, Brian and Sylvia Lambert, Boy George along with several other members of the bell-ringing team, and Beryl standing beside Maria, Paul and Matt, who turned up in his fireman's uniform because he was supposed to be on duty.

"Harry and I'll be up to see you once you've settled in," said Iris, who had been worryingly stoical and businesslike all day. "Off you go now. Drive safely!"

She turned and walked away so quickly that Neil really didn't have chance to say goodbye, but when he ran after her, he was shocked to see that she was dabbing her eyes.

"I'm just being a silly old fool," she sobbed. "It's going to be very quiet around here once you three have gone."

"Oh, Iris, you know we'll enjoy the peace and quiet really," said Harry, coming up to put his arm round her. "You can come and sit in the sun as I potter round in the garden, and I can come and chat to you as you cook us both an evening meal. We'll rub along just fine, you and me."

And as a small smile returned to her face, Neil held her close and knew he would really miss her. Infuriating, meddling, opinionated she might be, but he loved his mum. He loved her very much indeed.

"Come on, Dad!" shouted Sam from the back seat of the car. "Mum's waiting!"

Minutes later, there were waves all round as the car pulled away, only to come to a sudden stop a few yards later as a small group ran round the corner shouting his name. It was Sonia, with Charlie in her arms, Jake running ahead and Rosie leading the way with a piece of paper in her hand. Neil wound down the window just as Rosie arrived, pink-cheeked and breathless, beside the car.

"You've got to take this!" she puffed. "He said he needs to go with you!"

Neil looked down at a picture of Rosie's angel.

"Thank you, Rosie," he smiled. "I'm definitely going to need him."

And with a rev of the engine and a final wave from Claire, the car moved round the corner and out of sight.

❧ EPILOGUE ❧

The vicarage at St Jude's really came into its own at Christmas. The solid old walls, the big log fires, the crisp frosts that painted the holly berries and ivy in their garden in shimmering white each morning, all seemed to complement Claire's natural talent for home-making, so that the house felt cosy and welcoming. As Neil arrived back from his visits that lunchtime, his mouth watered as he smelled the mince pies she was just taking out of the oven.

"The postie's been!"

Kissing her as he passed, he pulled a stool up to the kitchen table and began to sort through the pile of letters and cards he'd picked up from the front door mat. Discarding any that looked like bills, he began to look at the postmarks, recognizing several from the Dunbridge area. The address on the first one he opened was written by a hand he recognized immediately. It was from Peter Fellowes.

"Merry Christmas from everyone at St Stephen's!" was the cheery greeting on the front of the card above a group photo of the congregation he knew so well. All the familiar faces were there, gathered around an elderly minister who stood right in the middle of the crowd. Inside, Peter had enclosed a letter of his own. Scanning its contents, Neil turned to Claire,

saying she just had to stop whatever she was doing and listen
while he read it out loud.

Dear Neil and Claire,

*Val and I hope this card finds you fit and well, and that
you're not completely run off your feet as Christmas
approaches. Not as busy as last year, I imagine, and in
some ways that must be a blessing in itself!*

*We're soldiering on at St Stephen's, with the invaluable
help of the Reverend Michael Kerridge, as you see from
the photo. He's made so much time for us in spite of
the fact that he's supposed to be retired, but he'll be as
relieved as us when the announcement is made about
who will be our next rector. Apparently there are several
possible candidates in the frame. More than that, none
of us knows yet.*

*Anyway, in the hope that you may be missing us even
half as much as we're missing you, I've got a proposition
for the two of you. Several members of the congregation
rather fancy the idea of going on a pilgrimage. I remember
how you've mentioned pilgrimages in the past, and
wondered if the one we've chosen might appeal to you. It's
a Christian cruise at the end of May next year around the
coast of Britain, calling in at Iona, some of the Scottish
islands, Dublin, the Isles of Scilly, Guernsey and other
places you can see on the brochure I've enclosed. In many
ways, we will be following in the footsteps of the Celtic
saints, and I remember how much inspiration you always
took from the courage and words of those early Christians.*

*Anyway, Claire will be glad to know this trip promises
all the cosseting you'd expect on a cruise – nice cabins,
entertainment every evening, lots of interesting trips and
wonderful food with no washing-up, which Val says
will be her favourite treat! The difference is that there's
a Christian team onboard leading worship and offering
pastoral care. I've a feeling that the most important
pilgrimage will be the simple act of travelling together
with a delightfully mixed bunch of other Christians from
different parts of the country. A dozen or more of us
from St Stephen's have already signed up, and more might
follow. If it interests you, how about organizing a party to
join us from your new parish? We promise we won't spill
the beans on the more entertaining times you had in your
training here. Your secrets are safe with us!*

*Seriously, though, everyone would love such a perfect
opportunity to spend time with you and Claire. What
do you think? I can't tell you how much we're hoping
your answer will be yes.*

*Take care, dear friends, and we wish you every blessing
this Christmas and always.*

With our love,

Peter and Val

"Well?" asked Neil, turning to Claire. "What do you think?"

"You on the high seas wearing a captain's hat?" she
laughed. "Give him a ring and tell him we wouldn't miss it
for the world!"